WARRIOR WISEWOMAN 2

Edited by Roby James

Cover Images:
"Mademoiselle Mars" by Pierre-Jean David d'Angers (1825); "Head Of An Italian Girl" by Valentine Cameron Prinsep (1838-1904); "Figures in a Winter Landscape" by Barend Cornelis Koekkoek (1842); "Earth Flag" by Derrick Coetzee (Dcoetzee) (April 20, 2005); "Eta and Keyhole in the Carina Nebula" Copyright © 2006 by Brad Moore (March 16, 2006).

Cover Design Copyright © 2009 by Vera Nazarian

ISBN-13: 978-1-60762-028-0
ISBN-10: 1-60762-028-6

FIRST EDITION
Trade Paperback Edition

June 1, 2009

A Publication of
Norilana Books
P. O. Box 2188
Winnetka, CA 91396
www.norilana.com

Printed in the United States of America

ACKNOWLEDGMENTS

Introduction © 2009 by Roby James
"The Executioner" © 2009 by Jennifer Brissett
"Shop Talk" © 2009 by Ian Whates
"Working the High Steel" © 2009 by Jennifer R. Povey
"Changer" © 2009 by Ardath Mayhar
"The Last Nice Afternoon in October" © 2009 by Leslie Brown
"Lady Blaze" © 2009 by Lee Martindale
"The Making of Her" © 2009
        by Sarah Ellender & Michael O'Connor
"Sister Grass" © 2009 by Deborah Walker
"Heart Bowed Down" © 2009 by Jeff Crook
"Peacock Dancer" © 2009 by Catherine Mintz
"Bloody Albatross" © 2009 by David Bartell
"Gardens of Wind" © 2009 by Kate MacLeod
"Silent Whispers" © 2009
        by Karen Elizabeth Rigley & Ann Miller House
"Beneath the Alien Shield" © 2009 by Z. S. Adani
"Rainfire by Night" © 2009 by DJ Cockburn
About The Authors

Warrior Wisewoman 2

Norilana Books
Science Fiction

www.norilana.com

WARRIOR WISEWOMAN 2

Edited by

ROBY JAMES

CONTENTS

Contents

INTRODUCTION

by Roby James

On panels at more than one science fiction convention, I've been asked—and watched other people being asked—"What's the difference between SF and fantasy?" That's a question that can be posed in a variety of ways, and it may be asked with some frequency, but it is hardly an idle question.

There are, indeed, similarities between the two types of fiction, in that both can be subsumed into an overarching genre called "speculative fiction," which also contains "magical realism," a term coined by literary critics to avoid having to call SF or fantasy by their real names.

I've heard the question about fantasy versus SF answered like this: "One has trees and spells; the other has rockets and ray guns." That's a relatively facile definition, but I don't believe it goes deep enough, or perhaps wide enough. Ursula LeGuin has provided a definition that I like better: "SF does not contradict the rules of science; fantasy makes up its own rules."

To me, fantasy is that for which no realistic explanation can exist. SF, on the other hand, can have a realistic explanation, even if that explanation is currently highly improbable. Note that I used the word "realistic." The science behind SF stories does not, in my world view, have to be *real* (though that would be the height of desirability); it doesn't so much have to *be* grounded in reality, in the universe of the known, it just has to *sound* and *feel* real, which is a working definition of "realistic."

This year the question took on special significance for *Warrior Wisewoman*. Nearly a third of the stories submitted for this volume were what I was forced to decline, because they were what I ended up calling "fantasies in space." They took place on alien worlds or on the rocket ships that could be considered characteristic of SF. Yet the only way the major problem of the story could be solved was by the use of what we call "magic." The solution did not appear to be grounded in any permutation of science, either hard or soft. There was no attempt to tie it, even tangentially or subliminally, to any of the sciences, to any technological advances, or even to such inexact disciplines as medicine or meteorology. It was futuristic fantasy.

There's nothing wrong with futuristic fantasy. It's just not what *Warrior Wisewoman* exists to present.

But speaking of LeGuin: Sometimes there are stories that have an element of fantasy hidden in a great deal of realistic SF. LeGuin's *The Lathe of Heaven* is one of these. George Orr's ability to change reality by dreaming is pure fantasy, but everything that comes after that and surrounds it to create the story is strongly realistic science fiction. Just as LeGuin could do this, with consummate skill, so can today's authors, if they work it correctly.

So it is possible that some fantasy may sneak into stories and be disguised enough by the trappings of science that they slip by. I leave it up to you to see if that's the case here.

There is no single theme in this volume, but a number of the stories deal with women as nurturers—a role in which it's sometimes necessary to be a warrior. Whether or not a woman is also wise in that role may depend on several things: what she chooses to nurture, how she chooses to nurture it, and what her actions cost herself and those around her.

In all cases, the underlying or the overarching science in the stories in this volume is realistic, to a greater or lesser degree. That science may not be plausible. But here are plausible characters in plausible stories that can stretch the imagination and stir the emotions. I hope you enjoy them as much as I do.

—Roby James

Traditionally, a woman's role is nurturing, life-giving. But sometimes women are put into the position of having to take life instead. Most commonly, those women who kill choose to take that path. The woman in this story did not choose it. Rather, it chose her.

THE EXECUTIONER

by Jennifer Brissett

The day of the execution was the first and only time I'd ever been in a prison. It was a lot bigger than I expected it to be. There was more light in it, too. I thought it would be a dark place with screaming inmates yelling at me as I passed through. But that's not how it was at all. Everyone was silent when they saw me. I was like Moses parting the Red Sea. Only the sea was people moving out of my way. There were guards on every side of me as I walked through the prison. They guided my way to the death house in the back yard. I was Death personified, and everyone knew it. I felt kind of powerful. I looked up and saw these big, tough men who were afraid—*of me*. That's what I was that day, Death personified.

I had been warned not to look in the eye of anyone who didn't work for the State. So I kept my head down. It was hard not to look up, feeling the heat of so many stares on me. But I did as I was told. I was a good citizen. This was what the State required. My name had come up, and when that happens, you do your duty. That was how my family raised me. You don't shy away from your responsibilities. You stand up and do what needs to be done. I took no joy in being there. I knew that this was nothing to be happy about either. This was just something that had to be done. And my name had come up. That was all there was to it.

They marched me into the back where there was a large green lawn. Inmates were working to cut the grass and they, too, stopped to stare at me as I passed by. The sky was unusually bright. It was clear and blue as far as the eye could see. And it was so quiet. As if the birds themselves knew that it was a solemn day.

I had just had my second child a few months before. I would have rather been home with her. She was such a little thing. And a really good baby. I could hand her to anyone and she wouldn't cry. She'd just look up at them with wonder and lean into their chests, calm and pleasant. I felt so lucky to have a good home and family. It was the State that kept us all safe from the likes of the one that I was going to put down. The way I looked at it, this was little to ask from a citizen to whom the State had given so much.

The death house looked like an old chapel, with its small "A" roof and peeling window wallpaper made to resemble stained glass. Inside was quiet, and people spoke in hushed tones. There were prison guards everywhere. They, like the prisoners, stilled when they saw me.

The warden was there to greet me. He was friendly enough—businesslike, though. He shook my hand and escorted me to the lunchroom where a fine meal was waiting for me. The State had sent a packet to my house with a return form requesting that I list the meal I would like to be served. I must admit that they got everything just right. Funny, I can remember enjoying the meal, but I don't remember the meal itself. It's like I have a memory of a memory about it.

While I sat and ate, the warden and the prison guards watched. It felt strange to be the only one eating. The warden told me to eat up, since I wouldn't be able to eat again until the next day. It's the way the drugs worked. If you tried to eat right after taking them, they could make you really sick to your stomach.

When I was done eating, the warden and I had coffee together. This time the three guards with us joined in. It felt like I had become part of a ritual of theirs. I wondered how many of these executions they had attended. I wanted to ask, but didn't. We just all sat quietly together sipping at our coffee until it was gone or got cold.

The warden took off his glasses and rubbed his eyes. For a moment I thought that he was crying. When he looked up, I saw that he wasn't. He just looked tired. He put his glasses back on and laid his palms out flat on the table. "Did you read the packet that the State sent you?" he asked.

Yes, I nodded.

"Good. Well, I'm going to briefly go over the basics again of what's going to happen tonight. Please stop me at any time if there's something you don't understand or if you have a question."

I nodded again.

"We will take a little bit of your blood now. It will be used to create the drug cocktail. It will be prepared and injected into you in about an hour. Once you receive the injection, you are the State's agent of execution. The drug will only affect the condemned. It is coded with his DNA and yours. You cannot harm any other person with your touch. Do you understand?"

I nodded.

"You have to answer verbally. It's the law."

I said, "Yes."

The warden continued, "We will wait until midnight for any last-minute reprieve. If there is none, you will be escorted to the death chamber by these guards to face the condemned. Myself and the minister for the condemned will be in the room. A family member and a witness for the condemned may also be in the death chamber. He will be strapped down securely onto a gurney. You will be perfectly safe."

I instinctively looked at the guards sitting with us. One of them lowered his head to avoid my eyes.

"He will be allowed to say his last words," the warden said.

"Will he say anything to me?"

"The law states that a prisoner has the right to face his executioner. So he may say something to you." The warden took off his glasses again and spoke softly. "My advice to you is to pay no attention to what he says. He doesn't know you and you don't know him. Remember, you are not his judge or his jury. You didn't determine his guilt or innocence. Others performed that function. You are his executioner. You are just performing your lawful civic duty."

I must admit that I always just assumed that the man was guilty. I didn't even know what he had been condemned for. The packet from the State suggested that I not research the case, so I didn't. Sometimes I think that was a mistake.

"When you feel ready, you are to physically touch the condemned."

"How am I supposed to touch him?" I asked.

"Any way you see fit," the warden said. "I've known some who hugged them and others who have just put a pinky on them. There is no right or wrong way, as long as there is physical contact."

"And that's all it takes?"

"Yes, ma'am. Death will commence at that point."

"How long will it take?" It felt ghoulish asking, but I really wanted to know.

"Death may occur within a few moments. You are legally required to remain with the condemned until he is dead. Then you are free to go."

જી⊂ଓଛ૭ଅ

The night passed slowly. The lab technician who had mixed the drug cocktail was also the one to administer my injection. He made me roll up my sleeve and rubbed my arm with cool alcohol. "This may sting," he warned.

It did.

"You may get a slight fever tomorrow," he said. "It will pass. You'll be fine in a day or two."

I unrolled my sleeve as he put his needles and things away. The area where I was injected felt sore and began to throb. My arm ached for several days after that. Such a small price to pay.

"At least you won't ever be asked to do this again. The drug only works once. It will never work in you again. At least that's something."

"At least that's something," I repeated.

CR8Oso

I spent the rest of the afternoon in the lunchroom with the guards. They were good people. We talked about our families and showed each other pictures of our kids. We played cards and dominos to while away the time. I couldn't help constantly looking up at the clock. It seemed to be ticking more slowly than usual. I began to feel anxious as the sun came down. I had survived the weeks preceding that night by simply not thinking about ending a man's life. After the sun went down, all that changed. What I was about to do was all I could think about. I was just a small-town mother of two. How had I become this agent of death?

CR8Oso

By 9 PM, I was visibly shivering.

"I don't feel well," I said to my guards. "I want to go home."

They just looked down. One of them said to me, "You're just nervous. This happens to everyone."

"But I feel sick to my stomach," I said. It was no lie. My stomach was twisted into knots upon knots. I felt like I could throw up.

"That's normal," he said. "I feel like that every time I have to do one of these. Every single time."

ଔ൝ଔ

By 11:30 PM, the guards and I were all on our feet. The cordial feeling between us was gone. Now it was all business. The minutes passed like hours. Then it was finally time. The guards escorted me to the death chamber. My legs moved on their own, because I felt nothing. We entered the room and it was like the warden said it would be. He was there standing next to a minister. And there was the condemned man. He was on a gurney strapped down by many large belts. His arms were stretched out on two protruding extensions of the gurney so that he looked like a man on a cross. He was just a boy, really. Maybe he was in his late twenties. There was something about his expression that reminded me of my little brother. He physically looked nothing like my brother, but the way he held his face and moved his head was just like him.

I heard a whimpering as if it were coming from an injured animal. There were two women standing behind a glass window. They were holding each other. One looked elderly; the other was young.

"Do you have any last words?" the warden asked.

The boy craned his neck to see the two women through the window.

"I love you," he said. "I'm sorry, Momma."

I felt my knees begin to shake. I didn't want to be there. I didn't want to be there. I didn't want to be there. The boy looked back at me. He had soft brown eyes. He was not what I had expected at all.

The warden nodded to me that it was time. My legs went completely numb. I couldn't move. I could hardly catch my breath. My feet were like wet cement melting into the floor.

"When you're ready," the warden said.

Many moments went by, and I still didn't move. I stared at the boy. My heart pounded in my chest. No one said anything. It was deathly silent. It was all up to me, and I couldn't move.

The warden waited patiently for a time; then he looked at his watch. I saw him wave his hand to the guards. And these men, these good men, whom I had spent the whole day with and with whom I had shared pictures of my kids, grabbed me and forced me forward. It was then that I understood that the guards were not there just to protect me, but to force me if I tried to refuse.

I fought them. I fought them hard. I waved my arms and scratched like a cat. A wild animal rose in me that I never knew was there.

"Don't touch me!" I screamed. And they backed away. The women behind the glass looked at me with a kind of hope and sympathy. I felt a flush of guilt and shame. I felt naked before them. I straightened out my clothes and passed my hands over my hair. Then I slowly stepped towards the boy. He looked at me with eyes that tore at my soul. I went over to him.

I said, "I'm sorry." He nodded and swallowed.

I took his hand in mine. It was warm and soft. Then I backed away.

Minutes passed and nothing happened. I felt a wave of relief. I had read in the packet sent to my house that sometimes the drugs didn't take. I felt a joy then that I didn't think could be possible. The boy smiled at me. He looked over at this mother. And she weakly waved back at him. My face was completely wet at this point. I wiped away my tears. Then the boy jerked.

He convulsed for a few moments, twisting in his restraints. Little pockets of foam appeared at the corners of his mouth. His eyes turned back so that they were all white. His body shook for a minute. He let out a deep sigh and closed his eyes. He moaned a little as if he was having a troubled dream. I could see his chest still moving. Then he jerked again and he moved no more.

The warden came over and checked his pulse.

"Death occurred," he said and looked at his watch, "at 12:27 AM."

I can't explain the feeling I had then. It's a feeling that has never left me. I felt hollowed out like a Halloween pumpkin, all carved out with nothing left inside. I had killed a man. With my own hand, I killed him. I looked at his still body, and it was like there was nothing else. I couldn't hear anything. I couldn't feel anything. The guards unstrapped him and his slack body flopped. I looked away. I heard someone let out a loud cry. I thought it was the boy's mother. I was surprised to find that it was me.

⋘⋙

I could barely walk. The guards helped me out of the building and escorted me to the parking lot. Someone called to me. I turned around. It was the boy's mother. Her daughter was trying to hold her back. She was coming at me. The guards stood in her way.

"I want to speak to you," she said.

I said, "It's all right." Inside, I felt that even if she wanted to hit me, it was all right. The guards got out of the way and the daughter hesitantly let the old woman go. She was short, so that I had to look down to see her. She looked up at me. My legs buckled and I found myself on my knees before her. She took my hand—the hand that had just killed her son—and she held it in hers. Her small veiny hands cradled mine.

"This was not your fault," she said. "I will pray for you and your family."

Then she let my hand go and turned toward her daughter. They held each other and slowly walked into the night.

⋘⋙

My husband once told me that all the cells in a body completely change every seven years. Well, it's been seven years since then, and I still feel the same. There's not a day that goes by that I don't think about it. I don't talk about it with anyone. My husband knows to just leave it alone. I know I've been different. Quieter. I think about things more. I think about life more.

It's a warm day today. The sky is blue as far as the eyes can see. My eldest is playing in the yard with his little sister. I've been watching them laughing and tumbling around on the grass. They are so innocent. Their whole lives are in front of them. Their faces are filled with only possibilities. His momma must have had days like this. Days when she looked out at her children, laughing and playing, and dreamed of what they might be.

Growing up is never easy, because change is never easy. And when remaining the same is government policy, each person must decide if wisdom lies in compliance.

SHOP TALK

by Ian Whates

Gemma had obviously been running; she was gasping for breath, and her eyes in the doorscreen gleamed with excitement. Calli waited for a few seconds, watching with amusement as her friend shifted impatiently from foot to foot, before instructing the house to admit her.

"There's a new shop in town," Gemma said breathlessly as she came in, not even bothering to say 'hello'.

A new shop? Perhaps the day was not going to prove such a non-event after all. "Really? What's it stock?"

"Clothes."

"Oh." Another one. For a moment there she had been fooled by Gemma's excitement into hoping for the unusual.

"No, trust me, you want to see this. The clothes are zero degrees."

"Oh, sure." Calli gave a disdainful toss of her head. "As if clothes could ever be *that* cool?"

"These are. Really!" Gemma's voice betrayed her. She was clearly desperate to share her new discovery and at the same time afraid of being dismissed as a dweeb for getting so worked up over mere clothes.

Calli said nothing, just raised her eyebrows to produce her best 'I'm only tolerating you at this precise moment' look.

"Oh please, Cal." Gemma was openly pleading now. "You must come and see them. They're strange, they're wonderful . . . they're just so *different*."

It seemed that in the space of a moment the conversation had evolved into a personal crusade for Gemma, so determined was she to vindicate her enthusiasm. Calli felt a sudden mischievous urge to refuse, but dismissed the thought even as it occurred to her.

Instead she shrugged and smiled. "Okay, I'll come—if only to shut you up." After all, there was nothing better to do.

The two girls strolled out of the house, leaving it to seal itself and power down, through the wooden gate in the white picket fence and into the lane, heading towards town. Gemma, who was a head shorter than Calli, slightly stout to her slender, and dark blonde to her brunette, was gushing—initially with gratitude and then from sheer excitement.

"There's this old man who runs the place. He's a bit creepy, but don't worry, just ignore him."

Calli tuned out the other girl's voice and concentrated on simply enjoying the walk. It was a lovely day, exactly as the WET (Weather Engineering Trust) had promised. Things had gone pretty smoothly since they took over running the climate a couple of years ago. The previous lot, the ECC (Environment Control Consortium) had been a shambles: you never knew whether to pack a sunhat or an umbrella, whatever they scheduled.

Her dad had moaned constantly about the ECC. "Don't know how they got the job, it's a disgrace. How are the old land farmers supposed to cope when they've no idea what's coming? Just be grateful we're firmly in hydroponics."

Hydroponics: her future. How she hated that word.

"Lovely afternoon, isn't it, girls?" She glanced up to see the craggy smile of Davy Arthur.

They were passing the old schoolhouse, and Davy was lounging in the shade of its porch, pushing himself gently back and forth on a flimsy-looking rocker. Everyone knew Davy Arthur. He had been the town gardener for as long as Calli could remember. Now that she took the trouble, she could hear the persistent hum of the half-dozen mini-cutters he was currently supervising. The bird-sized 'bots were busy trimming the long privet hedge into neat uniformity, buzzing around its crown like giant metallic beetles, their silver carapaces glinting in the sun.

A tall figure emerged from the whitewashed building behind the old gardener. Calli's heart sank; it was Matt, Davy's son. Why did they have to bump into him, of all people?

"Hello, Calli."

"Matt," she acknowledged curtly.

"Just teaching Matt here the trade," Davy explained with obvious pride.

"Hello, Matt."

"Hi, Gemma."

Despite the greeting being so clearly an afterthought, Gemma went all moon-faced and stood there with such a ridiculous grin that Calli feared she was about to start drooling. "Must dash," she said, taking hold of her friend firmly by the elbow and propelling her in the direction of town. "There's this great new shop I simply *have* to see."

"I heard about that shop," Davy Arthur called after them. "You be careful; it's from out-of-town, you know."

The comment was so unexpected that Calli almost stopped and asked what he meant, but then she remembered Matt and strode on with greater purpose. "What an odd thing to say," she murmured.

"Did you see the way Matt looked at me?" Gemma asked.

Calli managed not to utter any of the several tempting responses that leapt to mind and, for once, stayed quiet. At least her friend's new preoccupation had stopped her wittering on about the wretched shop and its clothes.

Progress became disjointed once they reached the town proper, as they paused to exchange greetings first with the

Gallagher twins, then with Mrs. Clement and finally with Mr. Turnbull, who nearly bowled them over as he strode with unaccustomed haste out of a shop, clutching his latest purchase like some newly discovered treasure.

"Look," he urged, eagerly thrusting his prize forward for them to admire.

It was all Calli could manage not to physically recoil from the leather-bound lump and its musty smell.

They were outside the book shop, she realised, with its austere brickwork façade and its leaded-glass windows in mock-wood frames, complete with flaking paint. The venerable old shop had been a feature of the town for over a month now. Not that either girl had deigned to set foot inside—they would never have been seen dead in a place like that.

"Real paper, mind, none of your digital rubbish," Turnbull was saying. "Used to be in the library at the Vatican, this book did."

Suddenly Calli found the prospect of looking at clothes—*any* clothes—highly exciting.

They excused themselves, an impatient Gemma tugging at Calli's hand, and ran off down the street, giggling.

"Books? Can you believe it?" Gemma exclaimed when they were safely out of earshot.

"I know. How many people down the centuries do you suppose have read that thing? Just the thought of all those grubby hands pawing over the words and turning the pages gives me the creeps. Unhygienic, or what?"

"Gross!"

The girls stopped, suddenly aware of a vibration rapidly building through the air and the ground—a deep humming that crept towards a whine, climbing perceptibly in both pitch and volume as they listened.

The singing crystal shop, Calli realised. It was about to leave. She turned to find that its windows were already opaque and continued to watch as the shop began to shimmer, waiting for the vibration to reach a crescendo, which it did almost at once, cutting off abruptly with a sharp 'pop' as air rushed into the sudden void. The shop had vanished, leaving an empty lot in its place, ready for the next retailer.

"I wonder where it's going," she said wistfully.

"The Middle East," replied Mrs. Lundy, who must have joined them whilst she was preoccupied, "and then on to China. They'll be back in the spring, though, stocked with the finest crystals from around the world, Sunita promised."

The two girls exchanged glances. They had visited the singing crystal shop together when it first arrived and shared an opinion of its wares: same old tat given an exotic spin.

Calli even harboured doubts about the shop's keeper, suspecting that her skin colour was artificially augmented to enhance the exotic image. Her real name was probably Sharon.

"Come on," Gemma said as soon as Mrs. Lundy had continued on her way, "it's just around the corner."

And there it was: a small, neat shop-front, nestling between the Instant Eatery and Ernie's Entertainment Emporium, looking quite at home. Calli tried to remember what had been there immediately before, but couldn't.

The large plate-glass window displayed a single item: a beautiful flowing white dress of unusual cut and semi-translucent material, worn by a mannequin which walked casually on the spot, simulating a stroll along a sandy beach, the dress rippling in some imperceptible breeze. Simple and elegant. Class.

Gemma pushed the door open and beckoned her to follow. To her own considerable surprise, Calli was hooked even before she stepped inside.

She sensed at once that this was a friendly shop, that it would welcome your browsing through its stock all day if you chose to. And what stock. A mesmerising array of clothing confronted her, causing her gaze to flit like a confused butterfly from one point to another, uncertain where to settle.

"Welcome, young ladies, welcome." A portly middle-aged man approached, his face lit by a dazzling smile. There was something odd about that face, and it took Calli a moment to work out what it was: glasses, he was wearing old-fashioned glasses. Talk about taking an image to extreme. Yet, somehow, they worked, and managed to perch atop the bridge of his nose as if they belonged there.

"You arrive at a most propitious moment," the man continued. Calli realised that he had introduced himself but she had failed to catch the name—Donovan or some such. "The shop is about to give birth."

The two girls stared at each other in horror. "As in a *baby* shop?"

"Good gracious, no." The shopkeeper sounded as shocked as they felt. "That really would be something to see!" He chuckled. "To a new line of clothes."

"Oh, right."

"Cool."

Relief all 'round.

"They should be ready in a few minutes but in the meantime please look around." He gestured expansively, the sweep of his arm taking in a whole wall of outfits.

"Oh, wow, look at this, Cal," said Gemma, who was already on the case.

She held out an iridescent costume, which pulsed with shades of purple and blue, ripples of colour that coursed soothingly across the material as it moved. Calli went for a closer look but was distracted by another item—a bright orange sarong in a lacy material that proved deceptively substantial when she ran her hand along it.

"You have a good eye," Donovan said beside her.

She turned to see the man's round face once more graced with a warm and infectious smile that lent it genuine charm. She found herself smiling back and decided that she liked this portly shopkeeper. Could this really be the same person Gemma had described as creepy?

"What is it?" she asked, holding up the sarong. "I've never seen anything like it."

"No, you wouldn't have. It's Selith pupa; a single piece of material, uncut and, in a sense, still alive."

"Oh." Calli hastily let go, allowing the orange garment to settle back on its hanger.

"No, don't worry," the man said, still smiling. "It won't harm you—it's not alive in that sense—and nothing we're doing will hurt it. In adapting the material for clothing, all we've done is use it in the way nature intended, more or less. You see, the Selith produce these capes as protection for their young. Feel how warm it is and how strong?" He took up a corner and held it towards Calli. Still a little uncertain, the girl touched the cloth tentatively. It *was* warm, now that Donovan mentioned the fact, and she had already noted its surprising thickness.

"It has to be tough," the man continued, "in order to protect the Selith nymph for the first five years of its life, and adaptable, too. We've simply taken advantage of its natural characteristics. You can wear this as a sarong one day, a long-skirted one-piece the next and a short dress the day after that. It's programmed to conform to whatever you choose. In about five years the material will die and disintegrate, but until then it's fire-resistant, almost impossible to cut or tear and will keep you warm and looking beautiful."

She laughed at the blatant flattery. "You make a good salesman."

"I'm glad," he replied, chuckling. "After all, that's what I do."

A sudden thought interrupted her joyful mood. "You don't kill these Seli-thingamy-jig nymphs for this stuff, do you?"

"No, you needn't fear on that score," Donovan assured her. "The Selith are the dominant species on Reiggelis; they're sentient. We trade with them for the pupa material. Very expensive it is too, now that they're catching on to just how much it's sought after."

Calli didn't quite buy all this nonsense about other worlds and alien species—nobody came back from the colony worlds to Earth any more—but she loved the story anyway.

"You wouldn't catch me wearing that," said Gemma, who had come over to join them. "I don't want some creepy live thing crawling all over my body, thank you very much."

When put like that, the garment suddenly lost its appeal.

"My dear lady," Donovan responded, "it doesn't crawl, it cuddles." Which sounded much better.

At that point the shopkeeper paused, as if hearing something the two girls had missed. "Ah," he exclaimed, "the new range is ready. If you'll just excuse me for a second." With that he disappeared into the back of the shop.

"See what I mean?" Gemma whispered. "Creepy or what?"

"I think he's kind of sweet."

The two girls lost themselves in browsing through the clothes, marvelling at one garment after another. There was a formal dress, with a detachable skirt, this one in electric blue but available in a choice of colours. It peeled off to leave a risqué mini-skirt and when reattached, the outfit appeared completely seamless, even under the closest scrutiny. There was a whole rack of self-cleaning trousers in a material that neither girl had encountered before, and Calli was just about to satisfy her curiosity with regard to a display of self-warming underwear when Donovan reappeared.

"Ladies," he said with a flourish, "may I present our latest range."

Two mannequins stepped forward to stand beside him. Eerily lifelike, they adopted catwalk poses and suffered the girls' examination.

One wore a loosely belted swallowtail dress, dropping to mid-calf at the back and rising to just above the knee at the front. It was made from the most beautiful material Calli had ever seen, although she had reservations about the colour—a florally patterned burgundy. The second model wore black trousers and a seamless blouse of the same material, again in burgundy.

"What *is* this?" she asked, mesmerised.

"Silk," Donovan supplied, "a material sadly not seen on Earth in centuries. Our last stop was on Gaynor—a world where the silk worm still thrives, having been brought there by the first colonists. The shop learnt how to spin the material from observing the silkworms and this is our first range to feature it. What do you think?"

"It's lovely." Calli answered for both of them.

Donovan looked at her intently. "Do I sense a 'but'?"

"Well, it's just the colour. . . ."

"The colour?" He looked astonished. "But burgundy is all the rage, especially on Gaynor."

"Well, Gaynor can keep it," Calli told him, a little more sharply than intended. "I mean, I'm sure it's very beautiful, if you're into that sort of thing, but. . . ."

"She's right, you know," Gemma said, backing her friend up. "Stunning material; boring colour. Totally dull."

"Haven't you got it in something brighter?"

"Pastels, you mean?" Donovan studied the mannequins with a speculative eye.

"Anything, just so long as it's not burgundy." Calli knew she was doing a lousy job of expressing herself, so she tried again. "This material is so gorgeous, it deserves something more vibrant."

"You know, young madam, I think you might have a point." The shopkeeper looked at her with renewed respect. "You really do have a good eye. I saw that straight away. Have you ever considered a career in fashion?"

Calli's buoyant mood abruptly disintegrated, collapsing like a burst bubble.

"Did I say something wrong?" Donovan looked suddenly concerned.

"No, not really." She sighed. "It's just that I've already had my CAT and they've told me what I'm suited to."

"Which is?" the man asked, watching her closely.

"Hydroponics." She spat the word out like a bad taste. "I start the training course next week."

He smiled sympathetically. "You don't appear to be overly enamoured at the prospect. Do you have any great interest in plants or in farming?"

"No, none."

Gemma, who had wandered off to look at clothes again, chipped in with a distracted, "Boring."

"It's strange then, don't you think, that the CAT recommends you follow such a career?"

Calli shrugged. "It's what my father does, so I guess it's in the genes."

"Perhaps," the shopkeeper said, clearly unconvinced. "Tell me, what would you really like to do, if you could do absolutely anything?"

"Travel," she said instantly.

"Where?" he asked. "To other countries, or to the stars?"

Calli was about to answer, but stopped herself, wary of saying too much, of revealing her most-guarded dreams. Yet she knew that he could read the answer in her eyes.

"Hey, Cal, you *must* see this."

She excused herself, relieved, and hurried across to see what Gemma had uncovered. As the two girls continued to explore the shop's wares, she forgot her discomfort and almost recaptured the high spirits of earlier. Almost.

In the end Calli bought the Selith sarong—the very first item she had looked at—whilst Gemma bought a couple of skimpy tops and a water-repellent swimsuit. Donovan even gave them a discount as a reward for their helpful comments about the new silk range.

"If you come back tomorrow we'll have some silk items in the new 'vibrant' colours for you to try on."

"Great." Calli couldn't wait to feel that wondrous material against her skin. "We'll be here."

"Oh, I almost forgot," he stopped her as they were about to leave. "Take this home and have a look when you get the chance." He handed her an image card. "I've set it at the bit that I think will interest you, but by all means look at the whole thing."

"What is it?"

"Nothing much; it's just an info-prog about the Earth, a sort of travel guide for off-world visitors like me." He smiled that warm smile of his. "I thought you might like to find out what we think of you."

She took the small plastic card, slipped it into a pocket and promptly forgot about it.

"Thanks, Gem," she said to her friend once they were outside.

"Told you it was worth seeing."

"I know, and you were right. I'm really glad you bullied me into coming."

"Me, bully you?" Gemma cocked her head to one side. "I don't think so!"

Calli grinned. "Maybe not, but thanks anyway." They hugged and parted with a promise to meet again the following day.

On reaching home she went straight to her room, anxious to try on her new garment and to blog about the shop, but she never had the chance.

"Callisandra!"

Calli froze, and knew that she was in trouble. No one other than her mum ever called her *Callisandra* and then only when she had stepped firmly in the manure. She hurried to answer the summons, grabbing the sarong on the way in the vague hope that it might provide a distraction.

Both parents were waiting for her; not a good sign.

"What's this we hear about you going to a new shop today?"

"Oh, that? Sure; Gemma took me. It's really—"

"We would prefer it if you didn't go back there," her father cut in. They would never actually ban her from doing anything, which would be bad parenting, but this was as close as they ever came.

"Why?" She was genuinely astonished. "I mean, it's only a shop."

"Calli, dear, listen to your father."

"Perhaps, but it isn't like any other shop," he said gravely. "This one is dangerous."

"Dangerous? It sells *clothes*, Dad."

"What's that?" he asked, apparently spotting the sarong for the first time. "Is that from the shop?"

"Yes," she said, smiling and holding it out to show them. "See, it's just a—"

Her mum snatched it from her hand. "We'll have nothing like that in *this* house, young lady."

Calli had never seen her mum and dad like this before. It was not so much anger she saw in their eyes, but fear.

All of which gave her plenty to think about later that night. Until the encounter with her parents she had tended to dismiss Donovan's claims of coming from off-world as so much elaborate sales patter, despite the shop's many marvels. After all, he seemed just like a regular guy. A bit eccentric perhaps, but not *alien*. Okay, she knew that people from the colonies were still technically human, but they had not been born on Earth, which made them aliens in her book.

She remembered Davy Arthur's warning about the shop being from 'out-of-town,' which had so puzzled her at the time since all shops were from out-of-town by definition. She now realised that the words were not intended to be taken literally. The phrase was a euphemism for what he had been afraid to say: 'off-world.'

It seemed that everything Donovan had told her so casually might actually be true. She had stood and nattered about clothes with a man from another world. There were a thousand questions she wanted to ask—should have asked—if only she had taken him seriously.

The stars!

Calli had dreamed of going to the stars and visiting other worlds since she was small. Despite all their centuries of independence, the other worlds were still referred to as 'the colony worlds,' when they were mentioned at all. She supposed the vaguely derogatory term helped people maintain the illusion of Earth's significance, rather than face up to the reality of its true status as an isolated backwater.

It was still hard to believe the reaction of people—people she had known all her life, like Davy Arthur and even her own mum and dad. This was the first time she had ever encountered prejudice, and she found that she didn't like it.

Earth had severed all ties with its precocious children-worlds long ago. Apparently that was a good thing, or so they were told. What did seem certain was that Earth would never again reach out to colonise anywhere. It seemed ironic that the very first colonies were established in the latter half of the so-called 'Dark Ages'—the 20th through to the 22nd centuries. Yet the extravagances of that same period had left the Earth so denuded of natural resources that no further exodus from the mother-world would ever be possible, giving the new colonies free rein to claim the stars for themselves.

Calli had seen images from the Dark Ages; in fact they were required learning for every child. Roads choked with cars and the sky full of planes, all busy converting precious fossil fuels into pollution. What was wrong with the ancestors? Why couldn't they embrace the simple joys of walking? Instead, they had exhausted the Earth.

So the stars were out of reach. Visiting other worlds would never be anything more than a dream . . . but what a dream.

Calli fell asleep imagining what it must be like to live like Donovan, seeing all those exotic places and meeting so many different kinds of people.

␣ CRSO ␣

The next morning found her refreshed and in good spirits. She could hardly wait to visit the shop again and this time intended to go fully prepared with all those questions she had always wanted to ask.

In the cold light of day, the confrontation with her parents seemed little more than a bad dream. Already its impact was fading.

She gave Gemma a call first thing, anxious to make arrangements.

"Hello Cal." Her friend looked uncomfortable, embarrassed even.

"You okay?"

"Fine, but look, I won't to be able to make today."

"But what about the shop and trying on all that silk stuff?" Calli realised that she was now in danger of being the one who was pleading.

"Not a good idea. I'm not going near that place again. I told you the old man was creepy, but I never dreamt he was an *alien*."

So she hadn't believed him either.

"Parents?" Calli ventured.

"Heavy-time; yesterday, when I got home."

"Same here."

"Probably for the best. I think the word's out all over town. People are angry."

Angry, or afraid? Clearly it was not just her parents who were overreacting to all of this. By the sound of things, a lot of other people were as well.

"Sorry, Cal."

"No probs. We're cool. Talk tomorrow."

She knew there was little love wasted on the colony worlds but still found it hard to accept that feelings ran so deep. Did Donovan have any idea of the amount of resentment building up against his presence? Thinking of him reminded her of the image card he had handed her yesterday. What had she done with it? After a little rummaging around, she uncovered the presumably alien card and put it on the console, activating the program.

An image appeared in the centre of the room—the Earth seen from space. As Donovan had warned, this seemed to be part-way through the program, but she let it run, curious to find out what he had wanted her to see.

"In the aftermath of the Great Exodus, the authorities on Earth became obsessively concerned with stability, with restricting the opportunity for change." The unseen narrator's rich tones delivered the commentary with lecture-room precision.

"In theory, the huge advances in AI-based technology that we take so much for granted should enable the citizens of Earth to move around as freely as anyone else, but this has never been the case. The taboos against commuting which first arose in the late 21st century still persist, and society has been structured in many subtle ways to reinforce them.

"The authorities go to extraordinary lengths to provide everything anyone could want as locally as possible, thus avoiding the need for travel." The image switched to that of a typical high street, with shoppers strolling along. "Though no longer a relevant issue, the scarcity of fossil fuels provides a credible excuse for curtailing recreational travel. Where people would once drive to centralised malls or to large cities simply to go shopping, the stores now come to the people. Shops jump from town to town and from city to city, providing a never-ending variety of goods and opportunity for retail therapy.

"Rare on other worlds but common on Earth, the mobile shops are themselves semi-organic constructs, each housing an AI, though on Earth every Intelligence is heavily governed and able to operate only within strictly limited parameters. This remains the only contact that a typical Earthman is ever likely to have with an AI."

Calli sat open-mouthed. This was all new to her. A shop was just a shop; she had never considered what else it might represent.

If the section she had seen so far was a revelation, what followed was even more so. The scene shifted to the image of a girl lying down, with a familiar band of metal around her head.

"Central to the system of control is the Careers Aptitude Test, or CAT, which supposedly examines every individual to the depths of their psyche, determining which career path each person is ideally suited to. The resultant recommendations are adhered to with near-religious faith.

"CAT is a sham, designed to ensure that each person is found a job as close to their home as practicable, with the results tailored to fill vacant niches in the local work-force. This often leads to a trade or occupation being continued within the same family, generation to generation, thus simplifying the whole process.

"An immobile populace is a controllable populace."

Calli was stunned. CAT a *sham*? Yet it made sense. Her greatest dread was the prospect of spending the rest of her life as a hydroponics farmer, yet that was precisely what CAT had decreed for her, what it insisted she was best suited to.

She was not so naïve as to take everything said at face value, but much of what this program said rang uncomfortably true. One thing was apparent though: prejudices were not just restricted to the people on Earth. Colonials had a few of their own.

The images and the words continued, but she had stopped paying attention, no doubt having already viewed the section that Donovan had intended her to see. She still wanted to watch all of it, but not right now. There were more pressing matters to attend to.

Snatching the info-card from the console, she hurried out of the house and down the lane towards town.

A crowd was gathering on the green by the old schoolhouse, including several faces she recognised, Davy and Matt Arthur amongst them. Their mood appeared angry, and she ducked down behind the newly manicured privet hedge and hurried past, anxious not to be seen. Only once she was a little further down the lane did one face in particular register.

Surely that had not been her father?

Another shock awaited her at the clothes shop. Its façade was blackened around the door, as if by soot, and the window stood empty, the strolling mannequin nowhere to be seen. She tried the door, half fearing it would be locked, but it opened straight away.

Donovan was waiting inside, and she felt a flood of relief at seeing him unharmed.

"Hello again." His smile now seemed fragile and less certain.

"What happened?"

"Just a spot of bother last night." He gestured dismissively. "Not wholly unexpected, although I had hoped it might take a little longer than this. Somebody tried to burn the shop down."

The horror must have shown on her face. "Is it hurt?"

Donovan smiled. "Not really. Thank you for asking, but there's no need to worry yourself. The shop will heal in no time; look, the window's already re-grown."

"It's true then, about the shops being living things, I mean?"

"Oh yes. I thought you might have known that already." He shook his head, "It's very difficult not quite knowing what you people here on Earth have been told and what you haven't."

Wordlessly, she held out the image card.

"Ah." He accepted the plastic sliver. "You watched it, then. The question is, did you believe it?"

She hesitated, before nodding slowly.

"And do you still want to be a hydroponics farmer?"

She laughed, a little wearily, and shook her head. "No, I never did."

Suddenly he turned very serious. "Would you like to see the stars, Calli?"

"What?" In a day of shocks, this was the greatest yet. To her dismay she found herself shaking, her head reeling. "Are you serious?"

"That's why I'm here."

"You're here for me?"

"You, or someone very like you."

He pulled across a chair, which she slumped into gratefully, feeling numb from head to toe.

"It's all right, catch your breath and I'll explain." Another chair materialised, and he sat facing her. "Humanity has lost its way, Calli; it may even be dying. Very early stages as yet, and it's not apparent to most people, but the process has started.

"The colonies have stopped expanding, you see. In fact they've already begun to draw in on themselves. Pioneer worlds, where life is hard, are being abandoned in favour of the more settled and established planets—the softer option. Why should people struggle to eke out a living when they can be more comfortable on one of the inner worlds?

"Without growth a society inevitably stagnates. Earth is a prime example of that; and yet, paradoxically, Earth is also our richest resource: the strongest and purest human gene pool there is. Here humanity's heritage has not been blasted and fractured by exposure to a thousand radiations on as many different worlds, nor warped and bastardised by our own misguided tampering. Here too there is a fierce pride and spirit, even though it is currently suppressed and twisted. We desperately need you for both the purity of your genetic heritage and the ferocity of your spirit, without which humanity may well be doomed. We need the people of Earth to come to the stars, but they don't want to know."

She didn't want to hear any more, feeling like a sponge which had reached saturation point. "I'm sorry, but this is all too much to take in."

"I'm here to find the adventurous ones, the people who long to visit other worlds," Donovan continued. "I'm here to recruit the dreamers; and that's you, isn't it, Calli."

She stared at him in disbelief. "One man? All on your own you're going to gather enough people to save the colonies?"

"Of course not," he said, smiling. "I'm merely the first. Shops like this aren't as common on other worlds as they are here but they're not unknown, and this AI hasn't been restricted in the way that the ones on Earth are. Nor will it just be shops—we're only one of the approaches being considered. I'm here to scout out the possibilities, to test the waters, so to speak."

"Well if this is your idea of being inconspicuous, you've got problems," she said, grinning despite everything.

"It's a dilemma. I don't want to attract too much attention but at the same time I have to announce where I'm from in order to entice the free spirits . . . and another aspect of my mission is to gauge the reaction that such an incursion evokes from your authorities. Mind you," he admitted with a twinkle in his eye, "perhaps my technique could use a little refinement."

Suddenly they were both laughing.

"Actually, being noticed is essential," he continued as the merriment subsided. "Your government's control relies on ignorance and conditioning. People are angered by my presence because I represent the unknown, because I'm from outside."

Calli nodded. "I saw that in my own mum and dad yesterday."

"Exactly! The anger is just a manifestation of fear, which has its roots in a lack of understanding. Once people realise the implications, once they can see beyond their fear and realise that the stars are not in fact closed to them. . . ." His voice trailed off and for an instant he appeared lost in his own thoughts, as if unable to express the magnitude of what his mind's eye saw.

"Sorry," Calli said, before he could regain the thread of his words, "but I'm having a real problem getting my head around all this." A sudden thought occurred to her. "Are you really a shopkeeper or is this just part of the camouflage?"

"No, no, I genuinely am the custodian of this shop. Everything I told you about Gaynor, Reiggelis, and the Selith is entirely true. I've just been recruited to the cause, so to speak."

Calli felt overwhelmed, unable to think straight. All that she had ever wished for was suddenly being offered to her on a plate, but what about her parents, her friends? For the first time in her life, she had no idea what to do.

"Hydroponics or the stars, Calli; it's up to you."

It was unfair, asking her to make such a decision, to choose between everything she had ever known and everything she had ever dreamed of. "Can I get back to you on this? I really need to think."

A new voice spoke; gentle, feminine tones that seemed to emanate from the air itself. "*I am healed and ready to depart.*"

"I'm afraid that's your answer."

"Was that—?" She could not quite bring herself to complete the question.

He nodded. "The shop, yes. Last night's incident made it clear we've outstayed our welcome. We have only delayed our departure to allow time for full healing and in the hope that you might come back before we left." The man gazed at her, his gaze demanding a decision.

She took a deep breath. "If you're asking me to decide right now, the answer has to be . . . no. I can't commit to something like this on impulse. I just can't." Somewhere deep inside her, hope withered and died.

Donovan slumped. "I understand, But you're making a mistake." His voice was small, defeated.

A familiar deep vibration began.

"I know," she whispered and meant it, even as she stood and proceeded to walk out of the shop on unsteady legs, tears stinging her eyes.

To find herself confronted by an angry mob, led by Matt Davy.

"Calli?"

Her unexpected appearance gave them pause but she could almost smell the fear and the rage that emanated from the crowd, whilst her eyes registered clenched fists, clubs, the glint of steel, and hate-filled expressions all around. United by their prejudice, they had assumed the aspect of a single organism blindly reacting to a perceived threat, rather than a group of reasoning individuals.

"What do you think you're doing here, young lady? I told you to stay away from this shop!"

"Dad?" So it *had* been her father she saw with them at the old school house. How could *he* be a part of something like this, how could any of them? Rage welled-up inside her. Suddenly, these were not the people she knew anymore.

Hydroponics or the stars . . . the anger of the mob or the comfort of the shop. . . .

The shop was about to go, its tell-tale whine building rapidly. She whipped around and threw herself at the door, hoping against all reason that it would still open.

For a brief instant it seemed to resist her, but then it gave inward, and she fell inside, into the arms of the ever-smiling Donovan, who helped her to a chair.

The whine reached a peak and suddenly cut off. She guessed they were on their way. It was strange; she had seen shops vanish a hundred times, but had never been inside one when it did. There was no sense of movement, just a peculiar calm.

Donovan was laughing and hopping from foot to foot, almost doing a jig in his excitement and delight.

"Welcome, Calli," said the serene but nebulous voice of the AI. *"You are the first. The first of many."*

Calli felt exhilarated, buoyant, in total contrast to the despondency that had engulfed her a moment earlier when she thought she was walking away from her dreams forever.

Calli saw again the hate in the faces of the mob, in the eyes of people she knew and loved, and determined to do all she could to wipe away such fear and ignorance.

Only then could she ever come home again.

A woman in a traditional society has two choices: she can conform and do the work that society offers, or she can rebel and do what's considered "men's work." And sometimes she's very good at it, especially when confronted with an unusual challenge.

WORKING THE HIGH STEEL

by Jennifer R. Povey

"She can do the job."

Malisse heard that over her shoulder as she turned to walk away. That her ability to do construction work would be questioned, she was used to. She was not particularly tall, not particularly muscular and very particularly female.

In fact, if she had a dime for every time she had been questioned, belittled, told to go back to the reservation. . . . She shook her head. Her long, dark hair had been braided and then secured at the back of her neck in a style that practice had taught her worked on high buildings.

Or in microgravity. It was, Malisse supposed, inevitable that the tradition of working the high steel would lead her people's men to the highest steel of all.

"Go back to the reservation." Women were supposed to stay home, raise the children, mind the farm. Not be suiting up to get on a space plane to take part in the most ambitious construction project in human history.

Malisse had never been one to mind the farm.

The latest person to question whether she could do the job had been a button pusher.

She'd stepped into the port terminal to hear, "Wasn't there one more of those Mohawk guys?" from the suit.

"That," she said dryly, "would be me."

The surprise on his face as he turned was not positive. He didn't say "go back to the rez" with his mouth, but he did with his eyes, his manner. "M. Gray," he said, reading the name on her overalls. "Umm. Miss Gray."

She resisted the temptation to put her hands on her hips, leaving them instead loose by her sides. "I worked the Berlin arcology," was what she said, a defense that left most men stopping to think. Five men had died when a beam slipped. One of them should not have been there. Thomas should not have been there. Perhaps, one day, the robots really would make them obsolete. Until then, Mohawks would work the high steel. "And I worked Station Alpha."

"Miss Gray, I was. . . ."

And then the foreman had stepped in. "She can do the job."

She'd taken the opportunity to slip back out, to go to the staging area. She had checked in, had done her duty. Marshall was out there.

"Malisse," he said softly.

His voice stopped her in her tracks. "Oh, don't start. We're not breaking the rules."

"The elders still don't approve."

Screw the elders, she thought, but did not say. They had never approved of Malisse, of the handful of other Mohawk women who had chosen to join their men. It broke tradition. The men were supposed to be the ones taking the risks. "The numbers are fine, and nothing is going to happen to me."

She claimed the last word with that, turning and showing him her shoulders and braid as she walked to the prep room. *Screw the elders.*

೮೮ಬಿ೮೦೩೦

"The first problem we had to solve was the carbon nanotubing of the stalk itself. It took many attempts to get a material that could support its own weight. High Terminal helps. It's a counterweight. Its orbital speed will hold the stalk up . . . once it's finished."

Malisse listened. One had to understand the technology one was working with. But, she realized, it was a bridge. Just another bridge. Not that she was worried too much about the elevator.

"The problem is that until the stalk is under full tension . . . it has to be held up by independently motored robots. And as it won't be under tension until the two halves meet; we have to monitor those robots."

Yeah, yeah. This wasn't steelwork, babysitting robots? She'd rather focus on the station construction, familiar and less groundbreaking, but it was work that still needed humans to step outside into space, to face the long fall.

If you fall, you die. Those who said that to her as a way to motivate her to stop did not understand. Once you accepted that, you accepted your own death and embraced it. Only then were you free to live.

She felt eyes on her and turned, her attention drawn from the boring lecture. Marshall. He'd been looking at her a lot since they'd come up. Perhaps it was simply because the only other women on the skeletal station were . . . not Mohawks, for a start. And two of them may have been the first to have lesbian nookie in space. If she was wrong about that, it was because somebody on Station Alpha had beaten them to it.

Marshall, though.

As they maneuvered out of the room, he contrived to bump into her. "Mal, can we talk?"

He never called her Mal. She liked the nickname, which was most certainly why he never called her it. Sometimes he was like an annoying big brother. Most of the time she wanted to hit him. Occasionally she wanted to kiss him. Honestly, he made her de-age to about sixteen. "Sure," she said grudgingly. If she didn't agree to talk to him, then he would harass her until she did.

He ducked off into what would, eventually, be a lab. "Mal," he said finally.

They were both wearing pressure suits with no helmets, which was required. The parts of the station they were occupying had life support, but it was not stable, not certain. "Marshall? Just come out with it."

"I know you're tired of hearing it. I want you to go home after this."

Anger flashed within her. "I can do the job."

"Please. Hear me out."

There was little privacy. She kept her voice quiet. "Go ahead. Get it out of your system. But I won't promise I'll listen."

"That's what I love about you. . . ." He tailed off.

Had he really said love? "Marshall, for. . . ."

"I want you to go home with my ring on your finger, dammit."

It had to be the least romantic proposal ever made. Malisse's eyes widened. "You want. . . ."

"I've been in love with you for years, just waiting for you to fall out of love with the steel. I'm tired of waiting. I thought if I told you. . . ." He looked away.

Something inside her softened just a little. "I'll think about it."

It was all she was willing to give him. Yet, if she married anyone, there were few she would prefer.

Maybe none.

⋐⋑⋐⋑

Marshall shook his head. Maybe he had made a mistake blurting out his intentions to Malisse five months ago at the start of their shift. A man was supposed to be more subtle in his courting.

He was supposed to win her, not try to take her. Now she thought he was after her because the tribal council had asked him to rein in the wayward. The truth was, she really was the woman he wanted to marry.

Malisse, who insisted on keeping her long hair even in the difficult conditions in orbit, and succeeded with never a safety violation. Malisse, who groundside and off duty dressed as if she were on the reservation, but on duty pulled her weight and did her job, who honored and defied their traditions in equal measure.

He couldn't really imagine marrying anyone else. So he tried to overcome his initial mistake.

Of course everyone knew he was courting her. Sadly, the reaction seemed to consist of crude jokes about how she was the only "squaw" on the station. Not that Malisse was a woman to take that word as an insult. She responded to it with a tossed head and a "thank you."

She was not the only despair of the elders. It was all the influence of the white man, this erosion of roles. Yet she could do the job.

In any case, in less than a month, they would be groundside . . . and groundside in triumph. Today had been the day the two strands of ribbon, one snaking up from the Earth, the other down from the station, had met and fused together.

There was always a celebration when the span of a bridge met in the center. It was amazing how much alcohol had been sneaked onto a station that was supposed to be dry.

They were partying in what would eventually be the hangar bay for the orbital transfer vehicles. And yes, there was Malisse, trying to demonstrate the steps of a traditional dance in zero-G. It ended up more slapstick than dance.

He wondered how drunk she was. He himself was stone cold sober. The rum had killed his father, and he was not letting it kill him. It seemed, though, that he might be the only one.

Then she had stopped dancing and propelled herself over to him. "We're almost done here."

"Yeah. How do you follow a project like this?"

"I don't know," she admitted.

Maybe he could persuade her to retire, go home, have a couple of children. She could even come back afterwards. As long as they were his children. He opened his mouth to make the suggestion and closed it again.

He'd worked out Malisse all right. If you told her not to do something, then that would be the very thing she would do . . . and the reverse.

∛ℤ℠ℭ

They'd run every test they could think of. An empty pod had successfully made the full ascent and descent. Twelve hours ago, they had started the first loaded pod on its ascent. The stalk was carrying its first passengers. Right now, it took thirty-six hours to climb the stalk, the same to descend, and the pods could only go one way at a time.

Maybe, Marshall thought, that was the answer to what's next. Six months off to recover groundside fitness, then back up here to work on the second strand and the switching mechanism that would allow them to run down at the same time as up. They'd already talked about it.

Maybe they could increase the speed. Marshall headed to bed. He was not on duty and all the excitement was over. It would take a day and a half for the first passengers to get here. This wasn't the official grand opening. The three people in the pod were two test pilots and one crazy company official. Had to be crazy, to want to risk being the first up.

In fact, there was pretty much nothing for the workers to do. Once they had the stalk tested, then they would start to leave, crossing the bridge they had built. That was only fair. They could run five or six pods on the line at once, as long as they all went the same way.

So pretty much all there was to do now was play cards. High Terminal was not quite finished, but hey, they had to leave something for the next shift to do. Everyone was tired, everyone was a little grumpy.

Marshall caught up on his sleep, and then went to the observation lounge. Malisse was there, staring out at the stars.

This room was going to be furnished, soon enough, for wealthy travelers. For right now, it was still spartan and still open to everyone up there. The pod would be about a third of the way up now, and why was Marshall so worried? Because one always was, when one opened a new bridge. It was natural.

"Hey, Mal."

She didn't turn. "I don't know that I want to go back down."

The centripetal force at High Terminal, now that the stalk was tense, created a tiny bit of gravity. The Earth was now 'above' them, an odd twisting of world views and concepts. Both terminals were at the bottom of the stalk, and Marshall laughed. "No, it's not you. I was thinking that 'down' equals up and both ends are down and. . . ."

"Giving yourself a headache?" She finally turned to face him. "What will you do?"

"Thinking of coming back up for another shift when they start working on the second ribbon."

"Me too," she admitted.

He wanted, for a moment, to reach out to her. He did not. But that might not have been his own hesitation, for at that point the PA system crackled into life.

"We have a problem."

"Houston," Malisse murmured.

જાઉરઈ०ઠ

Houston was what one said when one knew things were bad before anyone admitted it. Malisse was not sure when the word had entered her vocabulary.

Houston was a good word for it. The telemetry indicated the pod was stationary. The robots on that part of the ribbon were nonresponsive. So was the intercom to the pod.

Something had gone badly wrong, and they could not even find out what. The robots and the intercom both got their information from wires running up through the ribbon. Maybe that would have to be changed. Maybe a wireless backup would be a good idea.

"Lost power," Pablo murmured.

She glanced at the Hispanic. That was the most obvious, and also the easiest to fix. In fact, she couldn't think of anything else. But it was for the engineers. Malisse shook her head. They'd fix it or they wouldn't. And if they didn't? She could do nothing about it.

Except that there were three people trapped on that pod.

She pushed through the crowd that had gathered, and out into the corridor. Aha. There was the person she was looking for. Amanda Wilcox liked her for, as far as she could tell, no better reason than the sisterhood of women in the society of men.

"What's actually going on?"

The blonde turned. "There's a break in the power beam. We got a robot down to about fifty feet above the pod and it died. We're sending another to try and find the problem now."

"How long do they have?"

"Three days. It's not a rush."

No, it wasn't, Malisse thought. "Keep me posted? You know me, I worry too much."

Amanda gave her an odd look. "You aren't thinking of doing anything crazy, right?"

"Doesn't seem like there's a crazy solution." But all Malisse could see was Tom falling, falling because she could not hold him. Because a 140-pound woman could not hold a 230-pound man. Nobody else had been near enough to try.

No, she would not cry. But she quietly, quietly made her way toward the bay where maintenance kept the robots. Just checking it out.

There was a guy operating the robot; he was quiet, wearing VR gear and headphones. No, it would take even the robot a little while to get there, unless . . . no. They'd use one already on the stalk.

"Merde," the man swore. French or Canadian? Quebecois?

"You lost it?" she asked softly.

"I can't get it close enough to see what the problem is. It's not a break in the stalk, it's something to do with the pod, some kind of interference shorting things out." He said that in Quebecois French.

She understood him well enough. She understood what had to be done.

ଔଔଔ

"Where the heck is Malisse?" Marshall demanded.

"She's not in her quarters?" Pablo asked. "I saw her stalk out of the room. I think she's. . . ."

"She takes accidents hard. She's probably sulking somewhere."

Except that Marshall was not convinced by his own words. She couldn't have done anything too crazy, because the stalled pod was a third of the way down the stalk.

You would need . . . hell. They had maintenance pods. She wouldn't have. She couldn't have. She would have. And maybe she could have. He knew where the pods were kept and he knew it was guarded, but . . . this was Malisse he was thinking about. And everyone was distracted by the potential public relations disaster. *Let's see, how easy would it be to sneak in?*

Easy. The person normally keeping a watch on the pods was staring at a monitor that showed the stalk arcing downward and, of course, nothing else. He walked right in.

There was a maintenance pod missing. "Malisse." He turned and left the room. He could only think of one person he could talk to. Amanda Wilcox. If anyone knew what Malisse was up to, she would.

He didn't want to call her on the intercom, and he found her in her office. Maybe things would formal up once they had passengers here, but for now he had no problem just knocking on her door. "Have you seen Malisse?"

"Not for a little while. She seemed worried about the pod, asked if I knew what was wrong."

"There's a maintenance pod missing. Somebody's running the stalk and I can't find her anywhere."

Amanda turned pale. "No."

"What?"

"The stalk has no power within fifty feet of the pod."

His eyes widened. "So the problem's actually fifty feet above the pod?"

"No, we think the problem's a short circuit from the pod itself. We're desperately trying to contact the occupants, hoping that one of them can EVA. The two test pilot types are both trained."

He knew now what Malisse was going to do. Had he pushed her to it? No. She had always had that need to prove herself, and ever since Tom had died, she had been even more that way. "She's going to walk it."

"She'll fall. She'll die."

Marshall found a confidence he had not known he possessed. Softly, he said, "Mohawks don't fall."

⋙⋘

The maintenance pod came to an abrupt stop. The lighter the pods were, the faster they ran. The fifty-pound-plus difference between her and any of the men meant she could get here before any of them, and she could use that as an excuse. But the reality was that Malisse had to make up for the past. But the pod had stopped fifty feet above those trapped. And nobody had ever made arrangements for this or even simulated it.

They would now. People always fixed things after the accident. She was in the atmosphere, but at this height, the atmosphere was almost a technicality. Exposure to the cold and the thin air would be lethal, so she put on the construction suit the pod carried. It was designed to be as light as possible. Bracing herself mentally and physically, she opened the outer airlock. The ribbon extended away from her in both directions, smooth and an odd dull gray in color. The only way she could belay herself was a line secured to the maintenance pod. She made sure it was firmly attached to both the pod and her suit.

The wind was tremendous. She had felt wind before, but nothing like this. She knew all about wind that could literally rip workers from a beam and cast them to the ground, but this wind. . . . For a moment she could not move, and she knew that without the suit she would not have been able to breathe. *You fall, you die.*

It was not quite true. She had a chance of survival if the line broke and she fell: secured between the air tanks of the suit was a parachute. *Yeah. Right.* If she attempted to skydive from this height, she would be caught by the jet stream, blown only the Great Spirit knew where. The sky above her was still black. Only the wind told her she was not still in space.

She moved down inch by inch. *You fall, you die.* She embraced her death and made it a part of her life; you didn't work the steel if you couldn't do that. The wind was as the breath of God. *Bit by bit—you don't rush these things; you appreciate them.* Every moment, she felt more and more alive, more and more real. Her life was this, and there was no way she could give it up. The sky, the air, the edge of the world and a drop so fierce that she could not see the bottom. Could not imagine the fall—and any fear faded away. She would not fall. She could not fall.

Her hand slipped on the line. She caught herself, she let the wind aid her, support her. The descent became an eternity. Fifty feet. A short distance and a long one, and then finally her boots touched the top of the pod. Now she needed to find the problem. Undoubtedly those inside had no clue she was here. She fiddled with her suit frequency. Nothing. A crackle, silence. She was on her own. Fine. She often was. She carefully attached a shorter line to the pod itself and released herself from the long line that had supported her as she descended the ribbon.

The pod's climbing mechanism looked okay, but it seemed to have stopped in motion, its crawlers touching the ribbon. She hoped nobody had been hurt in what must have been quite a jolt. She examined it carefully. Well, there was no power to the ribbon here. But why? She pulled herself against the wind to the power receiver. That was the first, most obvious check. If the ribbon itself were damaged, that should be visible.

She pulled the tools from the suit's utility belt and got to work, removing the cover—and a brilliant flash of sparks encased her vision.

γεΩεω

How she was still alive, Malisse was not sure. The splitting headache was clear evidence that she was. The suit had saved her, but the tint of its visor had not been enough to keep out all of the flash, and in lifting her arm to shield her eyes she had slid across the top of the pod and been saved only by the line, which held.

She clawed her way back to the mechanism. There was the problem—a major surge in the power-receiving unit that must have shorted out this section of the ribbon. But the sheer voltage—had she not been in a suit, she would probably have been electrocuted. And she was a construction worker, not an electrical engineer.

Think, woman, think, she told herself. She forced herself to look at the short. Within the case, it seemed that the flaring was increasing; thin as the air was, it was enough so that the fire was not being extinguished. She had to break the circuit, for starters. *Okay.* What did she have? She took a wire grabber, but it didn't seem long enough to reach the contact point—or was it? She had a second one, slightly thinner. *Okay.* She pulled out the roll of tape used to repair suit leaks, breathing harder. *Relax. Don't waste oxygen. Tape them together*, that was it. Could she look in if she squinted?

If she kept her eyes almost closed, she could see where the wires were touching. So small, but it was sending feedback up the ribbon. *There.* The sparking stopped; the harsh light vanished. She twisted, inching up the tool so she could reach in and tape over the hole in the insulation, and she stepped back. *Okay.*

The pod sat there. Well, what had she expected? Every circuit breaker had to have been blown by the short. She hoped none of them was inside. *If I were a circuit breaker, where would I be?*

The wind caught her again. This time it nearly did blow her off the pod, pulling the line so taut that she thought it might snap. She clung on. If she was going to fall, let it be after she got this thing moving.

She clung until the wind slackened a little, and then she inched around the center. *There.* There was the breaker panel. She eased it open. And yes, there were several breakers in the off position. *Flip, flip, flip.* She watched, waiting for them to flip back. And then the crawlers began to power up slowly. The short had been the problem—a piece of worn insulation.

As the pod began to ascend, she realized the full measure of her misjudgment.

ଔଛୡୠ

Marshall was going to kill Malisse. By the time anyone realized she was gone, there was no way to send someone after her. Maybe there never had been. The pod, running at full speed and with its intercom turned off, had sped down the cable, and then stopped at the top of the dead area.

She had to have walked it. Or she was already. . . .

"She may be fine. The suit in the pod was designed for the purpose," Amanda Wilcox said softly. "And she had a parachute."

"Which at that height. . . ."

"I know."

"Mohawks don't fall." He was saying that for himself now. As true as it was, nobody had tried to walk the cable. Walk was the wrong word anyway—it was vertical.

He was at the edge of the control center, a place he should not have been, but where he remained by tacit agreement. Because they all knew he had a thing for Malisse.

Then, a ragged cheer came up from some of the technicians. "It's moving!"

"She did it." But then someone remembered. "The maintenance pod."

"That's not moving—hell, they're going to collide." That was strong language from Wilcox. Assistant directors did not use language like that. "It'll trash the maintenance pod."

"Malisse. . . ." Marshall couldn't finish.

"Wouldn't be in it anyway. I'm sorry, but I don't really see that she could have stayed on when the passenger pod started moving."

"Somebody is going to pay for this," Marshall murmured. "Whoever's responsible for whatever design flaw made her have to go down there."

"She didn't have to."

"She thought she did. One person or three, and a successful test of the ribbon. That's a simple equation." He knew he was right.

"We're going to try and find her suit tracer. She may be retrievable."

Before she ran out of air? He doubted it. But this was Malisse.

The next ten hours were the worst of Marshall's life. They still could not communicate with the pod. It was climbing, yes, and the ribbon itself seemed undamaged, but whatever had happened seemed to have blown out a bunch of systems, including communications. They could not find Malisse. They would have no way of knowing anything until they got the passenger pod up there.

Half the station had gathered in the terminal area. They stared at the metal tube the pod would enter, and then the hole would be irised closed around the ribbon and the pod would slide into the docking area.

It arrived. There was blackening on its outside, but it seemed otherwise undamaged. Its airlock did not open.

Two of the station crew moved forward and forced the manual override. The outer door slid aside, then the inner, with a slight pop of equalizing pressure.

And there were four people inside the pod.

೮ೂ೧೩೯ೲ

"So," Mal said quietly, "when I made the repair, I realized that if the pod started to move, I would never make it back to the maintenance pod before they collided. Then I remembered—"

"The emergency airlock." Marshall interrupted her.

"Right. It's designed to be opened from the outside when the pod is stationery." She breathed in, then out. "I had about twenty seconds until the crawlers kicked in. We're going to need to. . . ."

Scott, one of the engineers, cut in. "It won't happen again. We're going to do a bunch of redesigns to prevent it, including equipment so that if we do have to get to a pod on the ribbon, nobody will have to risk falling."

Malisse smiled. "Mohawks don't fall."

He laughed. "Yeah, I guess you don't. But we're going to make very sure we don't have to test that."

Marshall kept looking at her. She could tell he wanted to hug her. Then, quietly, he said, "I can't ask you to. . . ."

"We have six months before the next shift. We have plenty of time."

Scott gave her the classic crazy look. "You're coming back after that?"

"It's come back or retire."

"You know," he said, "there's going to be another big project starting up about when medical would free you to come back up. We need the facility to build the interplanetary ships. It's going to be the largest space station yet."

Malisse glanced at Marshall. "You up for that?"

"How the hell could I not be?" He paused. "Do you mean. . . ."

"It means I'm thinking about it." That was all she would give him—yet.

She could tell that he had come, finally, to understand that this was who she was. And she knew she could do a lot worse.

Would females still be females in an alien culture? Would their values be the same? Their strengths? Their ability to love?

CHANGER

by Ardath Mayhar

Sashemi lay prone amid the golden grasses, waiting for her skin's adaptive pigments to replicate their colors. She had situated herself to peer, unseen, between the thickly grown stems, keeping watch on the path the aliens would follow as they returned to their shuttle after visiting her grandfather at the People's meeting place.

As she waited, she spread her sensory net widely, webbing its electrical field to catch sounds and motions, as well as appearances. Although this could not translate the alien tongue, through it she could often pick up mental images as they spoke and, in the time since their arrival, she had also studied their spoken language, while keeping unseen watch over them. She now understood a great deal of what they said and much of what they did not say.

Horami, her grandfather, did not precisely distrust the incomers, but he had lived a long life. Dealing with other clans on their own world had too often led to deception and hostility, though all their clans were connected through their sensory nets. These people possessed electrical fields, but it was clear that those were not capable of connecting their minds, even among themselves.

Horami had no intention of taking at their word these strange beings with skins of tan-pink and brown and dusty yellow. While they varied from each other, their skins did not change to blend with the landscape or to complement the decor of a room. Horami considered the newcomers, however polite, to be aesthetically unsound. For many reasons, he had assigned his granddaughter the task of being his unseen eyes and ears, and this seemed to her the most vital assignment he had given her so far.

Sashemi felt her flesh tingling as her skin-cells changed and her hair mingled with the silky strands of the grass. Now she saw through golden eyes, while the line of strangers moved along the path beneath the pala trees, brushing aside their long silver-green fronds. She could hear the murmur of their voices drawing nearer, the shush of their feet in the dust, and she focused her hearing into the web.

They paused in the fringe of shade before venturing out into the golden meadows before them. "The old man seems pretty trusting," said the brown-skinned male, who claimed to be their leader. "He never blinked when we asked for a site for a permanent base, though I'd have been more comfortable if he'd named his price up front instead of wanting to wait and consult with other leaders. That can often spell problems."

The pinkish female, who had hair like russet vines, shook her head. "You're spoiled, Potter, to easy negotiations and to unsuspecting . . . victims. How many bases have you imposed on worlds that were unprepared to cope with the changes they bring and the problems they create for native populations?"

The man made a strange sound like a snort. "As many as I've been assigned to get. The Consortium doesn't care what happens, as long as they have their bases and their trade routes and access to valuable minerals."

The yellowish human spoke. "What about the ore? Not ten worlds in the entire galaxy hold mercanium, and when the bosses learn that this one has it, they're going to want it, no matter what it takes to get it. A private source of that stuff would cut their fuel costs incredibly."

"That is going to be something of a problem," the woman said. The group, intent upon their conversation, now walked on, but very slowly, and Sashemi was grateful for that. As she watched, the woman looked back to make sure no one had followed them. Then she said, "You know that mining mercanium destroys the soil for miles around the site. I think these people won't like that at all. They seem to revere the land."

The leader shook his head. "That's their problem. What the Consortium wants, the Consortium gets!" He picked up his pace, and the group was soon out of hearing.

When they had disappeared from view, Sashemi drew in her sensory field, rose from her grassy hiding place, and shook out her hair. Her skin and hair began to grow darker, picking up streaks of silver-green from the foliage, pale blue from the sky, rusty copper from the rocks along the road into which she stepped. Now she was in harmony with her surroundings, as the People must always be, or they became irritable and incompetent.

She moved back toward the meeting place, her steps soft, her colors changing as she came to the gardens, then the houses of the farmers, and then the low stone wall surrounding the meeting place of the People. As she entered the arched doorway, she shifted her field, and her coloring became dim, a blend of subtle pastels.

Her grandfather came to meet her. The light within the place of meeting was muted and shifting, for this was a place of rest, allowing their pigments to settle and regenerate themselves. When the People met to discuss their problems and plans, it was best for them not to be distracted by constant changes in hues.

"Sashemi, did you overlook the newcomers? Did they say anything of interest?" he asked. His thin face flickered in shades of gray and silver as he led her to his great chair. At his advanced age, the stress of extending his own field so far would have exhausted him, but she felt his intense interest as she perched upon the stool at his feet and composed her mind.

"They asked for a place for their base?" she asked.

"They did. I did not say no, for I suspected that they may possess dangerous weapons that they might use on our people. I told them I must consult other leaders, though that was a lie. I was connected with the other clans through the net. We do not want those outlanders here on our world, Sashemi. Do you not agree?"

Thinking about what she had overheard, she knew he was right. "They said that their Consortium, whatever that may be, always gets what it wants. They also mentioned something called mercanium. Have you ever heard of that?"

Horami drew a sharp breath. All his pigments combined to make his face as pale as a midsummer cloud. "When you were a child, there came a traveler to Gulara from beyond the sky. He was old and wise, curious as a two-year-old. He walked every day around our country, then borrowed my riding beast to travel this continent.

"I almost forgot about him, for he was gone for several winters, but at last he returned, bringing me a new beast to replace the one that died on his journey. He spoke of a very valuable mineral that his people used to fuel their sky-ships, and he called it mercanium. He cautioned me never to allow anyone to mine it, for the operation destroys not only the soil but also the health of those who live nearby."

Sashemi shivered, feeling suddenly cold, though her people seldom covered their bodies except in the direst weather and did not normally feel cold or heat as discomfort. A sudden sense of her people's vulnerability before these unknown aliens filled her with foreboding. She meshed her aura with that of her grandfather, creating between them the web field that would convey their thoughts directly.

Sashemi had a thought. "My brother Lubeni is very near their craft. If he can enter it and listen to their private conversations, that would give us valuable information."

For a long while they sat frozen, their energies concentrated. If they knew almost nothing about the alien people, they knew everything about their own kind. Using their unique abilities, meshing the entire population into one powerful web, they would learn as much as possible about these newcomers; with that information, perhaps the Gulara could find a way to thwart their purposes.

☙❧☙❧

Togu Potter was a pragmatist. For that reason, his employers entrusted him with tasks that more ethical men might have failed to accomplish or might simply have refused to attempt. He was not entirely convinced that the old Gularan, Horami, was as simple and unsuspecting as he seemed. Potter preferred to use his special skills on younger, less seasoned leaders of worlds possessing things the Consortium coveted.

As he led his contact team into the shuttle craft that waited for them, he turned to Vallie, his second in command. "I think we ought to impress the hell out of these people, using the blasters on trees or animals. Even, maybe, on one of those geeks. Once they see the kind of equipment we have, how quickly we can make things too hot for anything we meet, I think it'll make them anxious to cooperate with us."

She nodded, her red braids flopping. "It never hurts to show you have teeth before you need to bite somebody," she chuckled. "I didn't see so much as a ceremonial spear in the entire place. I looked around while you talked with the old fellow. There were no guards, though you'd think even primitives like these would take some precautions when meeting with new kind from off-world."

Ho-Nin, the xenologist, clicked his recorder into its niche and strapped himself into his seat as if they were taking off, though they intended to camp here in the shuttle during their mission. "I tend to agree; these seem to be peaceful creatures, focused on agriculture and, strangely enough, art and aesthetics. The Consortium has dealt with such kinds before, always entirely successfully and without being censured by the

Interspecies Council. So long as the Council doesn't know what we're doing until too late, we're in business, and these primitives don't have technology of any kind, much less our trans-space communicators." He patted the small device at his belt, and the others smiled. "These have made our kind the masters of communication."

Lubeni, hidden in plain view, almost choked with amusement. He had already pilfered one of the things from their storage compartment and found it a poor substitute for the web.

Potter snorted. "Artistic types are always easy marks. All you have to do is fake a lot of philosophical garbage, and they fall for it every time. Farmers, on the other hand, are pretty limited to practical things, so it's easy to misdirect them while you get what you want. I don't know what the combination will be like, but it should be an easy deal to make. By the time they realize what's happening to them because of the mercanium mining, we'll be long gone and they'll be the Consortium's problem."

As the group dispersed to their tasks, Potter was left to his endless record-keeping, which kept him focused on the monitor forming the bulk of his desk. This was most fortunate for Lubeni, whose skin had taken on the color and texture of the shuttle's interior wall behind the desk, even to duplicating the chart and the photograph that decorated it. Having had the benefit of Sashemi's sensory mesh to gain familiarity with the alien language, the young Gularan was busily digesting the information gleaned from the exchange among the humans. There would be more, he was certain, as he continued to settle his body into the pattern of the wall. He would remain here, invisible to their unaccustomed eyes, while they made their plans and discussed the ways in which they hoped to impose their wills upon his people. When he meshed his web again with Horami and the other clans, they would learn much to their benefit.

ೞಌಔಔ೩

The web tingled with communication, as the different Gularan clans pondered this new situation. Bearing in mind the alien who had warned Horami, all those seasons past, they understood that they must move carefully. That warning had included cautions concerning the powers that sent people across the voids between suns.

"Those who send them do not value their own people's lives. Far less do they consider the lives or comfort of those whose property they covet. They will kill without thinking, if it suits their purposes, so be subtle and even deceitful, if you must deal with them. Make them believe that you are children, indeed, lacking the wit to understand what they want and what they intend. For those employed by these powers are as conscienceless as the powers themselves.

"Above all, do not threaten them overtly, for they will use that as an excuse to wipe out all your kind on this world. Though this is against all the laws governing trade between worlds, those who administer those laws are light-years distant and cannot know what occurs beyond their range of knowledge."

Those words had traveled throughout the web, to be absorbed by all the Gularans. Though a generation had grown up since, the words were still there in the very tissues of the people of the clans. Now was the time to take into account the alien and distressing matters they had mentioned, and now was the time when those who wove plans and created patterns must learn how to deal with these folk and their cruel Consortium.

Even as Lubeni slid imperceptibly away from his place on the wall, taking on the tints and patterns of the corridor through which he gained the portal leading out of the alien dwelling, he was considering the problem. Sashemi, the youngest of those who advised their clan, seemed to have a certain gift of visualizing matters as if they were happening before her eyes. The newcomers called this imagination, and Lubeni liked the word. It implied making images to act out scenarios, which was just what occurred when he and Sashemi linked for exchanging ideas.

Now as he waited for one of the aliens to open the portal, he was anxious to meet with her, to concentrate their minds, instead of diluting them with the web connection, and make plans for dealing with this dangerous development. There came a tingle of awareness, and he felt the approach of the man called Potter. That one was alert, aware, not easy to deceive with pattern and color. Lubeni melted against the curving wall, making even his self-awareness evaporate.

The portal sighed aside, and Potter stepped noisily out of the entryway, speaking into his communicator, which seemed to Lubeni a most ineffective substitute for the linkage of the web. "We'll be moving the shuttle tomorrow to the other side of the mountains," he was saying. "We'll wrap up our reports here, and I'll go and con the old guy out of his land this afternoon. We should be off this mudball in a few more days. This is like taking candy from a baby."

While some of his words seemed to be metaphorical, their meaning was all too clear to Lubeni. Today would see the final confrontation that could mean the survival or extinction of his people. Once outside, the Gularan sped toward the meeting place.

Even as he moved, the solution presented itself to Sashemi, once they linked through the sensory net. Her reaction combined shock, grief, and determination. "If our deaths are required, in order to inform their rulers of what they are doing, then so it must be. I go to Horami now to tell him of this, and I will join with him, when the time comes. Did you find it possible to take one of the communicators the aliens use?"

"I concealed it among the lariche bushes beside the track to the meeting place. You should find it easily. Take it to Horami and have him get one of the youngsters who play with such toys to learn to use it now. We must be able to convey to these aliens' home world what they propose and what we intend to do about it. This is the key to our strategy."

"I go at once!"

He could see in his mind the speed at which Sashemi was hurtling toward the hidden device and her kinsman. He sent along the web the details of what he had learned and the specifics of her plan, and a surge of grief and agreement returned to him along the linkage. All the clans of Gulara would be with them, this evening, as they faced this inimical alien. He could only hope that this desperate action would save them.

ଔଔ୧ଠ୭

Potter, Vallie, and Ho-Nin prepared carefully for their crucial visit to the meeting place. Their uniforms were special ones made for such use, invisibly armored against attack from almost any source, and their weapons were polished to blinding brightness. Even Vallie's untidy braids were smooth, and Potter had managed to screw his dour face into a semblance of pleasantness. He was satisfied that they were ready to achieve his goal, and he was determined to do that, whatever actions might be necessary. These fragile creatures hadn't a chance against any of his people, and his weapons should force the issue, no matter what happened.

The golden meadows and colorful woods did not hold his attention. Such matters were irrelevant. Only the welfare of the Consortium and his handsome commissions meant anything to him, and strangely enough, it had never occurred to him to wonder what he was going to spend those commissions on, when the time came. It was the idea of profit that drove him.

However, as he neared the meeting place, he was not thinking even of profit. Alert for any hint of hostility, he scanned the grassy fields, the ornamental trees, the subtle shape of the meeting place itself, without even glimpsing the throngs of Gulari whose chameleon-like skins blended with whatever backgrounds they chose for themselves.

Only when he approached the wide doorway did he see an individual, this one a slight, very tall one, a female he thought, who gestured for him to enter. Followed by Vallie and Ho-Nin, he found himself in a shadowy space that seemed alive with presences, though he could see no one except old Horami and a shimmer that might be the female.

Though he considered courtesies a waste of time, he went through the prepared spiel the Consortium required. The old man and the girl were joined, surprisingly, by another, a young man who seemed to appear from nowhere, and the three heard him out courteously, but before Potter was done he had a feeling that there was no agreement in any of them. "I understand that you cannot decide for all your people here and now, but we want you to speak with them and gain their agreement. This will bring prosperity to you all, in time. Be sure to tell them that."

Horami bent his neck to look down at Potter. "They have heard all your words. They heard the words of another of your kind, long ago, when he warned us of the destruction such mining brings to the land and its people. We share all through our web, for we are linked in ways you do not understand. We are agreed—we will not sign your agreement, and we will not allow your mining on our world."

Potter grimaced. Then he motioned to Vallie to use her weapon, and she incinerated a flowering bush.

Horami stepped forward. "No," he said. "We have stolen one of your devices for communicating with your world, and young Tellit has made it work. I am willing to die in order to show your Council what you are doing here. My kinsmen Sashemi and Lubeni stand beside me. Burn us with your weapons. Kill us here in our own place where you have no right to be. Even now the signal is crossing the void, carrying our words and actions to your home world."

Potter had never been so furious. Without pausing to think, he raised his weapon and destroyed the three standing before him. His own communicator began to hoot. That would be the Consortium, he knew, as his anger began to cool. The Council would soon have the situation in its data banks, and his own life was forfeit.

"Vallie! Ho-Nin! We'd better be off this world ten minutes ago. We're—" he choked and caught himself—"we're outlaws now, and we'd better steal the Consortium's ship before they can divert a patrol vessel to stop us."

ೞ೧೪೧ೞ

The Gulari, linked through the web, knew they had saved their world—for now. Though Horami and Sashemi and Lubeni were still present, as thoughts and memories, within their linkage, never again would they be active participants in the lives and decisions of their kind. Grief wrapped their world, but already the Gulari were debating their next action. Who would be chosen as Eldest? Who would replace the active mind of Sashemi? Those decisions must be made, and with their "primitive" communications abilities, they finished the task before sundown, while the alien ship zipped away desperately through a now hostile sky.

What makes women valuable to men? Their value to the species is undeniable, but what is their value to the other half of that species? Does it depend just on what an individual man wants? Men have been asking for centuries, "What do women want?" It's about time we turned the tables. But what would bring that about?

THE LAST NICE AFTERNOON IN OCTOBER

by Leslie Brown

We stepped out of the Dakota apartments into a crisp fall New York afternoon, a few feet from the spot where John Lennon had died. There were some of the customary tourists taking snapshots of the innocent pavement. Others were looking up at my apartment windows and snapping pictures of the closed blinds. My stalker, Ian, was there as well, pacing the sidewalk. Gregor, my bodyguard, preceded me, and Ian stepped forward, hands outstretched. I waited the required ten seconds and then emerged from the building casually and started strolling down the sidewalk, apparently unconnected in any way to Gregor. I was disguised as a young man, complete with spirit-gummed sideburns. As Gregor dealt with Ian, the rest of the planets aligned for me. A city bus was at the corner of 72nd and Central Park West, its door open, and I made for it, running on my toes so that my feet wouldn't slap the pavement and alert Gregor. I clutched the bus fare in my hand as I had every day for three weeks. I leapt into the bus and slammed the fare into the box by the driver. Sliding into the nearest available seat, I slouched down and pulled on a knit hat that Gregor had never seen me wear. I resisted the temptation to look back toward the Dakota.

A few inches from my nose, the back of the seat TV screen flashed to a reporter standing outside the Dakota. I started guiltily, thinking my escape was already headline news. Then I realized it was a taped story, probably done last week before the leaves had turned fully. Halfway down the block, I slipped off the jacket with its GPS device that they didn't think I knew about, and left it on the bus seat. I wore a heavy shirt of Gregor's under the jacket to hide my contours and to keep me from getting cold. It was a disguise I had faith in: Gregor and I had used it many times to walk incognito down the streets of New York City. I waited a few blocks and then rose and exited the bus.

I ducked into the doorway of a store to get out of sight. I looked up into the blank faces of sex dolls hanging like meat in the window. Their empty blue eyes and round 'o' mouths made me shudder. I lowered my head and walked with hunched shoulders into the lobby of an adjacent hotel. The doorman frowned at me and I faltered, frightened that he was seeing through my disguise, but then his eyes slid past to a wealthy couple entering behind me. I walked to a lobby chair and sat in it, waiting for Gregor. A few minutes later he ran past, a black box in one hand, reading the location of my jacket.

"This isn't the kind of hotel where we allow pickups," the doorman said from behind my chair. I ducked my head in apology.

"My feet were sore from walking. I was just taking a break," I told him, using my lower register.

"Take a break somewhere else," he said, and I left. I was drawing attention to myself and I wanted to avoid that.

There were two policemen waiting to cross Central Park West. I gave them plenty of room, keeping the traffic light post between us. I grimaced when I saw a poster on the switch box with me on it, one of the ones where I wore the blue robe of the Virgin Mary and had a faint halo behind my head. Someone had scrawled 'Whore' across the whole thing in black marker. The light changed, and the cops swaggered across, Uzis unslung, loose-limbed and ready for trouble. I slouched behind and then veered off down a path that went into the depths of Central Park. Gregor would be catching up with the bus by now, finding and clenching my jacket in frustration. I savored my freedom, the aloneness for the first time in ages. I patted my shirt pocket to make sure the paper bundle was still there and not lost during my mad escape.

It was lovely weather for October and everyone was enjoying it. A gaggle of transvestites passed me, purses swinging, smooth faces turned toward the sunlight. They looked like runway models, and I gaped in their wake. One saw me and hesitated. I shook my head, and he pivoted mockingly, showing a muscled flank under his short skirt. I turned away and caught the expression on an older man's face, a man of fifty or so. It was a curious mixture of despair, disgust and greed. He saw me looking at him and carefully wiped his expression into blankness.

I looked for a direction to take and saw a signpost with an arrow pointing to the Memorial Garden. I followed it past the lake and its view of my most recent home. The Dakota was empty now except for me and Gregor. The other residents had all died, one by one, and their bodyguards had packed away all their belongings and left. There was a time I had had more than one bodyguard. There had been Mike and Lewis, Robert-don't-call-me-Bob and Pete. They were reassigned when I received my diagnosis and was no longer the exception to the rule. I remember Pete had had tears in his eyes when he said good-bye. I still missed them, and I hoped the authorities would let me see them again before the end. They had stood by me through the riots and then fended off the wall of reaching hands and pleading faces of which Ian, my stalker, was the only remnant.

I slowed down. I didn't want to reach my goal too soon, because all that was left after that would be to go home again and face Gregor. I felt a twinge of guilt for what I was putting him through. If I had asked, he would have brought me here, but he never would have let me go in alone, as I needed to. I sat on a bench by the arched bridge. Some ducks waddled up onto shore in hopes of crumbs, and I shook my head at them ruefully. They did an annoyed about-face and plunked their fat little bodies back into the lake. Someone sat down at the far end of the bench, and I examined him from the corner of my eye to make sure it was not someone I knew. He was slim and young with a fragility about him. As I elliptically watched him, he buried his face in his hands, and his shoulders started shaking. I debated whether to leave him alone with his grief or not and then wondered if it was all an elaborate come-on. Gravity held me there and I waited, watching the ducks make little vees as they chugged across the lake.

The man kept weeping, and I began to get uncomfortable. This was fresh grief and most people's sorrows were several years old. Finally, I could stand it no longer.

"Do you need help?" I asked him quietly, speaking from my chest to keep my voice low and masculine.

He raised a tear-stained face to me, and I was struck by the intensity of his emotion. This was profound despair. I had seen that emotion before, many times, on TV, on the street, on the faces of some of my bodyguards, but it should not have been so fresh.

"Yeah, I need help. But there isn't any to be had, is there?"

"Did you lose someone?" I asked tentatively. "A mother, sister, wife?"

"Of course I've lost somebody, you idiot. No, this is a brand new problem." He threw something at me and I flinched. A piece of paper fluttered to my feet. I leaned forward and picked it up. I read it several times before I understood it. It had a government logo on the top: United States of America Health Services.

"You've been drafted," I ventured.

"Right on the nose, pal," he said and snatched the paper back from me. He crumpled it into a ball and stuffed it into a pocket.

"Not something you've ever considered, I take it."

"If I'd considered it, I'd be mincing down the sidewalks over there with that bunch of trannies. If I'd considered it, I'd have had the operation and be sitting in some rich man's lap right now." He buried his head in his hands again, his voice laden with disbelief. "How has it come to this already? How is it I suddenly have no rights?"

"As I understand it," I said carefully, "all the men who were willing to become women have done so. I thought they were still at the stage where they were offering huge cash bonuses to men who were willing to have the operation. I wasn't aware that they were forcing people to do it."

He raised his head again and stared closely at me. I fought the urge to pull my hat down.

"You're the same physical type as me, slim, little or no beard, hands like a woman. It's only a matter of time before you get your notice, pal. You should do what I should have done: run to Canada. I left it too late, ignored the rumors. Now I have to go willingly so I can at least get the cash. If I force them to do it, they'll put a chip in my shoulder so they can watch me for the rest of my life, then they'll sell me to the highest bidder who can afford to operate a harem. What kind of fucking life is that?"

"It's not so bad being a woman," I muttered, appalled by what he was saying.

"We'll see what you say after they strap you to a table and cut off your dick."

"Yes, I suppose you're right." I rose to go.

"Don't go. I'm sorry. Look, if you're interested, we could get a license together, say we're a couple. If we were declared homosexuals, we'd be exempt from the draft."

I looked down into his desperate face.

"Why is that?"

"There's lots of guys hooking up together now for family, companionship, whatever. They're becoming the majority now, a political force, and the government won't go after them. The rich guys that want women, they don't want to think about what their girlfriends used to be, and they particularly despise the gays. We'd be safe together until that kind of man dies out."

"If that's an acceptable solution for you, why haven't you asked people you know? Why proposition a complete stranger in Central Park?"

"I don't have anyone," he whispered. "My best friend lost his wife in Year Two of the virus and his daughter a year later, as soon as she hit puberty. He killed himself six months after that. There's no one else I could stomach to touch me and they check, to make sure it's not a charade. You seem nice, even pretty like a woman. I could manage, I think."

"No, I'm sorry," I told him.

"Please."

I turned and walked away as fast as I could. He didn't call after me. The afternoon had lost its savor. Suddenly I was aware again of the skin pulling tight on my right breast, the lump that grew and twisted there. My hand rose to knead and poke at the cancer as had become my habit the last month or so, and I forced my hand down into a fist at my side. I rounded a corner and saw the memorial garden stretching as far as I could see. Parallel bulletin boards zigzagged their way across the landscape. On them, thousands, millions of pieces of paper fluttered and flapped. I approached the nearest section. There was no space. The faces of women looked back at me: grandmothers, wives, teenagers, even photos from magazines of lipstick models. Many were yellowed and tattered by the wind, but a lot were new as well. I kept walking. There was face after face, with some of the pins having little flowers on the head, crowning the loved one. I kept going, but there was no opening in the wall of paper. I didn't want to cover someone else's picture.

There was an old man standing in front of a segment of bulletin board near to me. His pants were belted half way up his torso. He was beckoning to me.

"Come, come, come."

I went over cautiously.

"You looking for a place to put a picture? There's a place here beside my Ester and she won't mind. Or if she did mind, she never would say anything. Look, I'll move her over a bit. You got a snapshot?"

I pulled the photo from my pocket and before I could yank my hand back, he snatched it from me and busily pinned it to the bulletin board beside a picture of a sixty-something woman in a brown cardigan and shapeless dress. A slightly younger version of the man beside me stood with his arm protectively around her shoulders. In my photo, six women smiled at the camera—the Dakota Six—and I hoped the old man wouldn't recognize us.

"Ester will take care of them. All gone, are they?" he asked. Then unerringly one gnarled finger pointed at me. "Except for you, eh?"

I gathered myself to run but he shook his head quickly.

"Nah, nah. Don't worry. I won't tell. You want to walk in the sun like the rest of us, eh?"

"Just for this afternoon," I whispered. "Just to do this, so people won't forget us."

"You were the youngest, eh, they called you 'The Princess in the Tower?'"

"That's what the media called me, but the original Tower princess was a prisoner, and so was I. At least she got to go free eventually."

"Ah yes, the first Queen Elizabeth."

I raised my eyebrows and he chuckled.

"Some people still care about their history. Me, I was a professor of social history. I am living now, at the perfect time, during the biggest upheaval mankind has ever known. I am very pleased to meet you."

"I'm afraid I can't contribute anything more to your study of history. My story is well known."

"But not the ending."

"Yes, that too, I'm afraid. I have the cancer. The virus got me finally."

"Ah," his face sad, he patted my arm. "Sit, sit with me."

We sat on a bench together. Up and down the wall of bulletin boards, men came and went. Some to touch a photo, others to rest with their foreheads against the paper, hands balled up at their sides.

"You were a symbol of hope, that we wouldn't lose all of you."

"There might still be some women left alive in remote areas but the virus is everywhere, and sooner or later they'll all come into contact. The Dakota Six's immunity was an illusion, and we were a false hope. It's a relief, in a way, not to bear the expectations of the whole world any more and to not have to put up with the endless testing. Some of the doctors actually blamed us for their failure to discover why we weren't sick. I remember Greta. . . ." I trailed off, remembering my beautiful, angry friend.

"What did Greta do?"

"She told them where to go, where they could put their needles. They strapped her down, tranquillized her. That day, all illusion that we were cherished vanished. It's best I'm dying now. I don't want to be here alone any more."

"Nah, nah. Don't say that. There are those still who love you, heh? Those who would cry when you go? Remember, while there's life, there's hope."

"What hope is there left? I sat beside a young man today who's being forced to become a woman. And what's the point? This is the last generation of mankind. The last girl children are being held chemically in permanent childhood. What kind of life will they have? Already they have cults forming around them, just like mine."

"Can you blame men for trying to keep the idea of woman alive? It's bad business what they are doing with this 'draft,' but it will calm down when they find the demand isn't as great as they thought it would be. I am putting my faith in science. We'll have children again. Your children, too, for I think you gave eggs to be frozen like every other woman still alive in Year Two."

"Yes, of course. It was another gesture of hope. Do you know they tried to make me have a child? I was the only one left of child-bearing age. They thought that if I was resistant to the virus, a daughter might be too. I had no choice in the matter, and when I didn't conceive by artificial means, they wanted me to pick a man or three. I got the cancer before they could force me to choose. I thanked God for it. I couldn't watch a daughter die when she hit puberty, and that's the only test for a child of mine, to see if she was resistant. So now they've pulled everyone off my detail except for one bodyguard and a doctor on call. It's a deathwatch now."

"And now you've escaped. What will you do?" He pulled a stick of gum from his tattered sweater pocket and offered it to me. I shook my head.

"Go back. There's no freedom any more for a woman in this world."

"You choose to go out with a whimper and not a bang?"

"What kind of bang could I make?"

"A little bang, maybe one only you can hear."

I stared at him, but he was busy unwrapping his gum. He put the stick in his mouth and carefully folded the foil into a little square that he tucked back in his pocket. Without looking up, he nodded to my right.

"There's someone staring at you. Do you know him?"

I turned casually and met the eyes of the middle-aged man who had been staring before at the transvestites. His eyes widened, and he started shouting and pointing. "It's her, the last of the Dakota Six! There she is, right there!"

A crowd started to gather, and I felt sick. This was going to end badly, and Gregor would blame himself. My new friend stood up, and I thought he was going to flee, which would have been the smart thing to do. Instead, he took my arm in his and started walking me back the way I had come. The shouting man blocked us. He was so overwrought, spittle was flying from his lips. Over his shoulder I could see Gregor running down the path following by Ian, my stalker. Both men looked panicked.

"Please let the lady by," said my friend. The shouting man lunged forward, hands outstretched, and I gave a little shriek. Then there were five strangers between me and my attacker. He bounced off their chests and fell.

"She has no right to be alive. Not when my Mary's dead," he screamed from the ground. Two of my protectors knelt beside him, and one started patting his shoulder. My attacker buried his face in his hands, sobbing. Gregor and Ian reached us and were trying to get to me. My protectors surged back at them, thinking they were hostile.

"It's okay, let them through," I called in my normal voice and every head turned involuntarily. Gregor pushed through the gap my protectors had made and swept me up in a tight embrace.

"Damn it, Elaine."

"Sorry, sorry," I whispered into his neck. I felt him shaking. I had never realized his feelings for me: he had been the only bodyguard not to ask me to sleep with him, which was why I requested that he be the one to stay.

The old man had let go of my arm when Gregor had come but I heard him chuckle in my ear. "Nice looking young man. What does he think about bangs and whimpers?"

I laughed for the first time in what seemed a long while. I pulled a little out of Gregor's embrace. "Gregor, I want you to meet. . . ." But when I turned, the old man was gone. Ian was at my side, looking anxious. I gave him a fond smile, which made him blush. "Let's go home, guys. I'm done here."

We started walking back to the Dakota, escorted by a crowd grown quiet, reverent. Now and then I felt touches on my hair, shoulders and arms, like butterflies alighting. I spared one final glance toward the bulletin board at my five friends. And Ester stood guard over them, protected in turn by the man with his arm around her shoulders.

Just as men have no corner on heroism, they have no corner on wickedness. And sometimes both qualities exist in the same woman. If they do, they may have many effects, but one of those effects is to make the women in whom they reside a lot of fun to know.

LADY BLAZE

by Lee Martindale

Only some idiot in the middle of a testosterone fit would have named so sweet a ship the *Hercules*. It was the first thing I changed about her. It was also the least expensive part of the overhaul.

I had big plans for the *Lady Blaze*, plans intimately tied to the big plans I had for myself. And since those plans most definitely did not involve hauling cargo in-system or packing colonists in like cordwood and dumping them on Nowhere Prime, I told the refitters she was headed for service as a holiday ship. Which, come to think of it, wasn't too far off the truth.

Now that I've whetted your appetite, let's back up and get acquainted. A lot of people on a lot of planets call me by the name of my ship, and that's fine with me. It fits us pretty well. We're both big, majestic ladies who take up a lot of space. Neither of us is more than middling long, but we're both beamed wide and shapely. And we both trail a curtain of fire when we move.

In her case, it's a Dante drive and doublers. In mine . . . well, in my younger days, my hair was a 100% natural marvel, a mane of auburn curls that reached to my waist. It gave me two of my other names: the Red Amazon—and why they laid that one on me, I'll never know, given that *both* these beauties are right where they should be—or just plain Red. I still answer to that one, thanks to the planets where henna is a cash crop.

I've worked under more names than I can remember. If a house already had a "Caitlin," I didn't think twice about grabbing something not already on the menu. At one time or another, I've been every stone, precious and semi-precious, in the gem catalog, not to mention stars, planets, galaxies and goddesses. And don't even ask how many times I've answered to "the one with green eyes, the three-hourglass figure and all that hair."

If I think real hard, I can even remember the name I was given at birth. I can remember it, but it hasn't fit in a very long time.

By now, you've probably figured out what I do for a living, so let's get a few things clear right up front. I never had any illusions about what I was, what the job was about, or what I was selling. I don't have any illusions about what I'm selling now. There were never any dreams about using the job as a stepping stone to "better things"—meaning marriage—or that Prince Charming would stroll into the front parlor some evening and "take me away from all this." I didn't want to be taken away from "all this"; I liked "all this." If I didn't, I wouldn't have gone into the Profession in the first place.

By now, you've also figured out what those plans for the *Lady Blaze* involved. Not that I ever claimed it was an original idea; I knew better than that from firsthand experience. I never even claimed that a woman could pull it off better; I knew better than that, too. Women are just as capable of victimizing other women as men are, maybe more so. They have the advantage of that old myth about all women being sisters. Gives 'em a foot in the door, something of an edge.

The Profession has its problems, has had ever since the first Neanderthal bartered a hunk of mammoth for a piece of tail. One pleasure ship and a savvy madam aren't going to wipe out several millennia of meanness, greed and downright stupidity.

Besides, that qualifies as a "noble notion," and I haven't had one of those since . . . well, never mind. Let's just say that the *Blaze* was about free enterprise, profiting from sound business practices, and luck—by *my* definition of the word. Which is having the good sense to learn as much as you can about as much as you can whenever the opportunity arises, not wasting effort on revenge, and not wasting time and hope on what the odds are overwhelmingly stacked against. Oh yeah, and knowing when to throw those last two out, give it your best shot, and to hell with everything else.

Which is how we ended up making planetfall at Ysbet Tertiary one fine morning (local).

Ysbet wasn't the kind of place we'd normally consider a port of call. We generally preferred planets that had seen enough development to start building an economy and small-to-medium-sized centers of occupation, but not so much that the enterprising local talent had started operating as other than independent contractors. Cutting into the trade of established houses just isn't good business, and it plays hell with public relations.

Ysbet had seen development, all right, to the point that any Golden Age it might have had was generations past and long since gone none-too-gently to seed. It was a source of some amusement among travelers in that region that all three of its spaceports had been kept operational, although in the case of our destination, it was a definition of "operational" only masochists, jackleg mechanics, and folk engaged in less-than-legal pursuits could love. Which was precisely why it was our destination.

Like every other spaceport, there was a native quarter outside the gates of Ysbet Tertiary. BackGate had the reputation of being poor, dangerous, and a good place to stay away from unless you were suicidal or up to something on the shady side of legal. Me and mine were anything but suicidal, and what we did hadn't been illegal for centuries, except on a few worlds colonized by theocrats and kindred busybodies. What brought us to BackGate was the illegal nature of the activities practiced by the object of our search.

ଔ◌ଔଛଓ

Felicity Adams came aboard with references from one of the long-established houses in Nadim and a delicate beauty that would certainly appeal to the vast majority of my clientele. She was bright and funny, with an underlying—for want of a better phrase—nurturing quality that would have clients coming back and asking for her by name. And three minutes into the interview, I was fairly sure she'd never turned a trick in her life. Oh, she was doing a fair enough imitation of a higher-class working-girl in search of new opportunity, but "imitation" was the operative word here, one straight out of your better class of vidfiction.

Cutting to the chase saves time, especially in a business where time, along with a few other things, is money. "Okay," I said, at about three and a half minutes into the interview, "we both know you're not a whore, so why don't you tell what this is really about?"

She got points for not getting flustered, and more for not trying to play me any further than she already had. She just went very calm and met my eyes for the first time. "I'm trying to find my son."

She'd given her age at 25 Standard, and I was willing to bet she'd tacked on a couple of years in a wrong-headed effort to appear more "marketable." So we couldn't possibly be talking about someone old enough to have gotten an itch and run away. "How old?

"He's three."

And by Lilith's sunken dugs, hadn't I heard this sorry tale often enough. "The old man up and split with the kid one fine morning?"

This was where she was supposed to break down in tears, blubber out the whole story, and beg me to help her. She didn't.

"No," she answered. Just that one word, clear and calm and still looking me in the eye.

I silently called myself several kinds of old fool and a few less-flattering things. Then I suggested she tell me what had happened, preferably with a large helping of the truth.

Felicity Hellmanns had grown up on Arabi; Boris Adams had been one of a shipload of specialty colonists recruited to fill holes in the local talent pool. His specialty was pharmacology, which ended up translating to opening an apothecary in one of the suburbs of Nadim. They'd met when she'd applied for a bookkeeper's job, and married less than a year later. A year after that, their son had been born. They built a house "in the country," and enjoyed a happy, prosperous life. A happy, prosperous life that ended one night, a few weeks prior to the conversation in progress, in the roar of engines, the whine of energy bolts, and the screams of a toddler wrenched away from his mother's arms by strangers.

"When I came to," she continued, "Boris was dead, and Nathan was gone. Offworlders, the constable decided, already headed to a system where they could sell Nathan to someone who brokered 'adoptions.' He said Boris died immediately, didn't suffer, and that I'd been," her voice faltered for the first time since she'd started talking, "lucky."

I'd heard that sorry tale more than a few times, too. "You were," I said, my voice gentle. "And lucky it's me you tried to fool. I've got more scruples than most . . . and if you let that get out, I'll deny it." I looked her straight in the eye again. "You're alive and young and healthy. It doesn't feel like it right now, and it takes time, but life does go on." And didn't I know the truth of that one several times over. "Mourn your husband, mourn your son, and then get on with living. Besides," my voice got a little harder-edged, "you don't even know who took the kid, or where they were headed with him."

"That's true," she conceded, "but I overheard enough to know what I'm looking for, if not who."

"And that is?"

"Are there many brigand ships captained by a woman?"

There was a long pause, then I said something reverent and biologically improbable. And noticed, just incidentally, that she didn't even blink. Just looked hopeful. "There are a couple of things you need to agree to before I even think about taking you on. First, I may own this ship, but I don't and won't put anyone else in danger without their say-so. And I'll tell you right now that old myth about hookers with hearts of gold is just that . . . a myth. You're going to have to convince my people, all of them, to go along."

"Agreed."

"Second, this isn't a passenger transport or a ship full of merctroops. It's a bordello. You're going to have to earn your keep."

"He's my son. I'll do whatever's necessary."

I snorted, but let it go at that. "Finally, if we do this and we do find him—a long shot, at best—there won't be any charging in like avenging angels. We'll buy him back if we can, steal him back if there's an easy shot at doing that, or we'll walk away. No trying to get revenge for the death of your man. Understood?"

"Understood."

An hour later, the parlor cabin was stacked two deep with every living soul on board, except for one fabio standing watch, hooked in via audiolink. The *Blaze* wasn't due to open for several hours yet, and he was there to make sure our meeting remained "family business." Felicity told her story, and I'll be damned if that bunch didn't prove me a liar. Turns out they did have hearts of gold, or at least soft spots for widowed mothers of kidnapped kids. They were all for it. All but one, that is.

By the deal I'd struck with Felicity, that should have been enough to put the kabosh on things right there. And would have been, if I hadn't succumbed to a soft spot of my own. Jayla, the one holdout, opined, "I'm not interested in losing trade for the sake of some planet-hugging, goody-two-shoes housefrau who wouldn't give us the time of day if she didn't need something. And besides, we haven't a clue as to who took the brat."

"Actually, we do," I cut in smoothly. "Unless things have changed in the last few months, we know exactly who we're looking for. Sick Jenn Shick."

For a count of about three, there wasn't a sound. Then Jayla glanced at Felicity before looking at me with the smile that gladdened the hearts of submissives everywhere we landed. "I'm in."

Yeah, they proved me a liar. And I proved myself a softer touch than I'd prefer anyone realize. Having Felicity take over cashier duties and keeping the books would be more valuable to me than having her entertaining customers. At least it sounded business-like when I told her.

☙ ❧ ☙ ❧

We've all heard the stories about prostitutes who served as spies for one side or another in this or that or another war. Most people not engaged in my line of work figure them for lies. Most people not engaged in my line of work don't realize that hormones aren't the only things that run loose when a client's getting down to fun and a whore's getting down to business. Especially when she's the prettiest thing he's ever seen and ever likely to have. Especially when she hangs on every word, and is extremely skilled at asking extremely veiled questions.

We spent the next several months doing that kind of nosing around. Gathering seemingly unrelated bits of information in the course of plying our trade along a flight path that would have been called "meandering" by anyone interested in the wanderings of one mid-sized, privately owned pleasure ship. Every random remark, every rumor, every boast made by a client to impress one of my employees went into the information pool.

Funny thing: We rarely had to resort to nudging conversations onto the subject of Sick Jenn. If she'd made planetfall anywhere near where we were, she was the prime topic of pillow talk from most of the local heads on our pillows. It was about evenly split between those who thought she should be blown into molecules in an unmarked region of space and those who considered her some kind of folk hero. The one thing that surprised me was how many of our customers wanted role-playing that involved her. Jayla started catering to that crowd, with the net result of a tidy profit and solid leads brought in. But then Jayla always did have a strong stomach.

Be that as it may, the *Blaze* closed in on our quarry. Jenn Shick's *Vulture* was berthed three slots over when we put in at Ysbet Tertiary that morning.

೮ଓଅ୫୦๊

We landed declaring "repairs, rest, and relaxation" as our "reasons for visit," after my captain and engineer had seen to it we had enough of the first part to make it look plausible. As for the latter two, even someone who enjoys her work needs a break once in a while, and it gave us all an excuse for wandering around BackGate. There was even an answer for an off-hand and very deliberate query by the port inspector as to why Tertiary instead of one of the other two, better-appointed, spaceports: "It gives me an opportunity to visit old friends."

That last was almost true. One of the brothels in BackGate was owned by a woman I'd worked with years before, another by the parents of one of my current employees. Combined with the aforementioned good relations we had, thanks to that policy of not cutting into local business, and a series of encrypted vidlink exchanges during our long approach, we had assurances of warm welcomes—and allies—where we needed them.

Most of the employees went off to play tourist, with ears open and plenty of local currency to engender good will and unguarded conversation among local shopkeepers. The captain and my engineer were primed to do likewise among SpaceMil and civilian station personnel. Maria, Felicity and I headed for the establishment owned by Maria's folks.

Three experienced professionals, a loving daughter, and a bright, highly motivated amateur can put on quite a show when need be. The few casual observers in the common room saw three old friends, one loving daughter, and one protégée greeting each other after a long time apart, just as they were supposed to. Then we retired to the private living quarters—actually, to a meeting room deep under the building—and got down to the business at hand.

I'd been fond of Klinda M'bano back in the day and was glad to see she'd done well for herself, the nature of BackGate notwithstanding. And I liked Flossa Menderos-Simmons the moment I met her. I'd already been halfway to that opinion based on what I'd heard from—and observed of—Maria. My opinion crept higher as we chatted while waiting for Maria's father to join us. It settled comfortably in when we wasted no time getting down to business.

Klinda was the first to speak, looking at Felicity. "It's been confirmed; there were no children on board the *Vulture* when she made port last week. I'm sorry."

"Thank you," the young mother replied, carefully maintaining the demeanor of calm poise. She'd picked up a few tricks from us, it seemed. "Is there any information on where the ship's been?"

"Some," Billem Simmons answered. "although not nearly enough to backtrack her to Nadim. And nothing to determine what happened to your son. It's possible he was sold to a broker and adopted. It's just as possible . . ." his voice trailed off, reluctant to say the words.

Felicity supplied them herself. ". . . that he's dead. I understand. Knowing one way or the other would be a great help."

"If what I've heard of Shick is true," I put in, "she plays things as close to the vest with her crew as she does with anyone else. Which means no one person on the crew will know everything, even if each has a piece of it and can be made willing to share. The only one who's going to be able to give us the information we want is Sick Jenn herself."

There was a moment or two of general consensus on the difficulty of same, culminating on the equal difficulty of getting her separated from her crew long enough to try. It was Klinda who provided the bright spot on that last. "The crew of the *Vulture* will be getting entertained at my place tomorrow night. Private party, booked this morning, at an obscenely high fee. It's something she does the night before they head out for another raiding run."

Glances were exchanged around the table as slow smiles began to form. "And Shick herself?" I asked lightly.

". . . will be alone in the ship," Klinda replied, with a smile of her own, "except for one masseuse and a chaperone, also provided by me."

I'll give Felicity credit; she said nothing until we were back in the ship and in my office. And she didn't say anything immediately once there, because I cut her off as she was taking breath to speak. "No."

"Why not?"

"First, because you're too close. Second, we agreed from the beginning that there would be no getting revenge for your man, and I'm not sure I trust you to keep to that agreement when push comes to shove. Third, you could be recognized. And fourth, you aren't a trained masseuse."

She took a deep breath, and I watched her settle her features into a look of cool calm. Her voice was even when she spoke. "First, I am close to this, which is precisely why I *should* be there to question her. Second, revenge doesn't find out what happened to Nathan, and that's my only interest. Third, even if Shick saw me in town before the attack, I don't look at all now like I looked then. And fourth, Jayla's been teaching me several different styles of massage, and says I'm quite good at it."

We stood there, eyes locked, for a ridiculously long period of time. Then I gave a detailed listing, with footnotes, of the numerous ways she was a fool. An even more detailed list, with footnotes, of the even more numerous ways I was one, as well, followed. That tends to happen when I give in.

⚬⚬⚬

Jenn Shick's quarters in the *Vulture* didn't look like I expected, but then, neither did Jenn Shick. The former, in sharp contrast to what we'd seen of the ship as we were being escorted through, was clean, spacious, and rigged for understated luxury. Sick Jenn herself was tall and spare, and reminded me more than a little, in build and movement, of retired SpaceMil females I'd known. Not exactly what I expected from someone with the reputation of being a homicidal, psychotic outlaw.

Until she looked me over, hard and suspiciously. To say there was nothing human behind her eyes may seem a bit fanciful, but it's as close as I can come to describing what I saw. Or, rather, didn't see. She gestured for my identification, and I handed over the packet Klinda had given me, dropping my eyes in what I hoped she'd take for respect, submission, or anything that wouldn't be interpreted as a challenge. She scrutinized the documents carefully before handing the packet back to me with a dismissive nod.

She turned her attention to Felicity, and her eyes narrowed. One hand came up and grasped the younger woman's chin hard, holding her face in place as she examined it for an uncomfortably long time. *Blessed Magdalena*, I entreated silently, *keep the girl steady or we're both dead.*

Releasing her rough hold, Jenn stepped back and gestured for Felicity's papers, going over them even more carefully than she'd gone over mine. And I'll tell you right now, it was harder to maintain the posture—hell, it was harder to just keep breathing normally—than when it was me under the gun.

Finally and apparently satisfied, Jenn turned to our escort. "You're done here, Oyster. Join the others. Usual drill . . . make sure they know I'll gut any man who comes back to the ship before morning. Get 'em all back at oh-seven hundred local. We lift at oh-eight."

"Yes, ma'am," came the reply, before he nodded and left, closing the door. We heard retreating footsteps, followed by the echoing clang of the gangway hatch, and, finally, the scraping whir of it being dogged. All the while, Jenn watched us with undisguised suspicion.

At last, she gestured toward a luxury massage table—the kind one found in fancy passenger transports, fine hotels, and top-tier cat houses and, in all likelihood, pillaged from one such during a raid—set up in the middle of the cabin like an altar. "Make your preparations there. I'll be out of the shower in a few minutes." She turned and disappeared through another hatch.

Locking eyes with Felicity, I shook my head. Talking, at whatever volume, including whispering directly into each other's ear, was not a good idea. Signing, in any form, including the subtlest of Professional hand codes, probably wasn't either. But not conversing might also set off someone as viscerally paranoid as Jenn Shick. As Felicity pulled various massage oils and the like from the kit she'd carried, we made inane small talk, liberally seasoned with fear, awe and admiration for the woman in the next compartment. In other words, exactly the kind of thing Jenn would want to hear if she was eavesdropping.

The subject of our discussion appeared a few minutes later, short blond hair damp and slicked back, her body wrapped in a bath sheet. Her eyes swept over Felicity's preparation, and she nodded once, apparently satisfied, before dropping the covering and stretching out, face down, on the massage table. Felicity deftly floated a fresh drape over her, folded it down to expose the neck and shoulders, and began working the muscles under her hands. In nearly no time at all, the woman on the table began to visibly relax.

A few minutes later, she tensed up again as Felicity slapped a plegiapatch at the point where neck met shoulders and pushed the woman off the table and onto the floor. A string of profanity followed the thump of limp flesh hitting metal deck. That's the thing about getting supplies from unsavory sources; what you end up with is generally just as unsavory. The patch Felicity used was one of a type rumored to be used at times by not exactly official entities interrogating persons of particular interest. It completely cut off motor control signals to arms and legs, while leaving involuntary functions—like breathing and heartbeat, and sensory functions like feeling pain—entirely intact.

Felicity dragged Sick Jenn to one wall and propped her into a sitting position with her back against it. She stood for a moment regarding the still-cursing brigand before leveling a short, swift kick to her ribs. "Much better," she said, stepping back a bit and regarding the gasping woman for a moment. "Let's talk about the concept of family, *Captain*. On Arabi, where I grew up, it's something we learn at our mother's breast and carry into childhood. We take it to our marriage beds and our graves. There's nothing more important than family. We'll do whatever's necessary to protect it."

"Are you going to be getting to a point anytime before dawn, or should I call refreshments in?" Of the many things said about Sick Jenn Shick, that she was one tough bird seemed to be accurate.

"Indeed," Felicity replied in a conversational tone. "Do you recall a visit you made to Arabi some months back? Landing at Nadim . . . or rather, the outskirts of Nadim . . . killing a man, savaging his wife, and stealing their child?"

"What if I do?" Jenn growled.

"You're going to tell me what happened to the child. You're going to tell me where you left him."

Jenn snorted, then make a suggestion to Felicity that I was fairly sure the younger woman wouldn't be interested in. Felicity smiled coldly, then took a step forward and stomped down hard on an extended knee. The sound of bones being crushed was loud; the sound of screaming was louder.

Felicity waited for the screaming to subside. "Let's try that again, shall we? Where did you leave the boy?"

"I spaced him," Jenn snarled through gritted teeth. "Little bastard died before I could deliver him to a broker."

The second kneecap met the same fate as the first. "You can take that to mean that I don't believe you, Mother."

It takes quite a bit to surprise me. And apparently I wasn't the only one caught by surprise. "What the hell are you talking about?" Jenn barked when she'd stopped screaming.

"When I was a little girl, my parents sat me down and told me the story," Felicity replied. "How the midwife was called to a spacers' wayhouse one night, how she found a young woman in hard labor, how she delivered a healthy baby girl. How the midwife took the baby home with her, how she and her husband adopted her and loved her and raised her. Raised her to believe in the importance of family."

Felicity grew silent as she regarded the woman in front of her. "I loved the Hellmanns as if they were my own parents. They *were* my parents, in every way that matters. But I never understood how a woman could give up her baby, give away her own blood. I always wanted to ask you about that."

Jenn shrugged before meeting Felicity's eyes. "I didn't have much choice. Signed on as crew of a free trader, no place to raise a kid and no prospects of staying groundside to raise one, either. Signing you over for adoption to the Hellmanns gave you a better life than I could ever have hoped to give you if I'd kept you. Loved you enough to do that, I did."

Felicity's lips lifted in a slow smile. Then she lashed out with another kick to Jenn's ribcage. "You can take that to mean I don't believe that, either. You see, when my parents died, I

found the paper you signed that night. Not an adoption paper . . .
a bill of sale. 'In consideration of services rendered.' You sold
your own flesh and blood—me!—like a sack of surplus grain.
That's how I learned your name, Mother. That's when I started
hating you. And that's when I promised that, one day, I'd find
you, whatever it took. Your raid on the Adams place told me you
were still alive." Then she turned to me. "And you gave me the
way to find her."

"So," I spoke up at last, "that story you told me about
your husband being killed and your son being abducted was a
lie."

Felicity shook her head. "Not entirely. Her men killed
Boris Adams and took his son. Nathan's my nephew, my sister's
child." She crossed to the massage kit and pulled out a pistol,
leveling the muzzle at the woman against the wall. "One last
time. Where did you leave him?"

That Jenn could laugh, given the pain she must have been
in, amazed me. And a nastier laugh I hadn't heard in a very long
time. "You stupid cow," she taunted, "don't you know better
than to try to threaten someone who can't be threatened?"

"Who said anything about threatening you, Mother," she
said before squeezing the trigger.

Jenn's body stiffened as the energy bolt hit her in the gut,
and for a second or so, the two women locked eyes. Then Jenn's
eyes went wider as fire sizzled its way through her torso and she
incinerated from core to extremities. For five eternal seconds,
Sick Jenn Shick burned in agony, a screaming banshee suffering
the tortures of the helpless damned. Then it was over.

I looked at the pile of smoking, oily ash on the deck,
caught the reeking stench in my nose, bent over, and began
retching. Gentle hands took my shoulders, steered me into the
bathroom, and held my head as I threw up everything north of
my toenails.

"We'd better get out of here," I said after I'd recovered
enough to speak. I'd called everyone back to the *Blaze* before

we'd headed over to the *Vulture,* and we could leave port on fifteen minutes' notice.

"You'd better get out of here," Felicity corrected. "I'm staying. When the crew comes back, they'll be told that Jenn Shick decided to retire and passed the family business on to her daughter."

"And your nephew?"

"Between the logs and the crew, I'll find him."

"You probably will," I laughed. "You owe me one, you know."

Felicity returned my smile. "I owe you several. Now get going. And tell everyone I said thanks."

S20

We cleared a good three hours before dawn local, with no harm done except payment of a small bribe to a merctroop transport captain for swapping places on the lift list, and the promise of a bit of free "entertainment" the next time our ships hit port at the same time.

My people surprised me again, when I told them what Felicity had really been up to and a slightly modified version of what had transpired aboard the *Vulture*. I'd expected them to be upset that she'd lied. They weren't. "You do whatever's necessary to take care of family," seemed to be the consensus. And while they all were a bit sad to see Felicity gone, it was Jayla who missed her the hardest and longest. I don't even want to try figuring out the why of that one.

The *Blaze* continues to be about free enterprise, profiting from sound business practices, and luck—by *my* definition of the word. Which is having the good sense to learn as much as you can about as much as you can whenever the opportunity arises, not wasting effort on revenge, and not wasting time and hope on what the odds are overwhelmingly stacked against. Oh yeah— and knowing when to throw those last two out, giving it your best shot, and to hell with everything else.

There may come a time in the future when women are not all human. But they're still women.

THE MAKING OF HER

by Sarah Ellender
& Michael O'Connor

The light of the afternoon sun was heavy on the Sygia's back as she followed Lady Shaarel on the winding path which led through the forest to the harbour, hauling their luggage on a wheeled cart behind her. She wore her own version of the uniform of the palace's militia; the black trousers clung stickily to her legs, and sweat trickled down the inside of her silk shirt and over her stomach. Despite the heat, she still strode easily behind her mistress, ahead of the other servants. The Sygia's long, golden-furred tail hung low behind her, flicking slightly with her steps.

At the head of the procession, Lady Shaarel mentally rehearsed words of greeting for the meeting ahead. So much depended on it, and first impressions would be crucial. Her father had ordered that she should travel to the harbour on foot, despite the fact that the journey took over two hours that way. He did not want to risk offending their visitors' sensibilities with an overly ostentatious display of the Makers' art. He agreed that she could take a small entourage, consisting of six bodyguards and three maids. Shaarel's young telepath would also go, disguised as a pageboy, so that his talent could be discreetly employed to protect his mistress from any treachery on the part of the Outlanders. And, of course, it was inconceivable that the

Maker-Heiress would go anywhere without her Sygia, despite her father's qualms.

Shaarel hoped that the Outlanders would find nothing insulting in such a small party. Everything must be managed smoothly. It was the first meeting between the Techs and the Geneers in over a hundred years, and it was vital that the breach between them be healed. Not for the first time, Shaarel fought down the resentment that grew at the thought of placating such deluded people. Her Geneer ancestors had first grown uneasy when the Techs began to ravage the land in their endless quest for more fuels and minerals. Then it was found that the output from their refineries was killing tiny creatures that the Geneers believed might be sentient. When the unregulated Techs started to capture large numbers of an elusive and gentle native species on which to test their unnatural mechanical implants, the Geneers could bear it no longer and emigrated to another continent to set up their own strictly governed society.

Shaarel shuddered. She reminded herself that the Geneers and Techs had once all been the same race, set down on the planet several centuries earlier by a colony ship. She tried to concentrate on this fact to produce a more diplomatic frame of mind. Her thoughts were interrupted by her Sygia.

"Mistress, may we stop for a moment?"

The Maker-Heiress looked at her in surprise. The Sygia never tired before she did. "What is it?"

"Someone is coming through the trees, my lady." They were passing through a long stretch of forest, and the Sygia had become aware of an unfamiliar scent, growing stronger as they progressed. She pointed out the direction.

Four men from Shaarel's bodyguard quickly surrounded their mistress, dragging the luggage cart to form a barrier between her and the unseen people in the woods. The other two drew their swords and prepared to defend the maidservants and the telepath. The interlopers might just be innocent travellers, but rumours abounded that the lesser Houses were restless, and the Maker-Heiress could be a tempting target for political kidnappers.

The Sygia had already slid softly and swiftly into the trees to investigate. Flattening her body against the dark bark of an aged oak, she identified the scents of ten individuals, and the rustlings that her keen hearing picked up told her that they were spreading out in an arc around Lady Shaarel's party. One strongly built man passed within an arm's reach of her. He had his sword drawn, and was breathing heavily. The Sygia could smell the adrenaline pounding through his body. She crouched down and *sent* thoughts of her findings to the telepath. She was sure that Lady Shaarel, too, would pick up the message. Her mistress could not read the Sygia's thoughts ordinarily, but many years of practice and a natural affinity allowed her to catch some of the Sygia's deliberate *sendings* and to *send* to her.

She did not have to wait for the youth to convey it. Shaarel's response was immediate: "Attack!"

The command freed the beast that the Sygia kept pent within her heart and head. She felt the concealed claws extend from her strong, bony fingers and her retractable canine teeth descend. Though she tried to control it, to achieve some balance, the animal inside her raged through her body. It took command of her breath, her limbs, her flesh, driving out all considerations but the need to protect its mistress. She bounded after the man who had just passed her, sprang on his back and sank her teeth into the soft flesh of his neck. With ten to dispatch, there was no time for a suffocation hold, so the Sygia ripped out the artery. Hot, salty blood filled her mouth, and she swallowed it hungrily. The savage joy in her own strength fountained within her. With a loping, rhythmic stride, she took off after the second attacker.

This one saw her coming, but his movements were slow and clumsy. The Sygia ducked under his sword, and raked his abdomen with her claws, bringing him down for the death blow. The screaming man thrust a dagger into her thigh as he fell, but the Sygia barely noticed the pain as she took his life. The drumbeat of her heart drove her on the wild dance with three more of the horrified outlaws, their frantic struggles swiftly subdued by the savage onslaught of her teeth and claws.

She heard footsteps behind her. Snarling, she turned and leapt instinctively at her new foe. This creature was like one of the Born in shape and size, but covered all over with a thick black fur. Its features were dominated by a pointed snout bristling with teeth like splinters of broken glass. Sygia-Shaarel twisted aside in mid-air, her tail aiding the manoeuvre, and landed on all fours. This was another Sygia, no easy kill. She shuffled backwards swiftly, cunningly, contemplating the best method of attack.

A garbled sound came from the monstrous creature's mouth. Then, with surprising swiftness, it dropped to all fours and fled amongst the trees. Sygia-Shaarel remained crouched, too dazed to move. In a mouth not suited for speech, the creature had snarled, "Master yourself!"

After a moment, she shook her head, trying to clear it of confusing thoughts, and listened carefully. She could still hear the other Sygia crashing away through the undergrowth, and knew from similar sounds further off that the other assailants were also in flight. There were no remaining indications of conflict. Licking her lips, she returned to Lady Shaarel's entourage.

The Maker-Heiress was unharmed. Her servants, too, were safe, and no injuries had been sustained by the bodyguards. Satisfied that its duty had been fulfilled, the beast inside the Sygia suffered itself to be caged again. Its teeth and claws retracted. Once the beast was dormant, the guilt came, as it always did. She had killed five men.

The Sygia noticed that the Maker-Heiress was regarding her with a strictly regulated expression of disapproval. As self-awareness returned, Sygia-Shaarel realised that blood covered her face, and had streamed down her chin to soak her dark shirt.

She was sweating, and her exertions had brought an improper colour and undisciplined expression to her face.

"My thanks for your good work, Sygia," Lady Shaarel said coolly. "But your unkempt appearance is now most unsuitable for our meeting with the Outland Lords."

"There is a stream nearby, mistress. If I bathe there now, my clothes will dry by the time we have walked to the harbour."

"Despite this distressing incident, we must not give our visitors the insult of being late to greet them." Shaarel and the Sygia exchanged glances. Everyone in the group knew that it would be best if the Outland Lords knew little of Geneeron's internal troubles at this early stage. It might put the Geneers at a disadvantage in their negotiations.

Shaarel addressed her telepath. "*Send* a message to our House. Let them know what has happened here and ask them to investigate. My father will know what to do."

Turning back to the Sygia, Lady Shaarel spoke again. "The rest of us will continue our journey while you attend to your appearance. You may rejoin us when you are more presentable." With a dismissive gesture, Shaarel led her entourage away, one of the bodyguards taking over the task of pulling the luggage cart.

The smell of fresh water tingling in her nostrils, the Sygia quickly found the shallow stream and waded in, fully clothed. Kneeling down, she washed the red stains from her clothes and from her fair skin. She wished the heavy feeling inside her could be washed away so easily. Squatting in the water, watching it turn momentarily pink before carrying out of sight the residue of her slaughter, she knew that she must learn to control the beast, to bend it to her rational will. If she did not, she feared that one day it would take complete control of her.

But there was no time for her to loiter. Her thoughts continued to whirl in dark confusion as she sped after her companions. The other Sygia had been a rogue, apparently masterless. A rogue Sygia was the most reviled creature there was, the only living thing that was allowed to be killed on sight under Geneeron law. And this one had fled rather than fight her. She knew she should tell her mistress about it, but a surprising, stubborn part of her did not want it hunted down and killed. She felt a guilty companionship with it. Perhaps she would tell Shaarel later, when they had time to discuss the incident privately. In any event, it was too late to catch the creature now, and greeting their visitors on time was far more important.

She caught up just before the group left the woods to emerge into the glaring sunlight at the port, and reclaimed the baggage cart from the gruff bodyguard. She walked behind her silent mistress, head bowed, until they reached the harbour and had their first clear sight of the Outland Lords' gleaming steel ship.

Moments later, she followed Lady Shaarel up the heavy gangplank, several paces behind, and kept that distance when they stopped and the Maker-Heiress greeted the visitors. Beads of sweat dotted her brow. She glanced longingly at the cool green water, infinitely deeper than the stream she had so recently left, and wished that she could swim. Inhaling the tang of crisp sea air, she let go of the handle of the luggage trolley and looked around, stretching her slender back and flicking her tail.

Her mistress made a minute gesture with her hand. The Sygia smiled approvingly at the elegance of it, remembering the times in the classroom when she and Shaarel had made mirrors of each other to practise the approved movements and poses that were so important in their society. Obeying the unspoken command, the Sygia moved up behind her mistress to hear her saying, "And this is my Sygia."

The Outland Lord was staring at her. His dark hair blew about his face; his eyes were large and brown like coffee, with round pupils like those of the Born. The Sygia's own slit pupils narrowed as a pulse of alarm jumped in her belly. She stared back until the Outlander removed his gaze from her.

"Welcome aboard," he said uncomfortably.

CRLSO

Karam stood on the deck of his silver ship, straining for a sight of the strange continent he knew only by hearsay. Over his head, the glittering white solar sails were filled with air and sunlight, pushing the arrow-like vessel swiftly across the placid water. Flickering from every mast, brightly coloured silk banners bore embroidered words of greeting to the woman the ship sailed to meet.

At last land swelled into view over the horizon. Karam took a moment to compose himself, then triggered his com amulet and transmitted on his brother's frequency, "Hey, come and get your first glimpse of Geneeron."

The younger man arrived at a run, brushing long red-gold hair out of his eyes. Marn, who still had his enhancement implants, could clearly see the buildings, smooth white stone painted in pastel colours, linked and interlaced with arches, spiked with towers and topped with fat onion-shaped domes which shone silver in the sun. Wide roads wound through the town, some disappearing into the heavily wooded hills that rose behind, where the trees seemed to droop and sway lethargically in the heat. Karam's implants had all been removed on his father's advice, in case they upset the Geneers. He had to content himself with peering at the view through binoculars.

As the ship drew closer to shore, Karam and Marn could distinguish figures moving on the quayside and along the roads and paths which led down to it. Some were walking. Others rode enormous shaggy creatures laden with boxes lashed to their undulating bodies by a combination of intricate harnesses and makeshift ropes. More drove wagons and chariots. A few rode by on muscular, prancing animals with glossy spotted fur, long flexible necks and broad heads.

Karam pointed at these. "There, now that's a good example of the Beast-Makers' work. Those creatures are said to be capable of speeds exceeding a hundred kiloms an hour and of keeping that up for a whole day at a time."

Marn shrugged. "Our slowest scooter is faster than that," he said, running his eyes disdainfully over one of the animals, which had stopped to let its rider dismount. "Why would any of our people want one?"

"Our people occasionally ride horses," Karam replied with a smile. "Those creatures are supposed to be very intelligent and very loyal if they are treated well. And if you want a more practical reason, the only fuel you need is vegetation."

Marn wasn't really listening. He was watching a tall man add another crate to the precarious burden of a patient, kneeling beast. "If these people are such masters of genetic engineering why don't they make something useful?" he asked. "Like . . . oh, I don't know. Yes I do. Like a beautiful woman designed to pander to your every whim!"

"How predictably unimaginative. You'd soon get bored with a woman who did whatever you wanted and had no will of her own."

"Perhaps," said Marn, with a smile. "All right then. How about a talking guard-dog which could mix drinks, play chess and carry you home when you're drunk? If the Geneers could design something like that, I might be impressed."

Karam frowned. "You'd better watch what you say when we land. These people are obsessive about good manners and protocol. We can't risk offending anybody. We're supposed to be initiating diplomatic relations."

"And trading links. Yeah, yeah, you've told me. Father's told me. Everyone in the Techon Council's told me! I'll be as polite to them as they are to me," Marn said.

On shore, a small procession had emerged from the woods and was making its way through town to the dock. Marn focused on the lead figure. "Hey, that must be the Heiress-Maker," he said.

"You mean Maker-Heiress," Karam replied absently.

Marn's visual implant gave him a magnified view of the approaching party. "Whatever. Do you want to know what she looks like?"

"I'll know soon enough," Karam said. He swallowed and took a deep breath. Nervousness was stirring in his stomach. The importance of this meeting was immense. Complete separation between the Techon and Geneeron peoples had lasted for over a century, since the Techs had become disgusted with the unnatural biological work of the Geneers and driven them away. But four years ago, the Tech epidemics had begun, and all their machinery had proved useless in treating them. They needed the biological skills of the Geneers. A number of desperate Tech traders had made tentative attempts to re-establish contact, concealing their true reasons to avoid weakening their bargaining position. They were surprised to find their approaches received encouragingly, and it soon became obvious that an official ambassador would be welcomed. Karam's father, the Tech President, had been exchanging letters with the Maker-Lord of Geneeron for several months to arrange the terms of this first visit. Shortly before he set out, Karam had learnt that his father was relying on him to form the alliance on a very personal level.

"You look terrible," Marn said, nudging him in the ribs. "You can't get sea-sick now. We're about to dock."

Watchers on the shore stared and pointed excitedly as the stabilisation field was activated and the vessel came to a smooth stop. The metal gangway slid out and clattered down onto the stone quay. Karam and Marn took up their positions by its head to welcome their guests. Karam wiped his palms on his baggy blue trousers and tugged down his patterned tunic. He repeated the formal words of greeting under his breath.

Marn leaned forward and whispered, "Stop fidgeting and muttering. The Heiress-Maker will think you're a total idiot."

"Thank you for those encouraging words," Karam hissed back without turning his head. "And it's Maker-Heiress. Please try to make an effort. If we fail in this mission, it will be because of your irresponsibility!"

The Maker-Heiress led her entourage to the gangplank and was the first on board. She seemed to glide towards the brothers, looking neither to right nor left, and extended a graceful hand in greeting. In the distance, the woman's confident bearing and elegance had given her the appearance of maturity. Now that Karam saw her close up, he guessed that she could be little more than twenty. She was beautiful. The eyes that met his with a challenging gaze were summer-evening blue, her expression serene. She wore a simple, elegant, blue-grey robe. Beneath a slim silver tiara, her pale gold hair was elaborately plaited and intertwined with ribbons.

"I am Lady Shaarel of the House of Medrinne," she said softly, "Maker-Heiress of Geneeron." She made a tiny elegant gesture with one hand. A deferential figure stepped out from the waiting group and approached with a dancer's stride to stand a little distance behind her. "And this is my Sygia," Shaarel added.

At first glance, Karam thought that the Sygia was very like the Maker-Heiress. But as he continued to look, he found he was gazing at the most exotic woman he had ever seen. In contrast to Shaarel's cool grace, the Sygia seemed barely in control of her own energy. Summer-evening blue eyes stared back at him, almost identical to those of the Maker-Heiress herself. But these eyes had elongated pupils, like those of a cat or a snake. And was that a tail flicking behind her?

Karam forced himself to return his attention to Lady Shaarel. "Welcome aboard," he said uncomfortably, his carefully rehearsed speech forgotten.

ଔ*ଓ*ଓ

The Sygia was confused by the Outland Lord's curt greeting to her mistress. It seemed deplorably informal, but genial enough. Suddenly she became aware that the Heiress was *sending* a thought to her. "Salute! You have not saluted the Tech Lord."

The Sygia started, then drew her ceremonial sword shakily from its sheath and went down on one knee, wincing slightly at the pain in her thigh. She pointed her blade to the deck, and bent her head over the pommel. She stumbled through the ritual salutation for visitors from distant cities, uncertain whether it would mean anything to these people from another continent. The Outland Lord and his companion, a younger man, stared at her, but she could not read their faces. This made her even more uncomfortable. How could she protect her mistress from these strangers if she could not read them and anticipate their actions? She rose to her feet too quickly and sheathed her sword without finesse. The Maker-Heiress *sent* her a shiver of annoyance.

The older Lord addressed the Sygia directly: "You're injured. I'll get someone to help you."

The Sygia looked at her mistress for permission to reply, but Shaarel spoke instead, with a gracious smile. "My Sygia sustained a small wound during training this morning. Thank you for your kind offer of assistance, but I will attend to her myself."

A pair of sailors in brightly coloured baggy clothes, with moon-white smiles, gently ushered Shaarel's servants below deck. The Sygia was surprised that the men looked so normal: she had expected gigantic monsters made of metal and flesh. A small silver machine on wheels buzzed up to her and extended a grappling device, which it clamped to the handle of the luggage trolley and trundled away. The Sygia followed her Mistress as the Outlanders led them to their cabin. Blood dripped down her leg and left a trail on the deck behind her.

ఴ⊂Ꝝℰᕲ๛

"They're all safely tucked away in the best cabins," Marn said, finding Karam at the prow of the ship. "I'm glad Father didn't agree to let us get dragged off into the wilderness with them. Who knows what they might have turned us into? Did you see that weird cat-woman padding about behind her Ladyship?"

"That was her Sygia," Karam told him sharply, turning so that his back was to his brother, "as you'd know if you'd bothered listening. Sygias are considered to be the height of the Makers' art and are highly prized. Whenever a rich or powerful Geneer house is expecting a child, they somehow have one custom-made as a sort of bodyguard for the baby. They're very secretive about how they do it, though." He turned to face Marn and forced a smile. "I suppose the Lady Shaarel's bodyguard is largely decorative, but I have heard that some Sygias contain the DNA of bears or lions and are truly monstrous."

"The whole thing is monstrous!" snapped Marn. "Mixing animals and people in the same body. It's disgusting! It's no wonder the Council threw the Geneerons out when they made the first one."

Karam shrugged. "They probably think we're disgusting, mixing metal and flesh in the same body. Prizing machinery above nature. It's the same ancient argument. We're here to try and get over that. We need their medicines."

Marn scowled. "I know," he muttered. "We've got no choice. But I still think we should have invaded them fifty years ago, when we had enough strength left to do so. Wipe the mutants out and take their land and knowledge for free!"

"You weren't alive fifty years ago, and neither was I," Karam replied in an undertone, hoping his brother would take the hint to keep his own voice low. "So there's no point in questioning the Council's decisions. I'm glad they didn't invade. I can't believe you really approve of genocide, but if you want to take a purely selfish view, who knows how much knowledge would have been lost? We might be able to learn a lot from them."

"We're after their cures and the fuels buried in their untapped continent," Marn said, in a deliberately exaggerated whisper. "Don't try to elevate it into a philosophical matter to try and ennoble what we're doing. Father is trading you for an open gateway between Techon and Geneeron, that's all there is to it. It's fortunate for you that the Maker-Heiress looks normal. What if they'd wanted you to marry a bear?"

Karam sighed. "The Maker-Heiress is beautiful," he said softly. "The most beautiful woman I've ever seen." Marn felt he was lying, but thought it wise not to enquire further.

୫ଔଷଚ୨ଞ

After the ever-smiling sailors had escorted them to its door, Sygia-Shaarel had inspected her mistress's cabin before allowing her to enter. The compact rooms were pleasantly cool, but the furniture was formed from functional steel frames, and upholstered in bright pinks and blues that made the two Geneers wince. Someone had taken the trouble to drape white curtains over one of the walls, and, after stealing a look behind them, the Sygia realised that this was to conceal the built-in control panels and other technological equipment.

"I am pleased they have so much respect for my feelings," Shaarel told the Sygia. "But I will have to do something about his taste in upholstery."

"Where will you live when you marry the Outland Lord, Mistress?" the Sygia asked. She could not sit down until the Maker-Heiress had done so, and was sidling up and down the cabin with her tail flicking uncomfortably. Between her and Shaarel, in flickering *sendings*, passed images from the stories of Techon. A place with no growing things, covered in artificial stone. Cracked, dry land ravaged with craters where metal and fuel had been ripped from the ground. Foul water that could not be drunk. Polluted air that was hard to breathe. Men that were more machines than flesh.

"I am sure that all those stories cannot be true," Shaarel said aloud. "I have not yet decided to marry him, but he looks manlike enough." She blushed. "In fact, he is very handsome, do you not think?"

The Sygia shrugged her shoulders. "It does not matter what I think, Mistress," she said. "The decision is yours to make."

Shaarel had been rummaging in her luggage as she spoke. She now extracted her medicine bag and seated herself on a couch. She motioned the Sygia to sit on the floor in front of her, and began to clean her wound with a cloth from the bag.

"I will be the Maker-Lady when father dies," Shaarel said musingly, "and will then have a duty to ensure the best for our people. I must preserve the knowledge of the Makers, and protect it from misuse. What if I had been killed today?"

Sygia-Shaarel shivered, thinking again of the rogue Sygia she had encountered.

Lady Shaarel continued, "The smaller Houses are protesting that we will not share the secrets of making the Sygias. But we will only make for those who will honour the contract to own one, and will dedicate themselves to a life-long bond. Some Houses would use the knowledge to build armies for themselves, and civil war would be inevitable. We must keep developing our knowledge, but we must also stop it from falling into the wrong hands. The Techs have better and safer ways to store and distribute information than we do. They can help us to govern in a way that will keep our people together. There is much we can learn from them." She spread some pink mixture from the bag onto the Sygia's leg to speed the healing process. "So the decision to marry the Outlander is not really mine to make at all. It is little more than a formality."

The Sygia looked up at her mistress. "Yes, he is very handsome," she said.

The Maker-Heiress smiled and leaned forward to hug her companion. "Ever since I was born, you have always said and done whatever would make me happy, Sygia," she said. "Promise me you will always do so."

"I promise, Mistress," said the Sygia. But her eyes were troubled. "Mistress, was it right for me to kill those men today?" she asked.

"You were doing your duty, protecting me in the way that you thought best."

But I did not think at all, the Sygia reflected privately. *I acted on instinct.*

ಌಖಀೲ

A sumptuous meal in the ship's formal dining suite was the main event of the evening, but the Sygia only picked at her food. She felt as if her belly was already full, full of guilt and self-doubt.

She had been given her own cabin, with a connecting door to that of her mistress, but she and Shaarel always shared the same bedroom so that she could protect her mistress properly. When they retired, she dragged her mattress into the larger cabin, placing it on the floor a respectful distance from Shaarel's bed. However, she did not sleep well that night, despite the delicious coolness of the cabin, where the atmosphere was regulated by Outland machines. The battle in the forest had disturbed her, although it was far from the first time she had killed. When the beast was in control, she had no moderation and no moral judgement. She had to get rid of it; cage it permanently, kill it if there were no other choice. On the floor, she turned and twisted, trying to escape from her dark thoughts. Her mind seemed to pounce upon and then discard a thousand subjects. The rogue Sygia and its shocking words, her fellow Sygias in the palace at Medrinne, scenes from her childhood, the disturbing expression on the Outland Lord's face when he first saw her: these fragments eventually knotted themselves into disturbing dreams, from which she struggled to wake.

The next morning, a sailor brought a message to Lady Shaarel that breakfast was to be served on deck while the ship toured the coast to the big Geneeron pleasure park at Neresh. The Sygia was concealing her tiredness as she helped her mistress to arrange her hair. They exchanged disapproving glances at the casualness of the arrangement as they followed the cheerful messenger. But any fears that deliberate disrespect had been intended were dispelled by the warm greetings of Karam and Marn, who were already seated at a table set under a gaudy canvas awning. The Outland Lords themselves served Shaarel her food, while her servants timidly accepted dishes from a many-armed mechanical servitor.

The sun was still warm, but the wind gusted strongly, tearing droplets of spray from the crests of the waves. As she sat beside her mistress, the Sygia maintained the correct expression of mild pleasure, but inside she was thrilled by the rush of the silver boat over the water. She looked to her mistress for permission to address Karam, and when it was given she said, "My Lord, please forgive that I beg a favour of you. I would like to see more of your ship. May I speak to your sailors concerning its workings?"

The Outland Lord gave her one of his broad, undisciplined smiles. "I'll be happy to show you myself. And the Maker-Heiress, too, if she'd like?"

"I greatly regret that I cannot accept your kind invitation, my Lord," Shaarel said faintly. "I am suddenly feeling rather weary. You must excuse me. I shall return to my cabin. However, it would please me if you were to show your ship to my Sygia as she requested."

Both the Outland Lords bowed their heads as Shaarel and her Sygia stood up. Shaarel leaned heavily on her companion's arm as they walked slowly back to her cabin.

"Ugh. I have had sea-sickness before, but I do not ever remember feeling so terrible," the Maker-Heiress said when they were out of earshot. "I must get back to the cabin and lie down."

"If they have poisoned you, Mistress. . . ."

Shaarel smiled wanly. "Do not worry, Sygia. I am sure they have not, although death might be preferable to this! It is merely the speed of the ship that has upset me. It will pass shortly, I am sure. You must go with the Outland Lord and learn all you can."

"I do not like to leave you unprotected, Mistress."

"I am confident that these Techs mean us no harm. Young Lilm would have *sent* me a warning if there were any threat intended." The telepath had admitted to her that he could not read these strangers as clearly as his own people, but he could identify strong emotion and would recognise ill intent. "And I still have the rest of my bodyguard to call on, if I am wrong."

"Very well, Mistress." The Sygia still looked doubtful.

They entered the cabin. Shaarel slipped off her shoes, and stretched out on the comfortable bed. The Sygia brought a cold wet cloth, and laid it gently on her forehead.

"Another thing," Shaarel said. "These Outlanders seem a little uncomfortable with our manners. Try to be a little less formal today."

The Sygia raised her eyebrows. "I will try," she said.

"Good. Now go."

The Sygia paused at the door, and turned, an unguarded grin on her face. "Mistress, I have just remembered. On the morning after Lord Jarmel's party, you looked just as you do now. I recall that you felt better after a nice big greasy bacon sandwich. Perhaps the same cure would be effective?"

Shaarel pulled a face, then giggled. For a moment, they were young girls again, teasing each other in the corridors of the Palace. "Get out, you hateful creature," she said, flinging a shoe at the closing door.

cs CR EO so

Karam seemed to take genuine pleasure in showing off the ship. He took the Sygia everywhere, from the engine rooms, where she watched the turbines spinning, to the bridge, where she tried her hand at the wheel. When their tour was complete, Karam asked "So what do you think? Do you like my ship?"

The Sygia flinched from such a direct and improper enquiry into her opinions and feelings. As one of the Made, she was unaccustomed to such questions. But she recalled her mistress's instructions to be less formal, and said, "Your technology is fascinating, and far beyond my comprehension. But best of all, I like to stand at the prow, and hear the wind cracking the sails, and watch the water rush by, and feel the spray on my face. It is wonderful."

"Yes, it is, isn't it?" Karam beamed. He looked at the Sygia for a moment. Then he asked: "Have you ever played quoits?"

She shook her head, not recognising the word. Karam looked disappointed. "But I would like to try," she added, smiling shyly.

cs CR EO so

It was not until early evening that the Sygia returned to her mistress's cabin. She bounded in to make her report. "Oh Mistress, I have had such an interesting day! The ship is driven by light caught by the sails, which can be stored or used to drive the turbines of the great engines." She said this carefully, proud of remembering the new words. "And the Techs play games just as we do, and they appreciate humour. There are wonderful silver boxes that play music as though an entire orchestra was seated a few paces away. . . ."

"Do stop gabbling, Sygia," Shaarel said faintly. "I feel so dizzy, I do not need all of your nonsense to confuse me further."

"I am sorry, Mistress. May I bring you a drink, or perhaps some food?"

"No, the Lord Karam's sailors have looked after me well."

The Sygia hung her head, tail between her legs. "I have neglected my duties, Mistress. I will remain with you until you are better. Would you like me to read to you?" Shaarel nodded, so the Sygia sat by her mistress's bed, and took up her favourite book. But she was unusually restless, and wondered why a sudden rush of anticipation went through her each time a servant knocked at the door, to enquire after her mistress's health, or to bring the evening meal to the cabin.

Lady Shaarel was sipping delicately at some thin soup when there was another knock at the door, and Karam walked in. The Sygia felt a jolt akin to panic. She bowed deeply to the Lord. "I've come to ask after your health, my lady," Karam said carefully.

"I am feeling somewhat better, thank you. Your sailors have been most attentive. You really ought to instruct them not to go to so much trouble. I have my maids to attend to me."

"I must apologise. I've been neglecting you. Is there anything I can do to entertain you while you rest?"

"You could tell me stories of those who have been worse passengers than I. Or settle our debate concerning exactly which shade of green you imagine my complexion to be. My Sygia says it is sea-green, but I think that is merely her attempt at wit. I am maintaining it is pure emerald. It seems more dignified!"

Karam laughed, then noticed the book resting on the Sygia's lap. "I've interrupted your reading," he said. "Please, go on. I'll stay and listen."

The Sygia looked at her mistress, who nodded. She took up the book and read, then frowned, and pressed a hand against her forehead. She read lines twice and stumbled over the words.

"Whatever is the matter, Sygia?" asked the Maker-Heiress.

"I am sorry. I have a headache, Mistress."

"You should have said so at once! I will fetch some medicine. . . ."

"Do not worry Mistress," *sent* the Sygia. "I am perfectly well. This is an excuse to leave you alone with Lord Karam."

"Clever creature!" Shaarel *sent* back, concealing a smile.

"Please do not trouble yourself, Mistress. I will soon be well," the Sygia said aloud.

"Perhaps I could take over the reading from you?" Karam offered. The Sygia passed him the book, and she and Shaarel exchanged significant looks. Karam continued fluently from the place the Sygia had marked. Quickly, the Sygia said. "I beg your pardon, my Lord. Mistress, I believe a stroll on deck will refresh me."

Karam turned to look at her, an unreadable expression on his face.

"You may go," said Shaarel.

The Sygia left with a strangely bitter satisfaction that her object was achieved. Surely now Karam would take the opportunity to make his proposal of marriage.

⋘⋙⋘⋙

The moon hung low in the violet sky, bathing the ship in rich, cream light. Outside, the Sygia found her restlessness had redoubled. She felt a little as though she were thirsty and could find no water, and a little as though she had lost something precious. She padded up and down the deck, trying to make sense of it. Then she went down to her cabin and changed her clothes. But something drew her back to the prow of the ship.

⋘⋙⋘⋙

At the end of the chapter, Karam glanced up from the book to find that the Maker-Heiress was soundly asleep. He felt a guilty relief that he'd not been able to propose yet. He had braced himself for every eventuality that he could imagine: that the Maker-Heiress might be hundreds of years old, or repellently ugly, or scarcely human, or many other things which would repulse him. Before he set foot on the ship, he was calmly convinced he could do his duty whatever he was faced with in Geneeron. So why was he now finding it so difficult? He needed to take a walk, to look at the sea. He left the cabin quietly and sauntered up onto deck and towards the prow. When he got there, he knew that was where he had meant to go all the time.

The Sygia stood there. She had put on her travelling clothes, and her sword was buckled to her waist. She turned swiftly at his approach. Her face was milky-white in the moonlight, her eyes dark as thunder-clouds.

"I'm glad I found you," Karam said softly. "I knew you'd be here."

"Where is my Mistress?"

"She's asleep. I want to talk to you." He gazed at her, trying to imprint the strange, lovely sight of her on his memory. He took a faltering step towards her.

The Sygia stepped back, her eyes glittering. She could feel her animal nature waking again, pulling at the chain on which she kept it. Her whole body felt so sensitive that she thought she could feel the heat from his skin.

"I'm supposed to marry your mistress," Karam said. "I don't want to, but if I don't do it. . . ." His head swam as distracting visions flashed through his mind.

"Yes, I know," the Sygia said. She felt her hips start to sway forwards as though she were dancing, and she fought to regain control of herself.

Karam took another step towards her, and then a third. As though he were pulling her on a leash, Sygia-Shaarel mirrored his movements until the pair was no further apart than the weft of a single garment. His breath and hers mingled and intertwined as their lips drew closer together.

"Karam, there you are. I want to . . . oh!" Marn froze, confused by what he saw as he clattered onto the deck. At first he thought his brother was embracing the Maker-Heiress, but then he saw the long golden tail, lashing in agitation.

"I . . . errm . . . sorry!" He turned and left.

The Sygia pulled herself away. Inside, her beast roared. It wanted her to take this man in Pairing as it had wanted her to take those in the forest to their deaths. Her claws sprang from the ends of her fingers. Karam stepped back in alarm, his eyes wide, but the Sygia was only fighting with herself. She leapt several feet into the air and landed by the side-rail of the ship. Karam stared at her in astonishment. He had never seen anyone move so quickly or athletically.

"No, I am not like you," she said, her voice bitter. "But I feel as you do. I feel pain and love and hope. But most of all I feel loyalty. I was created for one purpose only: to serve my Mistress. My Mistress owns me; she controls me." The Sygia scowled, and looked away.

Karam held out a hand to her. "You have a life of your own, too. It can't be so wrong to leave your mistress. Couldn't I buy you from her?"

"So you wish to be my Master?" In a quiet voice, she hissed, "I cannot even master myself."

Karam wasn't listening. He said hastily, "When we get back to my people, under our laws you'd be a free woman. I can get your mistress another Sygia."

"You do not understand. You cannot get her another Sygia," she told him, biting each word. "I was Made from her and for her. When she was conceived, the Maker-Master took her DNA and mixed it with others to make me. Sygias are infertile, so each one is unique." In a softer tone, she continued, "Shaarel is my twin sister. I will not betray her." *The beast will not have its will this time*, she thought.

"But that's . . ." Karam bit back the word "horrible." He looked from left to right, as though seeking desperately for an answer. He knew he had no arguments, but he still said, "Come back with me. Even if I must marry your mistress, we'll work something out, some arrangement. I don't care about politics. I just want to be with you!"

"This is not meant to be," the Sygia said, her voice calmer now. "My Mistress explained it to me. You and she must be married. The future of our land depends on it. There is no other choice."

Karam stepped closer, reached out to take the Sygia's hand. She felt the beast striving to overcome her. She looked over the side of the ship to the rushing black water. "There is no other choice," she said and threw herself over the rails.

The water was a sudden shock as it gripped her in its cold embrace. She didn't struggle, but let herself sink, dragged down by the weight of her sword, boots and clothes. A stream of bright bubbles issued from her mouth and rushed towards the swiftly fading light overhead. Then all was blackness.

❦❧☙⁊

Karam's cries brought his brother and many of the crew to the deck. The sailors raked the surface of the water with powerful searchlights but could see nothing. Used to oceans so toxic that a single mouthful of their water meant instant death, the Techon crew followed the search procedures they were accustomed to.

Roused by one of her maids, Shaarel stood watching them, shivering in a light robe and drawing on every reserve of self-control she possessed. Seeing her there, Karam stumbled over to her. "Your . . . Sygia. She went into the water. It was my fault."

"Karam startled her, my Lady," interrupted Marn breathlessly, gripping his distraught brother tightly by the arm. "I saw the whole thing. She was sitting on the rail, probably to feel the wind in her hair. I used to take such risks myself when I was a boy. Karam's unexpected greeting when he came up behind her made her lose her grip and fall." He stared fixedly at his elder brother, silently enjoining him to say no more.

Shaarel looked at the Outlanders, her eyes troubled and full of doubt. "Lord Karam's grief is genuine, Mistress," *sent* Lilm from close behind her. "Almost excessive, since he scarcely knew her. The Techs did not kill Sygia-Shaarel."

Shaarel could see that the pain on Karam's face was not faked. She realised how desperately upset he was at having been the unwitting cause of the death of her lifelong companion. And she knew that she would be happy to marry a man of such tender sensibilities.

As the sailors switched off their searchlights and sadly returned to their cabins, Marn ushered his acquiescent brother and the Maker-Heiress out of the cold night air.

ఆ**CR**80ు

Deep beneath the waves, in impenetrable darkness, the beast raged and broke free of its bonds. It refused to die.

When the Sygia recovered her self-possession, she was on the surface, coughing up clear water and instinctively paddling towards the shore. She had kicked off her boots and unstrapped her sword. She could hear the commotion from the distant ship, but kept low in the water and did not turn to look back. Deliberately, she kept her mind closed to Shaarel and the telepath. She could not afford to risk them picking up her thoughts. Shaarel and Karam would console each other, in time perhaps even come to love each other, provided they both believed her dead.

She smiled painfully. The hated beast had kept her alive. Maybe she could learn to live in harmony with it. She thought of the words of the rogue Sygia in the woods, and suddenly she knew what they meant. She would seek out those who could show her how to do it, who could help her to be her own master.

With renewed vigour, the Sygia swam towards shore.

Women who are willing to make sacrifices sometimes have to learn what's worth sacrificing and what's worth holding onto no matter what. The sacrifice may make someone a warrior, but the holding onto may be what constitutes wisdom.

SISTER GRASS

by Deborah Walker

"Don't trust the aliens, that's all I'm saying," said Myra. Myra had been a good friend to Neve and Penny. She lived next door, in the prefabricated huts that were the refugees' accommodation. Neve had only been thirteen when they had first come to this Kristrall refugee world. Thirteen years old with a two-year-old sister to care for, she had been grateful for Myra's advice. But now, two years later, she found Myra's attitude oppressive.

"You know how hard I've saved for this, denied myself and Penny. I've worked every day running errands, doing odd jobs in the camp."

The refugees were given an allowance—call it pin money—to buy small luxuries, and Neve had saved every cent. Neve had begged for small jobs, earning a few cents here and there. There were always small jobs to be done. It was curious how restrained and lethargic the people in the refugee camp seemed to be. They had little to do all day, but still the small tasks, which should have been easily achieved, were left undone. There was weariness in the refugee camp; it hung in the air, the miasma of a captive people.

"I've been working and saving for a year to get the entrance fee for the games, and now I've finally got enough, are you saying that I should give up?" Neve couldn't understand

Myra's attitude; Myra had helped her, caring for her sister, while Neve worked to earn the money she needed.

"I'm saying that you should think about Penny."

"I think about my sister all the time. It's Penny I'm doing this for."

"Is it?"

Am I doing this for Penny, or am I doing it for myself, Neve wondered. *No, Myra's wrong. I'm doing this for both of us.* She *was* sure of her conviction. *And Myra is just like the rest of the people in this camp. She means well, but she's been worn out by this life.*

The Kristralls had been magnanimous in victory, offering a home to those displaced by the war. Perhaps they were a benevolent species, giving aid to all those who asked. But they were paternal hosts, limiting and confining their charges.

Neve looked at Myra then, really looked at her, a small woman dressed in the refugees' uniform. Had she always looked so tired? Had she always worn that fragrance of overwhelming defeat? Neve remembered her differently.

"I need the money, Myra. There's no other way to get it. I don't want to be a refugee all of my life. The Kristralls won't allow us to do real work, not until they believe that we are fully integrated into their society."

When the Kristralls believed that the refugees accepted their status, accepted the Kristralls' authority, things might change; the refugees would have more freedom, be allowed to work and to take on more responsibilities. But the administrators had made it quite plain that the process would take many generations. There was only one way for Neve to acquire money, real money, and that was to participate in one of the Kristralls' games. Winning the game would mean substantial prize-money, and Neve needed money.

"What exactly did they say?" asked Myra.

"They told me about the games, described them to me. I chose the lost game." In truth the game administrators had been rather vague. There had been many games to choose from—all ill-defined. When she asked for explanations, the game administrators were evasive.

"The games are defined by the players," one had said. What did that mean?

"Think about it," said Myra, grasping Neve's hand. "We're protected here; we have food, a safe home, more than we had on Earth."

"Can't you understand that I want more than all this?" Neve gestured to the sterile surroundings, an alien take on basic accommodation. Everything neutral-coloured and functional, everything standardised, the same furnishing in a million refugee homes. She noticed the camera in the corner of the room watching them both, and stopped talking. It was easy to forget that you were constantly monitored.

"I know you've been working for this, and it was good, good that you've had something to aim for. But now that you're going to do it, I'm frightened, Neve, about what they might do to you. They're not like us; they know things that we don't."

"They said that the game was fair, that I could win the game. I believe them. Whatever they've done to us, they've never lied to us."

"Don't forget who you are, where you came from, and who bought you here."

"I'm going to do it, Myra, no matter what you say. Wish me luck. It's important that you believe in me."

"I believe in you," said Myra, but she looked away and Neve saw the doubt in her eyes.

⋅⋅⋅⋅⋅⋅⋅⋅⋅⋅

The technicians took out their instruments and placed a silver cap of wires over her sister's head. *She looks so small,* thought Neve.

The technicians connected the cap to a monitor, talking all the time in their fluttering language. Neve didn't recognise their species–there were hundreds of species on this Kristrall refugee world. Two of the technicians laughed; they might have been sharing a joke. This was all in day's work for them.

"Please pay attention," said Neve. "She's very young; she's only four." If anything went wrong, Neve realized she would never forgive herself.

Neve looked over to Berka, the technician who spoke English. She had been explaining the technical procedures to Neve. Neve didn't know if Berka had been assigned by the Kristralls as a translator, but she was grateful for her help. Watching her sister undergoing these long procedures would have been more difficult without Berka's calm explanations.

"We will scan her memories now, and then they will be transferred to the storage file. When her mind is empty, we will put her body into stasis, until you claim her."

Two of the technicians exchanged glances.

"How will I do that?" asked Neve.

"Part of the lost game is not knowing—you must find your own way."

"Neve," said Penny, "I can see Mummy. She's pushing me on a swing." Neve was surprised. In the two years that they had been on this world, her sister's memories had faded. She rarely talked about their mother; she had adapted well to life in the refugee camp—too well, perhaps. The life of a perpetual refugee was not the life Neve wanted for her sister, nor for herself. Neve remembered her old life very well, but she pushed away those thoughts.

"The process sometimes activates old memories," said Berka. "There is no need for concern."

Neve watched until her sister's expression started to fade. Penny's face grew still, her personality draining away into the alien technology. Her body stilled, too, as the consciousness left her.

"Almost complete now," said Berka.

Neve took her sister's hand. "I'll see you soon, Penny, really soon. Remember, this is just a game."

Berka took a glass slide from the machine. "Look, these are your sister's patterns transferred onto this storage file." Neve looked at the slide. She could see holographic patterns moving in the glass.

"This is all Kristrall technology," said Berka. "They are a wonderfully advanced people."

"Wonderful," echoed Neve, staring at the changing patterns, her voice was so quiet.

"My people started as refugees, too," said Berka. "In a few generations, we have worked our way up to technician class. There is hope, you know."

Neve said nothing and Berka resumed her professional demeanour. "The files will be transferred to the gaming field now. You will have five hours to find your sister's pattern. Good luck."

;␣

There were a thousand patterns in the grass, the personalities of a thousand individuals scanned and transferred to this field. Were they here because no one had found them? Neve preferred to think that wasn't the case. She needed to find her sister's pattern before the time ran out: one blade of grass in a field, one pattern amongst a thousand.

The cameras embedded in the glass dome, transmitted her actions to a watching audience. The lost game was very popular in this sector, but Neve had never seen it. The refugee class were not allowed access to entertainment media. The refugee class were not allowed lots of things: they weren't allowed to leave the confines of their camp, they weren't allowed to meet in large groups, and they weren't allowed access to information about the world they lived on. This Kristrall refugee world was a mystery to Neve. She knew that it housed hundreds of species, but she knew little else about it. She didn't even know how far it was from Earth.

The lost game had seemed to offer her the strongest chance of success. All she had to do was find her sister, and she knew her sister so well. She had been a mother to Penny for two years now, ever since they left their mother behind on Earth, lost in the disarray of war.

Neve realized she had been searching the field for a long while—too long—and time was slipping by. She had started the game calmly, methodically, examining the grass, staring at one corner of the field, searching for clues in the patterns of the grasses to the holographic images she had seen on the slide. But as the game progressed, she became erratic, running from one side of the field to the other, not recognizing the pattern she had thought she could find easily. Now she stood in the middle of field and screamed, "Penny, Penny," over and over again, hoping for a response.

She smelled smoke. Part of the grass verge seemed to be smouldering. Was that a clue? She had often told her sister not to touch the open fires that burnt in the homes and streets of the refugee camp. It must be a clue. The fire was gathering air, sucking in the hot perfumed air of the dome. Neve ran to verge and plunged her arms into the burning grass, but her hands slipped through the holographic flames.

They had told her that she could recognise her sister's pattern. They had told her she could win the game. They had assured her that the game was fair. There must be some way of locating her sister's pattern, but she felt overwhelmed. She was playing a game, whose rules she really didn't understand. Now she was beginning to fear that her sister would be lost in the field forever.

"You have one hour left," said a voice over the games system. Only one hour! She had been in the game four hours now, and her turn was almost finished. Fear threw a grey cloak over Neve, and she stood immobile, but only for a few moments. *No! Not now,* she thought. *Save the fear for later.*

"Another player wishes to join. Accepting another player will lower the prize-money. Will you accept?"

"Yes, I accept." The prize money seemed irrelevant now; she was fighting the fear of losing Penny. The administrators had explained that rule quite explicitly.

A figure materialised in the corner of the field. It was a member of the Kristrall race. Was this some sort of trick?

Bone white and elegant, he stood for a moment, possibly to allow the audience to admire his manifestation. When he moved, it was with a fluid grace, muscles working under skin in a refined sufficiency. He was at home here in the waving grasslands, at home with the advanced technology that had taken her sister, and in tune with the conventions of the game. But those thoughts didn't bring hope, they bought more fear.

He knows all, and I know nothing. My ignorance is his foil; he will use me to his advantage. No. She pushed down those thoughts. *He is here, and I can use him to find Penny.*

She ran over to him. "I need help, my sister is missing, and I've just got one hour to find her."

"My name is Greenstem, and I am honoured to meet you. Yes. Where shall we start?" He was unhurried. His presence, his elegance, created a reaction in Neve. She felt small, dirty, and insignificant. He magnified her flaws. It wasn't just his physical splendour—there was more, an aura of coherence and purpose that overwhelmed her. *No wonder they won the war. They are so much better than we are.*

The Kristralls always created this response in the human refugees, and perhaps in other species, too. The Kristralls often visited the human camps. Neve had seen them, chatting as they walked, taking in the sights, offering a word or two to the conquered peoples. They created this sense of wonder, as they passed.

No. Would her thoughts never be still? She was here now. She needed to find Penny; that was all that mattered. She subsumed her awe, ignored the hypnotic admiration he created. She *would* find Penny. "Can you show me how to find my sister?"

"And your name?" Greenstem did not seem to sense her urgency.

"Neve. Please help me. They said my sister was a type eight pattern. I thought I saw an overlay of butterflies or hearts—they're her favourite things. She's only four."

"I am also four years."

"Four Earth years, I mean."

"Ah, that is young. We measure time differently, you know. We relate to the Kristrall system."

"Right, of course. But can you help me find her?"

Greenstem looked towards the cameras, transmitting his actions to the audience. "I will do it," he said.

He walked over to a section of the grass and extended his arm, stretching and stretching the flesh until it lost its cohesion and became a protrusion of cytoplasm extending into the waving blades. This was the first time Neve had seen this transformation, though she knew that the Kristralls could mutate their flesh. There was endless discussion about the Kristralls in the camps. To Neve's eyes, the spectacle of his changing body was disturbing, and it diminished him, removed some of his glamour. *He is truly alien,* she thought as she saw his arms shape to the command of his mind. With their humanoid appearance, it was sometimes easy to forget how different these creatures were.

"There is an old creature here. I have met him before," said Greenstem. "I think no one searches for him now, but he is content to be here."

He moved his arm with its web of cytoplasm over another section of grass. "Is your sister related to you?"

"Yes, yes, we share parents, two parents." He was searching the grass, reading the memories of the individuals hidden within, but he was using his body to do it. Was that what it took to find Penny? For her, it was impossible, but the administrators had said that the game was fair.

"With equal chance of genetic exchange?"

"I guess."

He was moving more quickly now, waving his deformed hands in the grass. She thought that he would help her, that he would find her sister if she could not.

"Then she may not be genetically close to you. There is a high variation in your species, I believe."

"That's not the point," said Neve. "She's my sister, she's only four, and I want her back."

She looked over his shoulder as he continued his graceful movement. "What can you sense? Do you see her?"

"There is a colony; your people might call them ants. The old queen guards them well. Did you say that you sister likes ants?"

"No, butterflies, she likes butterflies."

"Ah, I will continue, then."

He moved away from the colony to another part of the field. "Do you like the Kristrall refugee world?"

Did she like it? Did she like living on this strange world as a refugee, her father dead, her mother left on Earth, light years away? Did she like being fifteen and mother to her sister? Did she like the feeling of dependence, the fact that she must be eternally grateful for the Kristralls for every mouth of food, for every breath of air?

"Yes," said Neve. "Your world is very beautiful, and you are a gracious people." Neve thought that was what he would want to hear.

She moved away from Greenstem. She lay in the soft grass. *I will do as he does.* She stretched out, not her body, but her mind, trying to read meaning into the impenetrable grasses, extending her mind outwards, outwards. *Penny, Penny, where are you, darling?* And then she touched a soft place; she reached another mind. It was not her sister, and she wanted to move away but it was immeasurably attractive. She didn't know the species—it was old, and it seemed to speak directly into her bones.

"I will tell you a thousand secrets, stories buried in a shell and hidden in the wreath of stars. There is a particular treasure that will help your people. I lost it many years ago and it is well armed, but I will tell you a mystery. . . ."

She felt something shaking her, and the touch of alien skin bought her to her senses.

"You've been lying there for many minutes. Have you found her?" It was Greenstem, standing over her.

"No." Neve was confused. "It was a voice telling me about a treasure, it was telling me secrets." She got to her feet.

"It was probably one of the game traps."

"You have fifteen minutes left," the games system announced. "Failure to find the pattern will mean that it stays here until you do."

"I've got to find her."

"Does she mean so much to you?"

"Yes."

"Then why did you allow her to enter the game?"

"We need the money."

"But refugees are provided with food, housing and limited education, all at our expense."

"I know," said Neve. "But we still need more, and Penny is too young to find me. This is our best chance."

"You need money to buy things?"

"Yes, all right, don't judge me." There was no need to tell Greenstem and the watching audience what she really wanted money for. There were always opportunities for people with money, on any world. Perhaps she could even acquire enough wealth to buy an illegal passage back to Earth, maybe even find her mother again.

"I do not judge," said Greenstem. "I simply observe. And offer a bargain, if you agree. I can find her. If not, she will remain here until you get enough money to play again. Perhaps you never will. Perhaps you will choose to spend your money on things. I do not judge."

Neve thought of her sister's body remaining frozen, never growing older, while her mind grew in strange directions by contact with alien thoughts. Even the one Neve had contacted here in the field had almost absorbed her. One day would be too long for Penny. "I'll do anything," she said.

"Merge with me. Then I will have the information to find her."

"I don't merge." Neve had seen men and women who had merged with the Kristralls, forlorn relics, their minds immediately tuned to alien thoughts, unable to function as humans any longer and cast out by the other refugees. She needed to care for Penny, and she couldn't do that if she merged with Greenstem.

He said, "It may be your only opportunity to find your sister at this point. And you will have the money you desire."

"I just want her back."

"It can be a difficult game for those who don't understand the consequences." Greenstem stretched out his strange hands towards her. "That is why the game always seeks new players, new species. The audience likes the fresh emotions you younger species generate."

"And you?" asked Neve. "What do you like?"

"I am a collector. If you merge with me, I will find her. Your memories will remain with me, and I will gift you with my memories."

The Kristralls, she thought, *set a trap for me and I've walked into—like an idiot. Was this all designed to trap me? They're watching me now, on their cameras. Watching me.*

She thought she had no choice, that she had to do it. She had to save her sister, even if it meant that someone else would become a mother to Penny. If she extended a trembling hand to his, she would be changed forever. He would flood her with a lifetime of his memories, the sea of his experiences passing through her. She would swim in his alien memories; his hopes, dreams, and experiences would inundate her soul. For a moment she would be him, and then their memories would bind together, all while the audience watched.

Her only consolation was that her mother wasn't here, wouldn't know that she had been changed, wouldn't know that she had fallen into a trap and nearly lost Penny. She'd tried not to think about her mother, since she'd lost her, had tried to be a mother to Penny. But she missed her mother so much, and so did Penny.

Her mother! That was who Penny would seek, that was where she would be. Neve ran back to the place where Greenstem said he had found the colony of ants.

There is a hive mind, a Queen guarding her children. That's what Penny would seek—a mother figure.

And yes! She was here. Neve could feel the patterns of her sister's mind. "I found her!" she shouted triumphantly to the cameras. "I've won your game! Now give her back to me!"

Greenstem came over to her. "You will achieve your acquisition of money."

"Yes." She would have the money, but she realized the price had been too high, the hazard to her sister had been too great. Neve had been naive, and she hadn't understood the game. In her overwhelming desire to escape this world, she had risked too much. But even as she thought that, a voice spoke inside her, insisting, *I won. I won the game. I escaped the traps, and Greenstem and his machinations.*

She was stunned to see her sister materialise in the grass sheltered, for a moment, by a huge shape with a small triangular head, which faded. Neve ran to hug her, but her body had no substance.

"It's a holograph," said Greenstem. "Your sister's body is in stasis where you left her. You can collect her soon enough." He seemed to sigh. "You could have had my memories, and I could have had yours. I live a long time, and you could have shared that with me."

"Is that what you brought us here for? To eat our memories?"

Greenstem shrugged. "You are a new species, and your value to our games is high. But there are many of you, and you breed quickly. I suggest that you play as often as you can if you wish to gain money. The value of the human mind will soon be diminished."

She knew she would never play again. She would seek new ways to make her way back to Earth. And, somehow, now, she felt sure that there would be other ways, that she could find them.

The holographic image shimmered. "Did we win?" asked Penny.

"Yes, we won their game. I'll come get you, and we'll go back to the camp."

And she had won something else as well—the confidence that the Kristralls were not infallible, and that the games could indeed be won by humans. That message would spread through the refugee camp like fire through grass.

We think of artificial intelligence as sexless, but what happens if a robot is given the shape of a woman and an assignment that involves nurturance? What if it begins thinking of itself as "she"?

HEART BOWED DOWN

by Jeff Crook

From the inside, the city's shield was as green as a certain gentleman's eye, fading to black at the center, in which a few stars shone weakly. Joan's head rolled in a wobbly semicircle and came to rest on her cheek. She looked down the alley at the girl running away in terror. Rain dripped from the singed stubble of her eyelashes and collected in the crease of her lips. "Don't be afraid," she called after the girl. "I'm not human."

Foam-flecked tidal water crept up the alley. She couldn't see enough of her surroundings to match the area to the archival postal geoseg files in her memory. Flickers of unseen lightning illuminated the buildings, and a dim, distant roll of thunder sent static waves rippling across the translucent surface of the force dome high overhead. What could she do without a body? She might shout for help. But if she were discovered by the wrong faction, someone might be able to break into her memory core and discover her mission. Better to be melted in an incinerator or washed out to sea.

The water inched closer as the rain pounded down—soon it lapped at her chin and invaded the cauterized circuitry of her severed neck. Her buoyant head drew a shallow draft in the tide. Lighter bits of garbage raced by, while she knocked against the heavier items floating at the sluggish edges. As she bobbed along, she recognized signs of orbital bombardment, and some buildings appeared to have been recently damaged. She passed an occasional glowing yellow sign that pointed to an emergency shelter.

Joan crossed an empty street, swirled for a moment at its center, then hurried into another alley. The current there was riotous, the air filled with spray as the tide water smashed and heaved between piles of rubble. The flood then poured into a huge crater, descending in a whirlpool as it was sucked down into the bowels of the city.

Joan's head raced past a dozen ragged humans perched around the rim of the crater, busily fishing out bits of salvageable flotsam. They began to fight for her as soon as they saw her. A hooked pole shot out, only to be knocked aside by another hook. While these two fenced for position, a netted pole dipped beneath both and swooped her head from the whirlpool. One of the hooked poles then tried to steal her away, only to be foiled by a deft flip that trapped Joan's head firmly at the bottom of the net. She was quickly hauled to shore, where the winner, a ragged urchin wearing an oily rag tied over the lower half of his face, dragged her into the protective circle of his arms. The boy gloated over her, glaring at the others while he backed away from the crater. They closed in around him, grim and silent.

He turned and darted through the doorless portal of a ruined warehouse. The roof of this building was pierced by more than a dozen large blast holes, through which rainwater fell in noisy, smoking cataracts. The boy fled across the chamber, his too-big boots splashing through the deeper streams of runoff. An ancient steel door hanging by one hinge noisily gave way before him, opening into a narrow street running between gray faceless rows of long-abandoned worker housing.

The boy paused at a corner to make sure he wasn't being followed, then continued on his way. He dismantled his net pole into three sections, tucking two into the grimy duffle bag that hung from his waist, while carrying the third, with its hoop, net, and the head of Joan Tramp, over his shoulder.

For the moment, Joan decided not to reveal her functionality for fear of frightening the boy. She had never been programmed with the kind of mothering behaviors necessary to put a child at ease. He might abandon her (as the girl had done), or he might see the value of her intact cranial hardware and decide to trade her to the Pythonians.

After following the street through several turnings, the boy arrived at an old transport post huddled in the shadow of a sprawling mineral extraction plant. A dark-haired man sat cross-legged on a bench beneath the shattered plastiform roof. He wore a gray coat that might once have been part of some uniform—it certainly appeared to be in better condition than the clothing of any other humans Joan had seen so far. Bundles of optical wire were stacked head-high on the bench beside him, while beneath the bench a sewer grate growled and belched with tidewater. The air here had a bitter metallic tang in addition to the usual chlorine smell of the sea.

The boy lifted out Joan's head out of the net and laid it triumphantly on the man's lap, face heavenward. "Look what I caught today, Cassius," the boy said.

The man's familiar green eyes flickered over Joan's face for an instant. "She's a nice one, Kevin. Where'd you find it?"

"Fished it out of the pool," the boy said proudly.

"Good catch," the man said.

"Don't you think it looks kinda like. . . ."

"They all look the same with their hair and eyebrows gone. But I can use her. Thanks," he said with a forced smile.

"I'll go see if any more of it washes up," the boy said as he skipped away with his net.

"You do that," the man said, already turning his attention to the head lying in his lap. He gnawed his chapped lower lip as he explored the stump of her neck with his fingers. After a few moments, he laughed and slapped Joan's ear with the flat of his palm.

"Wake up!" he said. "You're not deactivated."

"No, I am not," Joan said.

He looked her over, taking in her features with a sharp, appraising eye. "Combat model?" he asked.

Her servos whirred in an unconscious nod reaction. "Yes," she said.

"I didn't think you were one of the old service or comfort models. Where's the rest of you?"

"I don't know."

"What happened?"

"Some sort of destruction beam. Part of a trap, I think."

"I see." He chuckled, shaking his head. His dark hair was long and damp, framing his face as he looked down at her. "So that was you. What's your mission?"

"Classified," she said.

"No, I'd say your mission is over." He stuck his fingers into her neck and she knew no more.

ෆ⊙ℛℰⓄৡ

Her internal chronometer failed to record time. When she awoke, her systems immediately alerted her to this fact, as well as to the complete absence of sensory data during her deactivation. She didn't know she *could* be deactivated in any manner short of total destruction. Her design documentation mentioned no such possibility.

So she had been turned off. She had not dreamed, she had not recorded, she had done nothing—true oblivion. Though she didn't know fear, Joan Tramp found this experience unsettling, as it violated seven primary system functions. There had never been a moment in her six-year service career that she couldn't later access for study and reflection.

What was more, she couldn't see. Her eyes were equipped with ultraviolet and infrared sensors, as well as a limited ability to detect in the X-ray spectrum. She had never been blind, not even in total darkness, until now. If she had still been trying to pass for human, she might have screamed. That would have been the most appropriate reaction. Her diagnostics told her that her vision had been disconnected. She accepted this as but one more obstacle to the completion of her mission.

"Remarkable," a voice said near her. It was him—the scavenger who had deactivated her. "You really can see almost everything with these."

"What are you doing?" Joan asked. Her sight returned and she blinked reflexively at the bright light under which she lay.

"Examining your systems," he answered as he leaned over a work bench and flicked through some loose wires until he found the lead he sought. Shelves behind him were littered with scavenged electronics. "You really are a remarkable piece of work. I had no idea we had advanced this far."

"We?" Joan asked.

"Humans. The Republic," he said, then laughed. "Oh, you thought I was an android! No, I'm quite human, though sometimes I wonder if it's worth it."

"Who are you? Where is this place?" Joan asked. The room was a small, cramped chamber that, by the closeness of the air, suggested it lay deep beneath the city. The small reflector lamp hanging over the work station shed the only light. The walls were composed almost entirely of pipes of various sizes and ages, many of them thrumming with rushing water. A small stamped metal sign hung above the entrance. The lettering was not in any accepted Republican cipher. It was Pythonian—a script not unlike ancient Earth cuneiform. It read:

Emergency Bunker Level 9—Seti Quad Residents Only
Slaves Forbidden

"My name is Cassius," he said. "You go by the name Joan Tramp, I know. I've accessed your identification files, so there's no need for an introduction. I can't seem to access your primary or secondary function files. Your logic and motivator systems are encrypted, as is your mission directive. Plus, there is a huge chunk of resident memory that appears to have no purpose I can identify."

"What do you intend to do with me?" she asked.

"I *was* intending to scavenge you," he said as he dropped a probe to the floor in disgust. "But I can't even get into your systems deep enough to erase your memory. Not with these tools."

"Unfortunate," Joan said. "You are skilled for a scavenger."

"I used to work here. We're beneath the old Illium Mineral Processing Plant."

"Then you are one of the original inhabitants?"

"One of the founders," he said. He pushed his hair back from his face and glanced around at the dripping pipes. "I designed this place. I designed the shield that keeps out the poisonous atmosphere of this planet."

A window opened in Joan's memory, a codeword trigger that, until spoken, she hadn't even been aware of. "You must be Dr. Cassius Brees."

"You've heard of me?" he asked in surprise.

Her neck servos whirred again, trying to nod. "I was supposed to find you," she said. "But I don't know why. You have the key needed to unlock my mission parameters."

"Mission?" He laughed. "Whatever it was, it's over now. With your combat chassis gone, you're not much good, are you?" He crossed the small room and warmed his hands against one of the sweating pipes. "Besides, what possible reason. . . ."

"Stand by," she interrupted. The memory gate continued to open, revealing unsuspected possibilities for the completion of her mission. Her last priority memory was of performing an emergency dump of harvested data, mission objectives, and parameters to secured hardware before the energy beam disintegrated her body.

"There was a bombardment," she said.

"There are always bombardments," Cassius answered. "There have been daily bombardments since the Pythonians captured this planet. You don't know what I have to do to keep the shield up."

"You're protecting them," Joan said.

"I'm protecting us," he said. "The Republic can kill as many Pythonians as it likes. But every time they damage my shield, we do the dying, not the Pythonians. They are too well protected. It's the people on the surface who are vaporized by your cannons or suffocated by chlorine gas seeping through the weakened shields."

"We're at war," Joan said. She scanned her newly opened memory banks for information about Cassius Brees.

"It's not my war," he fumed. "My war ended when the Republic abandoned us to the Pythonians. We had no choice but to let them in or they would have destroyed the shield. There were over a million people living here then."

"And now?" Joan asked.

He shrugged. "You never see more than a dozen at a time. Mostly scavengers. I've seen cannibalism, people hunting people for food. The central districts might be different, but I never get far from the perimeter except to scavenge the parts I need to keep the shield up."

"Speaking of scavenging parts. . . ." Joan began.

"You're useless," he interrupted, as he ran his fingers through the dark tangles of his hair. "I'd have to cut you apart just to get at your systems and find out why they're so heavily protected, but that would likely destroy them. Your head is combat hardened. I've never seen anything like it. Whoever designed you really had a plasma coil up his butt."

Cassius looked at her for a while, biting a full lower lip that was raw and chapped by his nervous habit. "I could melt you down," he said. "You've probably got some metals I could use."

"I've completed accessing your files," Joan said. "I have information that you might find of interest."

He stretched and leaned against the stool beside his workbench, hiding his surprise with a casual yawn. "OK. Shoot," he said.

"CommandSAC is fully aware of the danger of bringing down the shield dome via bombardment, but they have had little choice since they were unable to make contact with you. That's why I was sent—to find you and discover the shield's frequency."

"So why did you try to destroy my shield?" he asked.

"I wasn't trying to destroy it. I only wanted to get your attention."

"Well, you got it," he said. "I designed that trap to clean off the Republic's energy parasites."

"The Republic couldn't be sure that you hadn't gone over to the Pythonians, either willingly or through brain implants. All that CommandSAC knows is that someone altered the shield frequency from the specs on file at Homeworld."

"And if I were working with the Pythonians?"

"My orders were to discover the frequency and deliver it to the fleet currently stationed in orbit," she said flatly.

"Meaning you were to extract that information if I didn't volunteer it."

"Information extraction is not within my current parameters. I'm a C/E model, combat and espionage. I would have subdued you."

"Subdued how?"

"I have ways, some more subtle than others."

"I'll bet. And then?"

"I was to extract you from the situation and deliver you to the fleet."

"How? I doubt even you could fly a Pythonian ship."

"I have a ship of my own," she said.

"A ship?" Cassius's grimy face brightened. "Where is it? What's its transport capacity?"

"In the sea outside the shield, enough room for two. If you'll help me, I can get you off planet. There's a full complement of military, scientific and diplomatic ships up there. I'm certain the Republic would be more than delighted to have you back. At the same time, I'd like to be able to complete my mission. I've never failed before. This is a new experience for me."

His face darkened. "You know I can't go outside the shield. I wouldn't last twenty seconds in this planet's atmosphere. The Pythonians confiscated all the salvageable breathers when they took over, and there isn't any way to make new filters, or batteries to power portable shields. They don't have to worry about the shield because they know I'll keep it up if I want to stay alive."

"My back-up can pilot the ship to us," Joan said.

"You have a back-up?" The color seemed to leach from his face for a moment. He bit his lip and reached for a bundle of wires.

"Standard duplicate model. She's deactivated, but if I can contact my ship, I can boot up her systems remotely."

"Well, it doesn't matter. Nothing passes through my shield, not even gasses," Cassius said, not without a touch of pride.

"That's why we need the frequency. Our ships' shields are based on your designs," Joan said, noting the small smile of pleasure this brought to his chapped lips. "If my ship's shield frequency is 180 degrees out of phase to the city's shield, the two will cancel each other out without bringing down either. I can fly my ship through the shield remotely, pick us up, and get us into orbit before the Pythonians know what happened."

"And of course the fleet will use the frequency to swoop right in and invade the city, killing thousands of refugees. No thanks, Joan Tramp 9912C/E. Too many people have died already," he said.

"Including your wife," she said. He glared at her in stunned silence, his reddened lower lip trembling. "I have a complete file on Deanna Brees as well," she added.

"You heartless plastic bitch," he said. He jerked a probe from a tangle of wires on his worktable.

"If you force them to continue conventional bombardment, sooner or later they'll hit the shield in a place you can't fix, and how many will die then?" Joan asked. "This outpost is too important to the Republic's overall security, its minerals vital to shield production."

"It's not my war, and I won't help you fight it," he said as he picked up her head.

"It is your war. You are here. The war won't stop just because you want it to, Dr. Brees," Joan said.

"I may not be able to stop the war," he said as he inserted the probe into her neck stump. "But I can damn sure stop you."

Joan opened her mouth to respond, but there was nothing to say, and nothing to say it with.

ଔୠୡ

When next she awoke, Joan was vastly altered. Her mind had expanded a thousandfold and her body grown to titanic proportions. She felt herself breathing involuntarily when she had never before taken a breath that wasn't part of a preprogrammed simulation of human behavior. She experienced the enormous functioning of her extended being, its consumption of fuel, processing of raw materials, and expiration of waste.

But more than that, she felt the life moving within her. At first she thought they were parasites, feeding on the byproducts of her functions, draining her energy for their own needs. Yet they were also monitoring her health and making repairs to damaged and worn systems. They were caring for her, even as she took care of them, gave them life and warmth and safety.

"What's happening to me?" she asked in a soft voice. She couldn't feel awe, but the enormity of her expanded consciousness and her awareness of the number of lives depending on her produced a sensation that her programmers had never intended. She had been designed to learn and evolve, but never like this. It was almost beyond her ability to process. She sensed a breakdown in logic and automatically initiated repairs.

"I've hooked you into the city shield," Cassius said from somewhere below and behind her. "The Pythonians allow me limited access to the city's operational computers so I can maintain the shield, but my passwords will only get me so far. I didn't change the shield frequency—they did, and they don't tell me what it is, probably to stop anyone from doing what you plan to do."

"Have you changed your mind?" Joan asked as she allowed her consciousness to spread out and explore its new environs. The shield's design was marvelously simple in concept. No wonder its designer was able to maintain it with little more than scavenged parts against the full might of the Republican attack fleet.

"No, I'm changing your mind," he said. "In exchange for my help, you'll give us two planetary days to find shelter."

"Seventeen hours?" she asked. "I don't have the authority to postpone the attack, but I'll certainly make the recommendation. It's a reasonable request." Something had changed inside her. She didn't want to see these people die, not if it could be helped, even if it meant countermanding her own programming in order to choose the least efficient means of completing her assignment. She stopped the repairs to her logic and concentrated on gaining control of the shields.

"That's not a request," Cassius said as she worked. "If the shield is breached by one ship before I'm ready, the Pythonians will receive notification of exactly what's happening and they'll change the frequency, trapping any ships already inside and blocking the others out. The Republic will only get one chance at this, so they'd better do exactly what I say."

It didn't take her long to find the security walls blocking access to sensitive Pythonian systems. Getting by them presented little difficulty, but at the same time she had to protect herself from counter-infiltration.

"I'll relay your demands," Joan said. "I have the frequency." She had sent a false damage alarm to the Pythonian main computer, followed by a simple reboot request to reestablish the shield dome. It didn't require a password, and because she wasn't intruding into their primary defense grid, there was little chance of detection.

"Already?" Cassius asked. "I could have used something like you before now." He stood beside the workbench, brushed a dank lock of hair from his face with one gloved hand, and smiled down at her.

"I'm patching into my ship's com via the shield's proximity detection array."

"Clever. Just make sure you deliver my demands before you tell them the frequency. I don't trust those guys any more than I do the Pythonians."

"Acknowledged," Joan said. For a few moments, her face went slack. Then she said, "Message received. Your demand is reasonable and will be honored. Every effort will be made to limit civilian human casualties. Thank you for your assistance, Dr. Brees. The Republic looks forward to your return."

"You mean they look forward to me working for them again," he said.

"Just one more . . ." Joan paused, her face going slack, then she resumed, ". . . thing. That should do it. I'll continue to monitor. . . ."

"What the hell just happened?" Cassius asked.

"Did something happen?" she said.

"You zoned out for a second. Are you being probed? Have you been detected?" He grabbed the bundle of wires sprouting from her neck and spiraling down behind the worktable.

"Negative. All systems nominal," she said. "While speaking just now, I performed a data dump to a backup aboard my ship. It's possible that the primitive nature of the shield's proximity detector array slowed that link." Something *had* happened, but she didn't know what.

"I hope so," he said. He started to pack his tools, shoving them into a greasy black duffel bad. "If they suspect I'm aiding you . . . have you ever seen a Pythonian, Joan? Ever seen one angry?"

"I've taken part in four major engagements against the Pythonian empire since my inception date," she said.

"Then you know what they are capable of, their cruelty," he said.

"Moral judgments impair my efficiency," she said, then added, "But I can understand now why you're afraid. I am not capable of fear, but I respect their ability as warriors, and I know that you're afraid for the other people living here."

"You don't know what they did when they first took over this city, after the Republic pulled out," Cassius said in a trembling voice.

"Rumors have reached the Republic."

"You can't imagine the things I've seen. If they thought for a second I was helping the Republic, they'd drop the shield and kill us all."

"But that would kill them as well. The Pythonians aren't any more immune to chlorine gas than humans," Joan said.

"They have an inner shield, separate from the one you're controlling. I built it after the bombardments began, after they promised to allow us inside during the Republic's attacks. But at that time, there were still resistance fighters in the city. They carried out acts of sabotage and assassination. One day, the Pythonians ordered select personnel into the center of the city for a 'distribution of needed supplies'—people like me, engineers essential to the maintenance of the extraction plants, as well as religious leaders. They promised fresh food and water, and not just for us. There were cargo containers stacked in the street waiting for us, and they promised that we would be allowed to distribute the contents. But when we opened them, they were empty. Pythonian guards forced us inside."

Cassius paused, his fingers tightening around the spanner in his hand. "That's when they dropped the outer shield. The inner shield protected us, but everyone outside it was exposed to the planet's atmosphere. It only took a minute at most, and then they let us out. We had to dispose of the bodies, burn them in the furnaces—thousands of them . . . children . . . women. . . ." His voice caught in his throat and he turned away. "It took weeks."

"I am sorry," Joan said. While he had been talking, she had searched for records of the event. The Pythonians, being ever meticulous, had made a thorough account of the dead.

"All because a few dozen malcontents couldn't leave well enough alone, couldn't try to make the best of things, wait for the Republic to return. They had to fight, resist the invaders. I don't know how many died. The Pythonians estimated three hundred thousand. You can be sure that's a conservative number." It was, very conservative.

"Your wife was one of them," she said. Now she knew why the engineers had given her a strange new female face before this mission began—a face unlike the usual models. They hadn't told her who she would be impersonating, but now she knew. She had seen herself in the computer's records. "I understand your reluctance to aid the Republic," she said.

"Yeah," he laughed grimly. "Well, it's done now. I've got seventeen hours to spread the word and make sure history doesn't repeat itself." He slung the bag over his shoulder and turned to check Joan's connections to the Pythonian computer grid.

"I'll leave you hooked up," he said. "You should be ok here until I get back. The others know better than to come scavenging down here. I have the whole place rigged with traps like the one that cut off your head."

"I wouldn't leave if I were you," Joan's voice said. Joan tried to stop it, but an outside program with higher authority than any she had ever encountered had assumed control. She was helpless against it.

"I have to go. We don't have the luxury of com systems around here. News travels by word of mouth."

"You had better stay indoors," Joan's voice advised. The Republic had detected the breakdown in her logic and overridden her. Now they were shutting her down, wiping her memory, booting up her replacement. She felt herself cut off from the shield, felt the life force ripped out of her, leaving her small and alone and blind, a cold disconnected lump of alloys and severed flesh.

"Why?" he said.

In answer, a bone-jarring thump shook condensation from the overhead pipes, spattering them with oily drops. Another followed, rattling the remaining tools on the worktable.

"Fleet Admiral Inoshi regrets to inform you that she has overruled the agreement to meet your demands and orders all ships' defensive systems modulated to pass through the shield. The attack has begun," Joan's voice stated.

The duffle bag slid from his shoulder and clanked to the ground. "Didn't you hear anything I said? They'll drop the shield!" he said. "They'll kill everybody."

"Negative. The inner shield has already been knocked out. The Pythonians have ordered soldiers to find you. They can't drop the outer shield without exposing themselves to the atmosphere."

"But the people! They've no protection from the bombardment!"

"Acceptable losses."

"Not to me!"

"My orders are clear," Joan's voice said, without her volition.

"You used me. You used me and betrayed me. I trusted you."

"Because I look like your wife," Joan said. Her voice was her own again. An explosion rocked the room, staggering him. Joan's head rolled off the worktable and hung upside down by the wires connecting it to the computer network.

"I had no choice. My programming was overridden. But—" She paused, watching as he dragged a homemade machete from a hidden sheath beneath the table. "I would have honored your request."

"That's nice to know," Cassius said as he swung. The machete blade, fashioned from a piece of heat dissipation pipe, sliced through the wires and bit deeply into the table top. Joan's head tumbled to the floor and came to rest against his left boot.

"You're going to take me to your ship," he said as he started for the door. A narrow staircase led up through a tangle of blast-damaged ducts and twisted bulkheads. "How do we get there?"

She didn't answer. He slowed as he neared the top of the stairs to deactivate a trap. Distant explosions shook moisture from the ceiling. Shifting the machete to his left hand, he grabbed a handful of Joan's wires and held her up to his face. "Where's your ship?"

But her face had gone slack, this time for good. Her eyes gazed sightlessly in different directions. "Tramp?" he said, shaking her by the wires. "Tramp!"

A hot stab of pain, like a wasp sting, flashed in the back of his neck. Dropping her head, he clapped a hand over the tiny dart and stared incredulously at the dark figure framed in the doorway leading to the upper levels of the plant above his workshop.

The drug, a nerve toxin, worked swiftly. Knees giving out beneath him, he sank to the floor. He watched in dull horror as the figure quickly approached, heavy boots ringing on the metal floor, and stooped, lifting him in one motion over her shoulder. She was tall, powerful, beautiful, familiar. Unable to resist, his mind addled by the drug and by the familiar face of his attacker, he lay against her back, his arms hanging limp from his shoulders.

"Deanna?" he mumbled through numbed lips. "You're alive?" She carried him outside and started down the street. Lances of plasma streaked overhead, flashing against the inside wall of the dome shield.

"Dr. Brees, my name is Joan Tramp," Joan said to him. "My ship is nearby. We will be there shortly." She ducked through a newly blasted hole in a warehouse wall. The edges of the hole glowed red and steamed in the chlorine-laced mist.

"But you're dead," he groaned.

"I've come to take you home." Joan Tramp quoted from her mission file.

Both men and women who love their work hate having to give it up and move on to something else. Some careers are shockingly short; but there is no age limit on the creation of beauty.

PEACOCK DANCER

by Catherine Mintz

I rake a metal-shod foot on the floor with a menacing rasp, flex my arms and step into the courtyard as a riff of rain splatters its gray stone and makes the torches gutter. Alone, I move to the constant peal of the water chimes, testing the linkages. In the puddles, my reflection follows, foot-to-foot, hand to hand. That twin and I are as one, perfectly mirrored.

Tomorrow I will dance my last dance. Sumalee is ten years younger than I, but we are twins. She was created and raised to take my place. I should be proud they think so highly of me, but my art is my own, not something written in my genes. I lower my arms and hear the hiss of raw power meeting water. Vowing I will not spoil this moment with anger, I vibrate my metal-decked arms until they sing true.

I invoke phantom drums. Five beats I wait, turn my head left, right, left, and wait again. Right, left, right. The imaginary flute enters and I light my suit, spread my peacock tail. The courtyard flames with purples, greens, and blues. If it were not for the insistent rhythm in my head, I would be shocked still. Palm leaves drip gems and stone carvings glisten.

With a tremolo like nothing that has ever been played, I am the peacock, dancing the universe into being. Raindrops become stars. Splashing water spins into galaxies. My feet rasp the measured pace of time. I dance until there is no beat but the drumming of my heart, and the suit's power is exhausted.

Fading, I sink onto the paving in the rain and weep, not for sadness, but because it was so beautiful.

The clop of wet hands applauding spoils the moment. I shiver with disgust. I know who it is: Administrator Pravat, drawn here by the light. My face as impassive as I can make it, I bow to my unwanted audience and walk off, into the rain, into the darkness, stripping off my suit as I go. I am tempted to let the pieces fall where they may but I resist. I will give them nothing to complain about.

Why should I do what they want? I ask myself. I will not dance tomorrow or ever again: a small revolt against the iron rule of the Benevolent Autocracy. Leaving my suit in my room, I don coarse clothes, slip through the doors, and start down the road I climbed so many years ago. I came crying and I leave crying.

The road is rough-paved, with stones on either side. I lurch from marker to marker, near blind with rain and tears. My heart aches, not because I must go—I have always known this would come—but because my final dance for myself has been spoiled. I will never wear my suit—their suit—again. I wanted to dance one last time for no one but myself.

Administrator Pravat took that away from me. I loathe his red hair, his beak of a nose, and his thick hands. Most of all I hate his false name, chosen to be easy to pronounce, as if we were tongue-tied fools. He may rule us, but he has no business among us. Why can't he leave us alone!

His people find mine quaint, ethnic, and amusing. For them the great market of the port is a tourist paradise. For us it is an economic necessity. We need hard cash for new crops, medicines, and the communication feed that tells us market prices. In the Autocracy, everything must be profitable.

I wish he had never seen me. Month after month, he has come and asked if it was time for me to retire, was my replacement ready, when would it be. I must not wail aloud. Someone might think I was possessed, *phi pob*. Such people are driven up into the hills, to live among their own kind. As a child I wondered what it was like. As an adult—sixteen standard years—I don't want to know.

Lowering my battered hat, biting a fold of my shirt to keep myself silent, I walk on through stinging rain. I smell the farm long before I can see it. My family fattens pigs, and there are overripe bananas in the trough in the hog house. My nose twitches at the stench, but I knock on the door.

"You are early," my father says, lifting a light to see me better.

"Early is better than late or not at all," I reply. It's like a password back into my childhood; one I wish I did not have to give.

He smiles his thin, hard smile. Father did very well by selling me as a dancer. They came and auditioned me, as they do most of the girls, but for me he got a fee, in gold, that doubled the size of the holding.

His eyes soften a little, probably with the memory of how well he did then. "Tonight, drink tea and go to bed. I will expect you up with the others in the morning."

"Yes," I say, head bowed, demure. It would never occur to him that I have been taught to behave one way and think another.

"She has soft hands," says one of my stepmothers from her place in darkness. Light takes power. Farmers do not waste power.

"They will harden," my father replies.

"She is not ugly," she answers. "We might do better if—"

Then I am out of hearing. The kitchen is bright and hot, although most of the work is done. I remember the cook, although not well. A stout, brisk woman who cooks for twenty or more people, Rajini seldom has a moment to herself. She keeps congee on the simmer all night long and water near the boil for the emergencies, big and small, of so large a holding.

The methane-powered steamer that prepares garbage for pig food stands gleaming, ready for the morning.

She asks, "Have you eaten?"

"No," I say.

Without a word, she cracks an egg into a bowl, ladles in simmering congee. Then she adds shredded roast pork, green onion, and a dot of chili paste. Finally, she places the bowl on the rough kitchen table, puts down a spoon, and indicates a stool. I draw up the seat and sit in my wet clothes, which have begun to steam. I try to fill the hollow in me with food. It is not hunger that makes me empty, but I feel better when I am done.

"You're wet and dirty," says the cook, rinsing my bowl. "It's too late for a bath or laundry. There's sacking piled there. Sleep near the hearth and feed the fire. That charcoal should last past dawn. I'll want a hot, bright blaze for the morning tea."

"Yes," I say, and Rajini is gone. No telling where. I can hardly complain at being pressed into service, since she fed me better than my father thought necessary: rough but not unkind. I wonder what she dreams or if she dreams at all. Out in the yard, a peacock screams, and fusses back to sleep. My eyes tear, and I remember.

Mother wasn't really beautiful, of course, just beautiful as all mothers are to their children. She was uncommonly graceful and, when the day's chores were done, she would show me this or that dance step, or sit, laughing, my baby brother in her arms, while I made up my own. I had been some time at the Hall before I understood how carefully she trained me.

I lost her, and my brother died during one of the periods when the Autocracy suspended trade and no medicines were available for perpetually cash-poor farmers. My father had brought home chickens the week before, a strain that would reach market size faster. They were gorgeous.

My brother, intrigued by the cocks' red wings and blue-black tail feathers, chased one of them through the kitchen and into the house. Father had to let him keep that one as a pet to get him to leave the rest alone. When it grew ill and then died, my father didn't think much of it. Chickens pick up human diseases easily.

Then my brother fell sick. My mother nursed him constantly until she caught influenza also. They both died on the same night. Two weeks later, I was tested and on my way to the Hall, arm stinging with a vaccination. My father's messages, never very long, grew infrequent, and then ceased. When I heard he had married again, two sisters, I thought I would never return home.

Yet here I am. The compound is quiet, except for an occasional grunt from the hogs and a sleepy cackle from the hens, still penned near the house, theft being rated a greater risk than disease. A gust of damp air carries the ammonic reek of chicken manure to me, and I cough.

I feed charcoal to the fire, bit by bit, tucking the pieces into the coals as my mother once did, while the rain dies away. When I look out, there is moon-glow behind the clouds. My clothes are dry. I take a tiffin box, fill one layer with cold rice and tuck pickled chilies in the center. There's nothing handy to put in the other, so I add more rice. It will be a long walk.

I am not unknown in the city. It seems likely I can do better for myself than my stepmothers might. Tiffin box in hand, I slip out the door and begin the walk to Chiang Dao, Star City, the place of spirits. Ghost-faced foreigners call it Mongkut Starport.

The lower valley is spangled with fires: farmers out harvesting for market, delayed by the rain. I can smell smoke, bananas, and papaya. The wind is rising and the clouds drifting away. I am beyond my family's land when I pause, look back, and see what I had taken for the rising moon is the glow from the hall on the mountain. The place is ablaze with lights.

For an instant, I think stars in the sky are moving. Helies are seldom used at night, but there are a least a dozen in the sky. I look toward the city. There is nothing on the road before me.

There is nothing on the road back. I am alone and highly visible. Without thinking, I crouch behind a stone, listening.

The light hits me like a slap. I stand, ashamed to be caught huddled in the dark. "JAIDEE!" My name, roaring out of the sky like thunder.

"Yes," I say and feel foolish. My voice is so soft.

"WHAT ARE YOU DOING?"

"I'm going to the city." I might as well say it. The road ends at the city. There's nothing beyond it but the paved plain where shuttles land and leave, hammering their way to low orbit.

"DON'T MOVE. WE'RE COMING DOWN."

With a blast of hot air, the heli settles to the road. Guards pour out of it like water from a broken jug. They have me by the arms before I can react, lift and carry me to the heli before I think to resist. The voice was that of Administrator Pravat. "You've put me to a lot of trouble," he says, "Why?"

"I went home."

He waits.

I wait, too.

"You didn't stay," he says.

"No."

"Sit there."

Like a dog, I sit in the indicated seat. The soldiers strap in. The heli lurches into the air, and turns east, toward the city.

"Where are we going?" I ask, startled. The worst I had expected would be that he would expect me to dance and accept defeat publicly. He ignores me, giving me plenty of time to struggle with my unhappy stomach as I take my first flight. I grip my tiffin box and wish I hadn't brought it.

The best thing I can say about it is the heli takes minutes to cover a distance I would take a day to walk. The worst is that I have utterly no dignity left when I stagger off. Despite the odor, the Administrator pays no attention. The soldiers are stoic.

I trip getting out and rice, red with chilies, is strewn everywhere. Someone stumbles on the mess and the dented box rolls off, clanging. I squat without thinking, trying to gather it together. The solders laugh and walk on. I sit back on my heels, carefully expressionless. I hadn't realized how much I wanted that taste of home until I saw it ground underfoot.

"Come," says the Administrator. "Come with me. There's nothing to be done about it." I look up. He offers me a hand, not flinching when I give him mine, which is filthy. "We go this way," he says when I start after the soldiers. I release his hand, but follow him.

The building is a maze crowded with shops. I smell fried fish, perfume, mangos, and something indefinable, perhaps from off-world. Punctuated by the clangor of metal-smiths, the din is staggering. A child wails and no one bothers to look. Everyone moves as if they were alone.

"This way," says the Administrator. "You can look around later." Then he really looks at me and adds, "If you want. It's not such a big place, once you know your way around." I follow him like a homeless puppy, through one door and then another. The smells and noise fade away. My lungs almost hurt with the cold, clean air, and I can hear our footsteps.

"Now," says Administrator Pravat, once we are seated in an office, "I had thought to talk to you after your final dance, but since you left early, it has taken me some effort to locate you." He pauses. He expects me to say I am sorry. I am not. He blinks, and cuts whatever he was going to say short. "I have something special in mind for you. Come."

I stay sitting just long enough to make him think I might not come, then rise like the dancer I am. We go through another door. I can hear the thud of a drum, the plink-plink of someone tuning, voices wailing and howling in warm-up. Administrator Pravat flinches and walks faster. I have a hard time keeping up gracefully. "Where are we going?" I ask.

He raps on a door and opens it without waiting. "Here," he says, and ushers me ahead of him. I start back and he laughs. The creature is taller than a tall man, and stands on four legs, with two large arms and two small ones. The hands have three digits. The head is grotesque, covered with bosses and spikes. Administrator Pravat slaps a switch and the projection fades, revealing a suit much like the one I dance the peacock dance in. "Put it on," he says.

It is not so much a matter of putting it on as fitting myself into it. I check the suit out thoroughly, locating all the contacts, the power packs, testing the joints and linkages. Finally I stand there caparisoned in metal and projectors. "Turn it on," says Administrator Pravat, and I do. He steps back, cautious. I move slowly, testing the strange form I wear. "Can you make it dance?" he asks.

"Yes," I say, and my four arms rise to an unheard drumbeat then fall as I make my first step. Without hurry, I begin improvising, testing. I had thought I would never again feel the smooth pivoting of powerful machinery at my command. The suit, mirrored in the safety screen, has a strange beauty.

I open my arms, and four cream-dappled arms open. I nod and a helmeted head nods. When I step, four tawny-stippled legs tap on the floor. I step again: there is sound. I turn, listening. The body made of light watches itself with great gold eyes. I am slow, but not awkward. I will be able to dance in this suit.

I began, something simple, listening to the staccato of my phantom feet on the floor. I clap two pairs of not quite hands, and they sound. I imagine a descant, like wind running over grass, through cane, through leaves. I crouch: this is a hunter's body. I spring, recover, crouch again, creep forward, slowly and silently.

Behind the safety screen, Administrator Pravat watches. "Stop," he says finally. "Good. Very good. Will you do it?"

"I don't know what you are asking."

"They," he points to the suit, "don't speak, although they do make noises. We think their language is gestures, but it might be something else. We need to find out. This may be the best way."

Securing the suit, I work myself out of it. I know I don't
want to say no. The feel of the machinery around me is too
welcome for that. There's a roughness in the way the suit moves,
something to work around. "I'll need to know more, to practice
with this, before I decide."

I am afraid to say yes. I know people who have dreamed
of going off-world: my father once did. Now he spends his days
in the orchards, packing fruit, fattening pigs and raising
chickens. I need time to think. "Will it be dangerous?" I ask, and
then, "Where is it? This place?"

Administrator Pravat doesn't bother to reply, just
gestures me to follow. My hair lashes my face as we walk
through a curtain of wind. Beyond the archway I see sunlight
and sniff a fragrance I cannot place. Administrator Pravat
motions that I should go first. I hesitate. He smiles. I stagger into
the sunshine. Behind me, he says, "It looks like this."

A fountain, its jets leaping to the music of wind chimes,
forms a backdrop for a dancing court, much like the one at the
Hall. After that, the resemblance to anything I have ever seen
ends. I take a deep, wondering breath. It is a world of beiges,
browns, tans, all dappled with light and striped with restless
shadows.

White flowers wider than my hand crowd the basin and
spill into the water. Feeling off-balance, I walk forward and
touch the silky cold surface. It is mountain water, nearly as cold
as ice, for all the stone under my feet is hot.

"You'll notice the gravity is lighter and the sun more
yellow," says Administrator Pravat. "You will need practice to
move well. There are about a hundred days until the ship leaves.
Maybe a hundred and fifty. If you don't want to go, perhaps you
can teach—"

I have no idea what my expression is, but he grins,
suddenly almost likeable. "Your room is over there. There are
recordings, notes, and communications. After you go through

those, if you need anything, ask. I'll see you tomorrow." With that, he walks through the curtain of wind.

In my coarse clothes, filthy with the dirt of this world, I sit on the edge of the fountain and look into the water. Pisciforms swim through the depths, indifferent to anything beyond their watery universe. The surface ripples with reflections: the exotic blossoms, the hologram of the foreign sun, and my own earnest face, framed by my farmer's hat.

Behind me stands my phantom second self, four-armed, four-legged and so real that I look around, startled. There's nothing there, of course. I can feel that body. It can run, fast and quiet. It can wait, without moving, watching the sun crawl across the sky. It hungers. It hates. It loves, and dreams, and dances.

I sniff my hands. They smell of rice, chilies, and earth. The other world won't smell like that. The food will be odd. The people will not be my people. It's frightening, thinking of all the differences. But I am a dancer. I rise, needing to don the suit that I will make my second self.

⊰⚬⚬⊱

Like hail on paving a hundred metal feet step in unison. I make it through the entire set without error and stand, panting, hoping not to be noticed. Not to be noticed is the greatest praise here. I must move at the will of the negotiator, who will sit safe in a cubicle, testing the reactions of the people we have come among, uninvited. All of the danger will be mine, but little of the glory. I am a tool and a poor one, at that.

My suit and I cannot move as *they* move. If I flex a limb, the motion is not and never can be right. That you can never do something more than acceptably is demoralizing. Still, muscles quivering, I stand ready. As the suits draw down their power supplies, they become harder to move, harder to hold in position. We've done well and are too tired to do better. Some days Sensei is merciful.

Not today.

"You are tired," she says in her meticulous Omlingual, "but you will have to work when you are tired and when you are sick. You have to learn how to keep going and to do everything precisely. There is no room for error. Ever."

There is a splash of metal on paving: a suit, unlinked.

Sensei's face does not change. It never changes when someone resigns. She gives us a moment while the name passes among us like wind through dry grass. Lisabet was a good dancer. Her resignation shakes us all. Trained to wring one more dance, one more sequence, one more step from unwilling bodies, we may not be all they want, but we are the best there is.

"Our future—and theirs—depends on your conveying meaning correctly. Again," says Sensei.

Minus one, once more our metal-shod feet step in unison.

I blush whenever I remember how graciously I accepted Administrator Pravat's invitation, how stunned I was when he said, "Good. Let's join the rest." He opened a door and there they were, fifty-three girls—women—all competing for positions.

I was young, and afraid to tell anyone I was frightened of failure. Death didn't seem nearly as scary, but that was before my first—and only—space flight, one long fall into darkness. Home is a long way away. There are only seventeen of us now. Some nights I dream of unlinking my suit and wake up crying, not knowing if I am happy or sad.

Class finishes. The others scatter singly to their rooms or jointly out into the city. At time-lived twenty, real-time thirty-one, I am younger than the rest, which makes me an outsider. Alone, I habitually go into the deserted garden and perform the dances I learned as a child—the lotus, the caterpillar, and the butterfly. If I am especially sad or happy, I dance the peacock.

I don't have my suit, of course, but children don't dance in suits. They wear bustles and wings of braided palm leaves that they make themselves. There are no palms here, but the covered basket of garden refuse at the gate always has plenty of leaves and stems. I enjoy the handiwork, like dancing with my fingers.

By now, I am nimble in my improvising. This afternoon, there are flowers heaped beside the trash, ripped from the beds and replaced. White, cream, and gold, their saffron pollen dusts my hands are I work them into patterns, making them beautiful one last time. I sniff; my hands smell of dust and something aromatic that makes my nose itch. I sneeze.

Listening to the wind chimes, I fasten my bustle and slide my wings on. Focused by tiny holes in my bustle and wings, minute suns spangle the pavement at my feet. In a shower of pollen, I begin the peacock dance, turning and turning, then stop and begin again. Frowning, I clap time for myself, a little slower than usual, a rhythm for late afternoon. I can leap high in the light gravity: it changes the pace of the dance.

My foot slides on the paving, and I am the peacock. My shadow follows, foot-to-foot, hand to hand. Suns swirl about me. My wings loose time winds, scattering saffron dust over the world I dance alive. The universe spins as I dance. Suns spill into the heart of the galaxy. Heavier, heavier, it sinks into darkness, then explodes into new glory.

I finish—wings flung wide, tail spread—and stand quivering as I return to time and place. Time and place and an odd tapping; I turn around. Someone has come into the garden wearing a suit. I blush furiously, drop my improvised costume, crush it in my arms, and bolt for the gate. With a smooth tap-tapping of feet on paving, the suit glides to block me.

Angry, I hold my armload high in front of me. I want out, even if I am undignified, because I'm going to cry. Which is why I am face to face, tears dripping off my chin, before I realize my audience is not wearing a suit. I gasp and drop the trash that was my costume.

The dapples and stipples are marks of rank, affiliation, and gender. The alien is very important. It would—I shiver—have to be important to be here, in our compound, unescorted. I see gold and garnets on its carapace. It reaches out—

Something touches my face, the velvety palp they use for fine touching. They don't speak, although frightened or hurt they can produce a shrill whistle. I back away. It rattles its feet on the paving, gathers up my armload and offers it to me with its lesser arms.

"Please," I say. "It's—not important."

It thrums its feet on the paving, demanding more. We know a few simple gestures and that is what this one means: do it again.

It was embarrassing to be caught out, frightening to find what my audience is, but—to perform. I bite my lip and swallow hard. I can't refuse. Everything I—everything *we*—everything *everyone*—has done up to now was to win this opportunity. At least I can't make a mistake, offend doing my own dance. Can I? It saw—

I take the offered armload, fearing the costume is too crushed to wear. My fingers fumble as I pull it into shape. I replace flowers almost at random until my legs can hold me. I put my costume on and close my eyes a moment to center myself. I slide one foot on the paving and I become—something new.

With a staccato rattle, my audience begins to dance, too. Suns swirl about us as our feet scatter saffron dust over the world we dance alive, into darkness, then into new glory while the wind chimes peal.

Sometimes women are the nurturers of memory, but they don't always ask themselves whether the memories are worthy of the nurturance.

BLOODY ALBATROSS

by David Bartell

A crowd was coming for Netty, not back on hysteria-wracked Earth before it was destroyed, but right here on the Moon, through the cold, flimsy corridors of Shoemaker Pod 4. Wild silhouettes of men and women from Shackleton crater flooded out of an airlock in slow motion, fists raised, shouting in that unintelligible language of dreams.

The mob swarmed over her and kept rushing by. They weren't coming for her after all, but were fleeing some unseen danger. As the pod administrator, she ran to seal the airlock, but when she got there, her limbs stiffened, and she could not raise her hands to the latch.

Netty awoke shivering. As the dread dissolved to reality, she was for the first time aware of the source of these nightmares.

It was the Bag, which was tucked in the storage shelf under her aluminum cot, so close to her head that she could practically hear it cursing her in her sleep. Though her room was larger than most—a private room at that—there was no closet or drawer to put the Bag in. She should have known that when you sleep with something insidious an arm's length away, it will poison your dreams.

She hadn't had the courage to look inside the black muslin bag since she'd packed it, some eight months prior, but every night, bloody memories not her own stole into her dreams.

She sat up halfway, and rearranged her bedding to put her head at the other end, farther from the bag. The cold, thin air bit at her arms and feet, until she drew the Mylar-lined blanket back around herself.

She groaned and wondered rhetorically why she had brought the damn thing to the Moon in the first place. But she had not forgotten the decision. As mayor of Philadelphia, she had been something of a celebrity even before. Then she decided to accept a post on the Moon, in anticipation of Big Bastard, the asteroid that later destroyed all life on planet Earth. So a lot of people sent her things to take with her. They were not presents, but precious objects that their doomed owners offered to posterity. She received so many packages that she eventually stopped looking at them, letting security pass along anything they felt worthy.

One day she opened a package from someone whose name was vaguely familiar. It was postmarked from Glendale, California, and had passed security with a code that indicated it came from a family member. A little larger than a shoebox, the package was heavy, and something hard clunked around inside it. It was from Jameson Grey, a distant cousin of hers who wrote that he had met her at the Thompson family reunion in Detroit. A postscript read simply, "Never forget," a favorite saying of her grandfather's.

She dug through the crumbling popcorn packaging and pulled out the most ghastly thing she had ever held in her hands. Immediately she knew that she would have to take it with her to the Moon.

೮೮ᏟᎡᏇᎧ౪౦

The morning after she realized the Bag was haunting her, Netty met her friend LaDonna in the mess hall for tea and biscuits. Jokingly called the Double-wide Diner because of its construction from two of the largest modules on the lunar base, the room served as a multi-purpose room as well as a mess.

When it was empty, it was stark white with grey trim. When it was occupied, it was the most colorful and interesting place anywhere in the pod.

"What I wouldn't give for some pancakes and sausage," LaDonna said. Like Netty, LaDonna was an American of color, in her late thirties. She had been tall and thin even before these months of measured rations.

"Rule number one: as a refugee on the Moon, never talk about food."

LaDonna pursed her lips into a comical sneer. "Oh, phooey."

"I'm serious. You keep that up, they're gonna pick up my stomach growling on a seismometer."

"All right, all right. I can take a hint."

"Thank you." Netty studied LaDonna's cornrows, thinking she needed her own redone. "Your hair still looks good."

"I keep lusting after Mekana's hair," LaDonna said, referring to a woman from Sri Lanka who had hair down to her knees. "She could crop it, give some to both of us for extensions, and still have it hang to her derrière."

"Make her an offer."

"When we're back on *terra firma*. You did a nice job braiding, for now. Which is good, because I volunteered to MC the show-and-tell tomorrow night."

"Oh, that."

"What do you mean, 'oh that'?" LaDonna asked, exaggerating the objection. "It's gonna be fun!"

"It does sound better than the Up and Atom Throat Singers we had last week," said Netty, "but I'm not in the mood for touchy-feely."

"You're homesick, ain'tcha? Every time they say we're clear to return to Earth, something comes up, and they postpone it. We're getting Moon fever up here. This'll do people some good. You're the administrator, so you have to come."

Netty had to admit that she really should attend, but she was not feeling charitable with her inner life at the moment. "What exactly is going to happen?"

"Everyone's going to bring their personal belongings, show them, and tell how they decided to bring them. You know, what it means to them."

"Ugh. How cathartic is that going to be!"

LaDonna narrowed her wide eyes and grinned. "Now, I know you brought your mother's earrings, because you wear them all the time. And you told me about your grandmother's wedding ring, which is waiting for a ripe opportunity. Then there's your Shake-and-Go wig, and maybe some clothes you're saving for Earth. But the way I figure it, you must have something else, to bring it up to the ten kilogram allowance."

"Oho, so you have me all figured out."

"Maybe as a PA you were allowed even more than ten, am I right?"

"No, just the ten."

"But there is something else, isn't there?"

"Of course. I have a little other jewelry, a knick-knack or two, a memento chip, and my pioneer clothes. Satisfied?"

LaDonna's eyes narrowed. "Antoinette Washington, I know you better than that. Come on, I'm your best friend."

Netty smiled. "You do know me." She was afraid to show the Bag, even though she had brought it for everyone to see. "There is something else," she said, "but it's gruesome, and now I'm not sure people will understand."

"What is it, Hitler's brain?"

Netty snuffled a laugh. "You're very perceptive."

"Scrumptious! Perfect for show and tell."

"I have a better idea. Why don't you let me be the MC?"

"So we don't get to see what you brought? Oh, no, sister, huh unh. You're showing it." LaDonna made a sweet and sinister smile. "I would appreciate it, also, if you'd make a brief opening remark."

CRITTO

The next day, the diner was full. Of the 120 people in the Shoemaker Pod 4 Moon Base, nearly a third seemed to have come to share their remembrances of their destroyed world. Virtually everyone not on duty crammed into the room, sitting on stools at the tiny tables and standing everywhere else. The wealthy Barajak family was noticeably absent, so Netty's curiosity over the contents of their personal spacecraft would have to remain unsatisfied. Netty and LaDonna stood at the front of the room, on the long step to the busing station. Netty felt oddly naked holding the black bag in public.

"Thank you all for coming," LaDonna said loudly. Her tall, thin frame seemed to tilt at impossible angles, thanks to the low gravity and her animated way of speaking. Netty had thought that her friend would be good at the performing arts, and she was right. "I see you all brought your things with you, and I have to admit, I can't wait to see what everyone has to show the rest of us!"

The men, women, and few children in the mess that doubled as a town hall clutched eagerly at their belongings, ready to share what was left of their shattered lives. Some of the objects were in bags or pouches, while others were already on proud display. This had been a good idea after all, Netty saw. Excellent.

"Since she's already up here," LaDonna said, "why don't we dispense with opening remarks, and just have our lovely pod administrator go first? Netty Washington, show us what you have in that interesting bag!"

I've been tricked, Netty thought. When she was a child, her brother once taunted her at the pool, because she was afraid the water was too cold. While she was endlessly bobbing her foot in the water like a nervous thermometer, he pushed her in. The water *was* cold, but the push was just what she needed. She remembered the shock and how it had erased her anger. "Thank you!" she had told her brother, and since that day, she had always been a little bolder when facing the unknown.

Netty shivered. "It's cold in here," she said. The heavy black bag hung in her hand, and she shifted it from right to left. Would people think she was crazy for bringing it? Since the nightmares, she wasn't so sure herself that it had been a good idea. If she wasn't convincing now, she could lose some all-important credibility as a leader.

"Listen," she said. "I don't want to take time away from the rest of you. You have to hear my voice all the time, and—"

"Just show us and be done with it," LaDonna interrupted. "You all want to see what she brought, don't you?"

The people cheered. It was the loudest single sound made by humans since the world died on Earth Zero. LaDonna leered happily at Netty.

Netty grew serious, cast her eyes at the floor, and then closed them. The room quieted. "Actually," she said, "what I'd like to share with you is not what I brought, but what I did not bring. That's just as important."

That brought murmurs of approval. She smiled politely at LaDonna, who glared back. She felt guilty, not for feeding LaDonna her own medicine, but for allowing the Bag to steal away a little of her courage.

"As you know, I used to be the mayor of Philadelphia, and I can tell you, one thing I didn't mind leaving behind was all the bureaucracy." She paused to let them laugh. "When it came out that I accepted the post as a pod administrator, a lot of people tried to contact me. You can imagine. And they sent me things, personal, precious things, asking, hoping, begging me to take them with me to sanctuary. You know what they were, because you brought a lot of them with you. Perhaps you brought something for someone else. If you did, you are the most noble people who have ever walked the face of any planet."

"What kinds of things did they send?" someone asked.

Netty looked over the audience and felt a wash of emotion ripple through her body. Her lip quivered. "Heirlooms, photographs, data chips, poetry, flags. Locks of hair."

A woman near the door held up an envelope. "A lock of hair," she said.

"Thank you."

"What else?"

"Oh my," said Netty, allowing memories to swim about her. "I received a Bible. It was signed throughout by thousands and thousands of witnesses. I couldn't bring that. Just imagine." And imagining brought a tear to her eye.

"I received a number of hand-made art objects," she continued. "The general theme was the beauty of the Earth. I got this one thing that was supposed to be a little model of the world, but it was all made of tiny seeds, real seeds, of different colors." She explained how the seeds were actually meant to be replanted on Earth, once it was able to sustain life again. "A lot of thought and care went into that one.

"The things I received almost never had a return address. They were babies on my doorstep. I think people did that on purpose—left off the address—to guilt me into taking them. I had to think that, because the only way I could leave so many things behind was by pretending that the people who sent them were not entirely sincere. But they were.

"Someone from Uruguay sent me a teddy bear that had been owned by a child who died of Trojan-HIV-X. I did not bring the bear, but I'll never forget it either. I wish I had a teddy bear for every child that—"

A moment of sniffing, for so many children. One woman repressed a sob with great effort, until a man behind her sobbed. That got her started, and others too.

"Oh," said Netty, retaining her composure, "and someone sent me a lei of silk flowers to place on the grave of one of the workers who died here on the Moon, building one of our bases. It was so light that I almost brought it, but it was one of those things I left in that wretched 'overweighting room.'"

"You are the noble one," a man said.

That cut into Netty, just like the word "Earth" whenever someone said it. They might not think her so noble if they knew she had brought with her a tangible reminder of things unpleasant.

Numbly, she went on, describing other things that had been sent to her, each one more heartbreaking than the last, but always leaving out the package from her distant cousin. And as she went on, the weight of that burden grew, as if the anorexic gravity of the Moon had somehow become voracious. She had to share the burden or it might crush her. Yet she could not. She did not know how.

Netty leaned on the wall, and LaDonna picked someone to tell his story. A man named Gleb stood, nervous and excited, as he held up a fishing kit, a practical tool, if any fish had survived Big Bastard. Netty's friend Oscar showed his father's hunting boots, an item both practical and sentimental. The Poitevins lamented that what they had to leave behind was *Française*, and no one blamed them. They declined to show their personal effects, and other than a ribald "oo-la-la!" no one blamed them for that either.

Never had such laughter and pathos erupted from these numbed people during their protracted months here. The pods were kept at low pressure to save resources, and the air was notoriously dry, so the many tears dried on cheeks, not finding the satisfaction of running their full courses. When it was time for a shift change, LaDonna had to disband the gathering, promising to make show-and-tell a weekly event. There had only been time for a fraction of the people to tell their stories.

The evaporated tears would be reclaimed and recycled into the water supply, so that people would drink them, and shed them again and again.

ങ‌ල‌ଃ‌ଠ‌ଙ

F or a long time, Netty had nightmares about the destruction of
the world. Now those fears were settling out of her dreams
and into her soul, only to be replaced by these new nightmares.
They were getting worse, so Netty decided to take the Bag out of
her room. There was a sort of treasure vault in another part of
the pod, a climate-controlled room in which were stored a
variety of treasures from Earth. She had not studied the
inventory, but she recalled that it contained everything from
ancient documents to modern works of art. The other pods had
similar rooms, and many more treasures were buried in strong
rooms under the Earth, in hopes that they would survive, along
with some of the people. The experts said that no one was left
alive on Earth (though they could not prove it), but that there
was a chance King Tut's sarcophagus and Babe Ruth's uniform
were safe in a vault somewhere at home. One of the original
Magna Carta copies and a Stradivarius were safe on the Moon.

As Netty left her room for the treasure room, black bag
in tow, an alarm sounded. Four short buzzes, and a long meant
radiation hazard. Obeying the emergency rules, she rushed to the
Double-wide Diner, the best-shielded compartment in the pod.
Behind the kitchen was a backup control center, a tiny room
from which the pod's main systems could be controlled
manually.

LaDonna's room was one ring inward, on the way, so
Netty stopped by, making her way through the rush of people
heading inward. She found herself constantly reminding
LaDonna of the importance of following the rules, especially if
Derrick, LaDonna's husband, was away on duty.

"What is it?" asked LaDonna.

"Probably sunspots. We'll see."

"I thought sunspots couldn't hurt us."

"Flares, that's the term I was looking for. When they
detect them, they turn on a magnetic shield, but the rules say we

go to the diner first, and then the safety team tells us what to do."

They paced carefully to the next ring in. The women often jogged together, but usually when the corridors were empty. With the low gravity, one could bound past several doors at once, which was dangerous with so many people flooding into the halls. LaDonna noticed the black bag.

"Whatcha got there?"

"You know," Netty said. "My albatross."

"Your what?"

"My burden. It's from an old poem."

"No wonder I never heard of it."

"Do you know the Monty Python skit with the albatross?"

"Who's Monty Python?"

"A British comedy team from the early days of television. My brother used to go around reciting them, word for word. He minored in Objective Humor at Cambridge. He'd go around with this corny accent, growling 'Albatross! Alba-bloody-tross!'"

LaDonna looked at her as if Netty had lost her mind. "If you say so." Then she softened. "Listen, why don't you let me carry it for a while? I won't peek, I promise."

Netty sighed, and handed over the bag. Her shoulder ached with relief. "I thought things would be lighter on the Moon, and they are, but somehow, you get just as tired carrying them around."

"Less weight, but the same mass," LaDonna said.

Netty looked at her with surprise. LaDonna was one of the least scientific people in the pod.

LaDonna smiled proudly. "My husband is an engineer, don't forget," she said. "If he keeps talking in his sleep, pretty soon I'll know everything he knows!"

Netty laughed. "Be careful what you wish for!"

They arrived at the diner. As they jostled with others through the door, LaDonna handed the bag back. Netty gripped it shut as if it held a spitting cobra. LaDonna followed her through the kitchen to the backup control room.

"Listen," Netty said, "I've got to check in, and make sure everything's all right."

"Okay, I'll just wait with the others."

"Thanks," said Netty, loosening her grip on the bag. "Here. Take this."

"Okay, sure. Don't worry, I won't peek."

"Oh, just go show it around. That's what you wanted to do."

"Seriously?"

"Better you than me."

"I better look first." LaDonna watched Netty's eyes. She slowly untwisted the top of the black muslin bag, waiting for Netty to object. Netty did not, so LaDonna opened the bag and looked inside. "What is that?" she asked.

"Take it out."

"Are you sure?"

"Hurry up, I've got to go!"

"Okay!" LaDonna pulled out a crude, misshapen object made of iron. It was a flat grey bar with loops at either end, huge rivets, and two links that were remnants of a chain. The metal was tarnished but not rusty, and it looked very manly, like something from an Old West blacksmith shop. "What is it?"

"Those are shackles, from the slave trade. They're hundreds of years old. They were actually used to bind the wrists of human beings."

LaDonna's face stretched into a silent scream. "This is real?"

"Yes, it is. It was actually used, many times."

"On real slaves, in America?"

Netty nodded. "There are 400 years of blood on those things!"

LaDonna thrust the object back into the bag. "Sweet Jesus, girl."

"I have to go now."

"Okay, go." LaDonna twisted up the neck of the sack, and looked away from it. "I won't show anyone, I swear. Oh my God!"

❧❦✦❦☙

After she was no longer needed in secondary control, Netty found LaDonna in the diner, still clutching the black bag.

"Everything OK?" LaDonna asked.

"The shield is up, but they want us to wait here a little longer, to make sure it's stable."

"Why don't they just keep it up all the time?"

"The shield generator keeps overheating."

"Do they have that problem over at main Shackleton?"

Netty bristled every time she heard or read the name of the larger complex of pods at Shackleton crater. *Shackle town*, a town of imprisoned refugees, unable to return to their homes. "Some of the pods keep their shields up, but most have trouble like ours. There are others with a different design. They built their water and refuse tanks into the ceiling, which protects them from flares."

"If our generator is overheating, why don't we just pump some of that heat into this icebox, and solve two problems at the same time?"

"Great idea. Get your brilliant husband on that one."

"What?" LaDonna asked with a harrumph. "And have him working all hours so I have to sleep in a cold bed?"

"All the more incentive."

LaDonna hefted the black bag. "What are you going to do with this?"

"I was just on my way to a storage vault, to get it out of my room. It gives me nightmares."

"And you brought this—why?"

"My grandfather used to say, never forget how our ancestors were enslaved, or it could happen again."

"DNC, girl," said LaDonna, impatience kindling in her voice. "Does Not Compute. You were always the one who wanted to put racism behind us. I can't tell you how many people you've told that to. We're starting over now, you said, and we're going to do it right this time."

"What's wrong with that?"

"Nothing's wrong with that. I'm all for it! But look at you! All that talk, and now you're the one who brings skeletons from the past right inside these walls?"

"Give me that," Netty said, seizing the bag. She checked her anger. "Don't you dare tell anyone about this."

"And let them see how insincere your vision is?" LaDonna waved her palm in the air, warding off the idea. "Not on your life would I tell anyone."

⸲⸱⸲⸱

Netty put the black bag in the treasure room, behind some other things, so no one would stumble on it. No rooms in the pod were ever locked. That was a safety measure—if there was catastrophic damage to a part of the base, no lock would ever prevent people from reaching safety. The room had been used as a temporary quarantine area when they first arrived. She thought that was a fitting precedent.

With the antique shackles well-hidden, she thought that her disturbing dreams would subside, but they did not. If anything, the recent attention she paid to them seemed to make them more powerful. She had nightmares of slaves manacled and tortured, with pulsing images of blood and the sound of screams. A family of runaways was caught as they tried to make their way on the Underground Railroad from Georgia to the North, and to freedom.

Then there was a man, beaten and bleeding, standing outside on the dark, icy Moon, wearing nothing but manacles on his wrists and shackles on his ankles. He was screaming for help, but she could not hear him. He was dying out there, impossibly slowly, and he pounded his arms on an airlock, but no one let him in.

His screams became her own, and she awoke shaking in the chilly air. Within seconds, several neighbors were at her door, which was nothing more than a Mylar curtain.

Someone came in and turned on her light. "Ms. Washington, are you all right?"

Then a general alert sounded. A scream in the night was not a thing to take lightly, not when there was radiation pouring down, and fallout from the asteroid impact still dropping on them from time to time.

"Yes, Enrique, I'm all right."

"You had a bad dream?"

She nodded. "Have someone cancel that alert."

"Of course."

Unable to sleep after that, she put on her shoes and went for a jog. LaDonna met her in B ring.

"I figured you wouldn't be able to get back to sleep," LaDonna said, ready to run. "You're always a bundle of nerves after an alert."

"I was a bundle before the alert." As they jogged, she told her friend about the dreams.

"Listen, Netty, this thing is too big for you. You've got to share the—what did your brother call it?"

"Albatross."

"*Bloody* albatross, wasn't it?"

"That's exactly what it is."

"Let's put it to rest, together."

They turned out to C ring, which made for longer laps. Netty was not jogging well, and she kept underestimating her footfalls, as if she had forgotten how to jog in the Moon's reduced gravity.

"Speaking of bloody albatrosses," LaDonna said, "I haven't had one since we came here. Have you?"

"What are you talking about?"

"You know, the *monthly* albatross?"

"Oh, that." Netty nearly hit the ceiling, and checked her jogging. "I've been spared that one, but that's to be expected."

"Maybe it's because the Moon doesn't have phases when you're on it."

"That's an old wives tale. The problem is that there are always lights on, which fools the body."

"Maybe, but things are different here. The Earth's pull is stronger than the Moon's was back on Earth."

"Hopefully we'll be out of here before we all synch up."

"Synching to oblivion!" LaDonna laughed loudly, and then grew serious. "I think I know why you brought the handcuffs," she said. "It's something you want to get rid of, but having an asteroid do it for you isn't good enough. We have to do it for ourselves."

Netty said nothing.

"Well?" LaDonna went on. "Or maybe we should melt it into something useful. That's a good chunk of metal there. We could make a little Statue of Liberty or something."

"Nothing good can ever be made out of this. It's haunted."

"Then let's just get rid of it."

"It's not just the shackles. Don't you see? The specter of slavery has followed us here. I'm worried that it will follow us, wherever we go."

"You're the one who brought it," said LaDonna.

"That's what scares me. Why did I do it? What made me?"

"Who was it that said we had to free ourselves from mental slavery? Was that King, or Mandela?"

"I think it was Bob Marley."

"Right, same era. And what had to happen before freedom really came? It didn't happen just because of Emancipation. It didn't happen just because of the Civil Rights era a century later. What had to happen was for the culture that dominated for hundreds of years to become just another minority itself."

Netty raised and wrinkled her eyebrows. "I'm not sure I subscribe to that line of reasoning."

"Once the so-called white values had to actually compete in society for the first time, the worst of them were finally weeded out."

"I've heard that before, but it's based on some fallacious assumptions about values. What ended racism was time. It just took a few generations of vigilance after Civil Rights for the stench to dissipate."

"Look, Netty, I'm not in your debate club. All I know is that if racism isn't a hundred percent gone, it's so far gone it ain't coming back. Especially now."

"The demons *could* come back, if we allow ourselves to forget about them."

"Do you think ignoring that hunk of metal would cause racism?" LaDonna asked with an exaggerated sneer.

Netty's face grew taut, and she forced a smile. She raised her voice. "Did you see me blaming racism for the problems in Philadelphia, or did you see me out there fixing them?"

"Thank you!" LaDonna said, even louder. "So what seems to be the issue? You want memories? We have the entire recorded history of the world, at the touch of a button."

"I'm sorry, LaDonna," Netty said. "I just can't seem to let it all go so easily."

"Well, I'm going back to my bed and my husband. You can go back to your albatross, or you can keep running in circles—if there's any difference!"

જી૦૮૩૭૦૪

Her jog spoiled, and unable to sleep, Netty sat at her desk in the round command center, which was sparsely peopled by the night shift. It was not really a desk; there was not even a margin on which to put her tired elbows. All she had was a keypad, a screen, and a speaker, with a wireless halo for private conversations. There was an open case, a request for transfer to Pod 3 from Doctor Simon, but she did not want to deal with that now.

She plugged in her memento chip and scanned to some video of her grandfather. She did not have any sound bites of his "never forget" philosophy on slavery, but she knew that by heart. Instead, she was looking for some other kernel of given wisdom that might help her. Back and forth she scanned, skipping around, unable to concentrate on even these precious memories. Felinity, a black cat smuggled to the Moon, rubbed against her leg.

A file of her grandmother whizzed past, and a new thought occurred to her. Maybe she had spent too much time trying to find something useful in her grandfather's files, when there were many other people who had influenced her life. She supposed that she would always favor Granddaddy Thompson, since he was the only grandfather she had ever known, and she had lost him when she was still growing up. Children do not know death, and when it first comes into their lives, it leaves an eternal smudge on the world. For Netty, her grandfather's passing defined death.

His wife had lived until the end of the world, and Netty thought about her last words with her Nana. Netty had gently hugged the stooped old woman. "I just need to hold you one more time," she told her, "so I can remember how you feel."

"I don't suppose I'm much to hug anymore, but thank you, dear," Nana Thompson said.

"I still remember how you used to hug me, when I was really small."

Nana laughed. "You should have seen me when I was young myself!"

Netty looked at her Nana's face, as if gazing through crystalline years. "How shall I remember you then?"

"There's only one good way to remember things of importance."

"How is that?"

"Through your actions."

⊰❈⊱

Rounded grey hills rose and fell like waves as they passed the window, lit by pale Earthshine that never fully graced the Moon's polar regions. Netty had commissioned an appleseeder, a small lunar rover used to place various objects on the surface. It wasn't a Rover 360, but it would do. During construction, seeders had been used to place survey transponders, power cable stays, and finally bags of bolts and such parts. By the time Netty had first arrived at Pod 4, that work was done.

This was her first venture outside since her inaugural tour, over eight months ago. She had trouble seeing the beauty that others had expressed in so many ways, since the first manned landings. Oh, the Moon was beautiful, of course, but it didn't *look* beautiful. Heaven itself would look ugly to anyone sent there by Big Bastard.

Passing the line of starfish return vehicles—now that was a lovely sight. There were six of them, plus the Barajaks' private ship.

The sight of the Jeepney rover, commonly called a "jaw rattler," bouncing beside the appleseeder was also comforting. Every excursion vehicle had to have at least one companion, for safety. The seeder was supposed to drive even more roughly than the jaw rattler, but she found them both uncomfortable.

Her driver, Pete, must have noticed. "This is easy terrain," he said. He looked completely at ease, despite his lack of a jacket. Most of the rovers were shirtsleeve environments, with detachable spacesuits mounted outside the vehicle, accessible by crawlways called moonholes. "Not as much traffic as Shackleton, either." He turned and grinned at Netty, who was in the cargo hold. "More bugs do get smeared on the windshield out here in the boonies though." The joke fell flat, because the image conjured by "traffic in Shackle town" threatened to awaken her nightmares.

Pete cleared his throat. "We're near the end of the plowed road. It'll get rougher after that. Where do you want me to go?"

"A little further."

"Say when."

The seeder leaned forward as it rolled on banded steel wheels down the slope of Shoemaker Crater. The view out the front opened up, and Pete pointed out the cables that led back down to the nuclear plant and the subsurface ice fields.

The seeder reached a turn in the plowed road. Following it led to Pod 2, but they went straight, off road, and into virgin dust. It was fitting. She would leave the manacles not only where no one had gone before, but also where no one would ever go again.

These wicked jaws had to be eliminated by the descendents of those whom they once had tormented. The seeder had a port on the bottom, which was meant for deploying or retrieving sensitive equipment. The port was air-locked, so Netty could dump the shackles onto the Moon's surface without having to wear a pressure suit.

Unlike LaDonna, Netty did not have a flair for the dramatic. Yet something felt wrong. She took the shackles out of the sack. Iron conducts heat better than aluminum, so if Netty's cot frame felt cold, the shackles were absolutely icy to the touch. She imagined the warmth of tortured arms, the slickness of unleashed blood, the cruel tyranny of heavy locks.

The seeder took a sudden dip. In one-eighth gravity, it hit bottom at an unexpected time, and Netty's stomach contracted, as if trying to clench onto something solid. Trying to ward off motion sickness, she fixed her eyes on the iron fiend on her lap. As it stole the warmth from her hands, she felt the grip of its archaic tyranny. In some unfathomable way, it still held her, as surely as it had held countless people in bondage over two centuries ago. It wasn't enough to drop it in some cranny; that was no different from leaving it on the Earth and letting nature have its way with it. She had to eviscerate its power.

Her stomach turned, her shoulders shivered, and her forearms lurched. The shackles jangled, snarling at her. Her mouth twitched from a firm, grim line to a purse of determination and back. "You son of a bitch," she muttered. "Not you, Pete," she quickly said, in case he had overheard.

Her hands shook as she tried to slide them into the heavy manacles. She could not do it. Once she had sworn to herself that no one would ever wear such things again. She exhaled loudly and tried again. Her hands just did not want to go into the loosened openings.

Netty was missing most of her left ring finger from a childhood accident, but now the stump seemed to represent the remnants of a whole people. She bared her teeth and punched her right arm through. Then the left.

She was wearing the shackles. More than half a millennium of torture, maiming, and death hugged her arms. The wordless cries from her dreams rose up in her throat. She swallowed hard. Anguished at not finding a voice, tormented ghosts screamed directly into her soul. Her head grew light. Maybe if she were to die wearing the shackles, they would pass away with her.

A fuzzy voice came from the radio speaker. "Which way now, Ms. Washington?" It was Alex, who was driving the jaw rattler.

Netty looked at her arms in disbelief. What kind of fashion statement was this supposed to be? Why had she brought these in the first place? All the effort to bring them, keep them safe, even take them back to Earth—all that was effort wasted on the past instead of being used to build a better future. This fragile refuge on the Moon depended on everyone trusting one another. The shackles embodied mistrust.

Disgusted with herself, she yanked at the manacles. To her surprise, they slid off with little more trouble than an itchy sweater. She had been wrong to think them an insidious, almighty evil. Like other once-omnipotent forces in history, this one was wholly spent.

Pete slowed the vehicle, and turned to her. "Which way, ma'am?"

Netty let out a great breath, feeling the warmth of it on her unfettered wrists. It was time to dump this albatross, like lead into the sea. "Let's head north," she said.

Pete laughed. "We're practically at the South Pole now. The only way to go is north."

She smiled. "North it is, then," she said. "To freedom."

Often women cannot control their own fate. They follow orders. But if they take their destiny into their own hands, they can risk losing everything—or winning it.

GARDENS OF WIND

by Kate MacLeod

The *Parjanya* approached from the nor'east. There was an outcry among the women for all of the last minute tasks that still remained to be done, but Akeli slipped away before her mother could assign her some duty. She knew this wasn't her father's ship approaching, nor her Brandon's ship either, but she still wanted to see it for herself before it docked. She climbed up between the hydroponics rafts to the catwalks that ran over the top of everything. She could still be seen through the glass roofs, but the gardens below were empty, all necessary chores finished early in anticipation of the arrival of the *Parjanya* and the festival to follow.

Akeli reached the end of the *al-Khátún* and leaned over the railing as far as she dared. The sky was clear, except of course for below, but still she could not see the *Parjanya*. She followed the rail to the balloon rigging, climbing to the very top. There was no rail here, no safety line, nothing between her and a fall to the earth far below save the grip of her hands on the rope ladder. She felt a twinge in her stomach she supposed was fear; that never used to be there. She risked using one hand to touch her chest, to make sure her locket was still safely tucked away, that it wouldn't fall and be lost forever in the clouds below. When she had satisfied herself that it was secure, she crept forward, her hands and knees pushing down on the balloon silk without quite letting her sink in.

She had nearly reached the point when the balloon silk descended once more when at last she saw it. It was a proper airship, sure enough, not a lashed together mess of rafts and balloons like the *al-Khátún*. You could go anywhere you wanted in such a ship, not simply float at the whims of the wind. You could descend below the cloud cover in such a ship without crashing. You could even land on the surface.

Those on crew duty were gathering at the rails below her, ready to toss and catch guidelines to make the *Parjanya* fast and help her people board their floating village. Akeli climbed back down the balloon, avoiding the crew by slipping through the gap between two rafts as she and Kahlil had done since they were little more than toddlers, climbing like monkeys in a children's story under everyone's unsuspecting feet. They had never once been caught at it, although Akeli supposed if they had her bottom would still be blistered. She paused for a moment, swinging her head far back to look toward the earth below her, lost under the clouds of brown and gray. Her arms soon tired, so she continued on until she reached the hydroponics raft nearest the room she shared with her mother. She slipped inside, but realized just as the door shut behind her that she was not alone.

Fortunately the arguing voices had not noticed the rush of wind or the click of the shutting door from the far side of the room. Akeli crouched under the cucumber plants, moving quickly and quietly away from the door just in case one of them had noticed but hadn't said anything.

Then she recognized the voices: her mother and her uncle Hyman, who was the captain of their vessel, such as it was, and the chieftain of their village. Akeli briefly considered sneaking back out the way she'd came, for she knew without even bothering to listen just what they would be fighting about at this auspicious moment, but she doubted she'd get lucky enough to pass unnoticed twice. She crept behind the tool cabinet, dangling tomato plants covering her like a curtain, and waited.

"She just needs time," her mother was saying.

"She's had time. It's been nearly a year," her uncle replied. "I am not without sympathy, sister. She may very well grieve the rest of her life, and I will think no less of her. But she can grieve and do her duty as well."

"I don't think she can. She took so long to find her Brandon—"

"All the more reason not to indulge her in long choosing this time around. In the end, it made her no happier letting her have her way."

"Hyman!"

"Well, it's true," her uncle said gruffly, although there was an undertone of contrition in his voice. Not that he would ever admit to feeling it; it was inconceivable that one such as he should apologize to his little sister even for the cruelest of words. "We must look to the future. We cannot survive if there are too few of us, and if every woman's son leaves us, who will care for us in our old age?"

"Our daughters."

"Oh, indeed."

"My son will return," her mother said in a very small voice.

"It is long past time you and Akeli gave up that dream," her uncle said. His boots echoed across the scaffolding, but he stopped and turned back at the door. "I will let it go for this last festival, but if she doesn't see her duty done this time, then I'll take care of it myself. Even if that means hailing every approaching ship and offering her to whomever is willing."

"You wouldn't! No, Hyman, you would not."

"What I will not do is provide food and shelter to someone who doesn't contribute to our common good. I suggest you speak to her."

Then he was gone. Akeli crawled out of the tomato vines, brushing the wrinkles from her festival clothes and realizing far too late that the flowers had been blown from her hair when she was out climbing in the cold wind.

"Oh, Akeli," her mother said with a weary sigh. "Come, let's rebraid your hair."

Her mother's fingers were fast and sure, and if she lamented that there were no flowers left to replace the ones Akeli had lost, she didn't say so. Instead, she took her own little box of treasures and brought out the jeweled butterfly she had never let Akeli so much as touch before.

"You know that I wore this the day I met your father," she said as she wove it into the end of Akeli's braid. "Perhaps there will be some luck in it for you. But please, Akeli, take good care of it. No going out into the wind and losing it. I could never forgive you for its loss."

Akeli nodded, pulling her braid forward over her shoulder to admire the blue and green stones set in the butterfly's little silver wings. She was certain they were just colored glass, not proper jewels, but she thought it much finer than the white and pink blooms she had lost.

The clang of the landing platform from the airship meeting the end of the dock of *al-Khátún* echoed through the hallways, and her mother caught her hand and pulled her to her feet, rushing with her to the open docking bay. The other women were already gathered around the railing there, some looking out for husbands making one of their all-too-infrequent visits, others just hoping to be the first to catch an unattached man's eye. Akeli pulled her hand free of her mother's grasp, preferring to linger at the back of the crowd.

The music started at once, and the women of her ship— her aunts and nieces and cousins and second cousins—took the men of the *Parjanya* by the arm and led them into the derelict zeppelin which was the only space large enough for all of them to gather together. The girders were swathed in garlands of plastic flowers. Akeli found them depressing. The light was dim enough for no one to see just how hideous they were, faded and cracked, too old to still be dragged out for every festival. But the bare girders were no atmosphere for a party either. The food at least would be delicious. All of the special treats they only had for festivals were laid out on mismatched pieces of bone china. The men of the *Parjanya* greeted the sight of all that food with even more enthusiasm than they had the sight of women.

Akeli lingered near the doorway, watching the women of her family load up plates for their guests, eating little themselves. The music still had a slow tempo, but soon it would turn rollicking, and all of the women would dance. Akeli hated dancing. No, that wasn't exactly true. She loved dancing, when it was just her and her cousins. She hated dancing when strangers were there, watching. But she didn't dare try slipping away again. She knew her Uncle Hyman meant what he had said.

Someone bumped her shoulder, a latecomer rushing to join the others. He took hold of her arm, as if afraid he had nearly knocked her down. He hadn't yet noticed how solid she was.

· "Sorry!" he said, letting her go, then brushing both hands through his flyaway blond hair. It flopped back down on his forehead, completely unmoved by his attempts to neaten it. He took a look around the room, at the people already formed up in pairs or in occasional threes and fours. Then he looked back at Akeli with a crooked smile. She could sense the work he was doing, trying to come up with something to say. She smiled back.

"Hey," he said at last. "What food here is good? Any meat? Man, I haven't had meat in ages."

Akeli shook her head, then crossed to the nearest table, filling a plate with little samples of everything. She brought it back to him. It was all finger food: little dumplings and samosas and vegetable pies. There was no meat; the *al-Khátún* wasn't large enough to keep animals, beyond a few reliable hens. Not like the massive floating cities she had heard crewmen from other airships tell her about. She had seen one once, far on the horizon, but villages usually kept a distrustful distance from them and each other.

"Thanks," he said, looking over the plate she had handed him, then choosing one of the pies and stuffing the whole thing in his mouth. Unfortunately it was the last thing that had reached the table and was still hot from the oven. Akeli covered her mouth to hide her smile as he hopped on his toes, eyes streaming, but still manfully chewing. "That's good," he said, although she was certain he had just burned every taste bud on his tongue. "There was some kind of spice in that; I don't know what it was but it was good. Oh, by the way," he shifted his plate to one hand and stuck the other out at her, "I'm Jason."

She took her hand down to show her smile and return his handshake. He looked at her quizzically. Then one of her cousins, who had been lingering nearby, stepped up to him, putting her hand beside her mouth to whisper in his ear. "Akeli doesn't talk," she said in a far too loud whisper. "But she's very nice otherwise." He didn't seem to notice her other hand squeezing his bicep. Akeli's smile faded away. If her cousin's means of assessing potential mates lacked subtlety, it was nothing compared to the totality of her dismissal of him among her prospects. She had turned and gone before the boy even managed to reply, leaving him to talk to the back of her head as she sashayed to the next crewman, a burly, top-heavy fellow guaranteed to sire many strapping sons.

With a touch of meanness, Akeli thought the big crewman looked dimwitted. Not that that mattered. Even if he took her cousin to wife, he wouldn't be around more than a few days at a time. Still, that was as likely to pass on to his sons as his beefy biceps. Akeli preferred the nervous warmth that emanated from Jason, even if it came with short stature and decidedly bony arms.

"That's all right then," Jason said, turning back to her. He had given up trying to speak to her cousin. "Akeli. That's a very pretty name." He flipped his hair out of his eyes but it settled back into place almost at once.

Eating gave way to dancing far too soon for Akeli's tastes. She could see her uncle shooting glances her way. She was still standing next to Jason, but he was completely focused on his eating and not her. She suspected it was more than just meat he hadn't had in ages.

The musicians started a new song, one of Akeli's favorites. She couldn't help bouncing to the beat.

"Hey, did you want to dance? I'm not keeping you, am I?" Jason asked. One of the cousins flitted by in a blast of colored skirts and a jingle of jewelry. When she was gone, his hands were quite plate-free. Akeli felt her uncle's eyes on her once more, but she only shook her head and willed herself to stop bouncing. "Well, how about a tour, then? This is the first floating village I've ever visited, though I've heard tons about them. I'd love a look around, if that's OK."

Akeli nodded and threaded her arm through his, leading him out of the zeppelin, over the enclosed walkway that attached it to the next section of the ship, the fuselage of an old airliner that had been stripped and then repartitioned into living quarters. He looked around at the little touches that made one woman's door different from any others; the pictures stenciled on the metal or the plastic flowers or beads. Akeli and her mother had made an intricate mosaic out of colored paper, which they glued right to the door. It was an abstract pattern, but parts of it just suggested the shape of a vine or a flower or a butterfly.

"Is this yours?" Jason asked when she stopped to touch it. She nodded. He leaned in to inspect it. "There must be thousands of little squares here. This must've taken days to finish." Akeli shrugged, then took his arm and led him on to the first of the hydroponics rafts.

The music, which was still audible down the length of the airliner, was drowned out completely when she opened the door to the walkway that led from airliner to raft. Akeli caught the tail of her braid before stepping out, mindful of her mother's butterfly, then let Jason go before her through the next door.

"Wow," he said, genuinely impressed. Akeli wasn't sure why; it was just a room full of plants dangling from long racks. The sky above the glass panels was darkening, but the stars had not yet appeared. It didn't look like anything. "You must have fresh food all the time, living in a place like this. I'm from space, you know. Born on a station up in orbit. I've only been down here in atmo for a couple of months on the *Parjanya*. I suppose I look like a total rube, geeked about fresh food, but by the time any of it works its way that far up the gravity well, it's pretty limp and nasty."

Akeli looked around until she spotted a row of strawberry plants. She plucked one ripe berry and handed it to him. He bit into it with undisguised pleasure. "That's good."

She led him through several more rafts of plants, occasionally pausing to let him sample something. He kept up a constant chatter about growing up on a station where he was always indoors, always in the dark, and about his life now on the *Parjanya* in the sun and wind. Akeli was listening so attentively she didn't realize until her feet were on the open deck that she had taken him clear to the other end of the ship, to the platform under one of the four enormous balloons that kept her village afloat.

Look, Akeli. It's a parachute! I'm going to find out what's down there. I'm going to find Dad. I know that's where he went, he was always talking about it. When I find him, I'll come back for you. The three of us can live together. Mom, too, if she wants. I'm going right now. Do you want to watch me jump, Akeli? Don't cry, sister. I'll be perfectly safe. It's a parachute! This is what it's made for. Watch me go, Akeli!

"Akeli?" She looked up when she heard Jason's voice, almost too soft over the wind. She caught her braid, remembering late again, but the butterfly was still there. She stepped back from the railing. There was nothing to see looking down anyway, nothing but the same brownish-gray clouds that covered everything. Jason leaned past her as if to see what she had been looking at.

"Ugly, isn't it? I don't care what they say, I don't think that's ever going away." He straightened and continued walking along the platform, around the corner to the next walkway. Akeli caught up with him in time to open the door for him.

By now the constant string of garden rooms had ceased to impress him, although he still looked around with great interest. "You know, a lot of the people up here are talking about leaving Earth. The colonies on Mars are growing lots of food now. It doesn't do us much good, of course; it takes longer to get here than your atmo food. They've got factories there that can process it so it doesn't rot before it gets to us, but it's still pretty tasteless. Actually, it's probably because it is processed." He winked at her as if looking for her to agree, but Akeli had never had food from a factory. "Lots of folks are talking about just moving to Mars. You can't go outside there, of course. No wind in your hair without bringing your own oxygen along, but they've put enough greenhouse gases in the atmo to make the temperature tolerable. Or so they say. My brother took his wife there a year ago. I'm waiting to hear from him what it's like before I make such a big move, though."

They reached the end of the line of rafts. One last plunge in and out of the wind, which was getting colder as the sky darkened, and they were back in the living section of the ship. It was all workshops and storage rooms here, and no one was about, but the music from the party reached them faintly. Akeli tried to figure out what song it was from the beat, as she couldn't make out the melody.

"Akeli," Jason said, catching her arm before she could lead the way back to the zeppelin, "listen, I've not done this before. I mean, I've done *that*, I've just never been to one of these floating village festivals. We have the opposite trouble back home: too many people and not enough room. Too many people moving up the well. I guess that leads to your problem being opposite, with everybody leaving all the time. Someone has to stay and grow the food." She sneaked a glance up at him and saw his cheeks were as red as she had suspected from his stammering voice. "I know it's expected, though, right?" he went on. "For the food you gave us? I mean, I ate a lot. Damn. The guys on the ship told me things, but I think they fixated on the wrong details. They assumed I knew how to get *started*."

Akeli listened, not quite looking at him. His hand was still on her arm, just above her bangles. Cheap plastic.

"I'm not sure if I'm even supposed to ask, but do you have a guy already? Like a guy on another ship or something?"

Akeli stared at the floor. He wasn't supposed to ask. At last she took his hand, dragging him behind her down the corridor away from the party, to the rooms used by the captain and those on crew duty. She took him to the far end of the narrow meeting room, with its long table, behind the big chair which was her uncle Hyman's. The wall was covered with photographs and lists of names. She didn't have to look to find Brandon's; she knew exactly where it was.

"Brandon Stone, *Matarisvan*. He was on the *Matarisvan*? Oh." It was a name of infamy. Airships were lost all the time. They would crash in storms or run into mechanical trouble far from help and disappear without a trace. Not the *Matarisvan*. The *Matarisvan* had exploded for no discernable reason shortly after leaving the village ship of *Vata*, in full sight of the *Vata* villagers and four other airships. The picture on the wall next to the list of names had been taken from one of the other airships. The fire had already consumed the balloon, and all that was visible were chunks of debris and little dots of crewmen plummeting to the brown clouds below.

She wondered, not for the first time, which dot was him. Or if had he been burnt to nothing in that first instant. Or if had he already fallen through the clouds by the time the man with the camera had taken the picture.

"Is that why you don't talk, then? Or were you born not talking?" Akeli just shook her head. She wasn't prepared to share everything, particularly not that.

Jason reached out and picked up the end of her braid, ostensibly to examine the little jeweled butterfly. "Akeli." She bit her lip. She thought about bringing him back to her room, but her mother wasn't so old that Uncle Hyman wouldn't expect her to do her duty as well. This was as good a place as any. He tugged gently at her braid, drawing her closer.

It wasn't like with her Brandon; it wasn't love. It wasn't exactly duty either. It was companionship, Akeli decided, and felt tears prick at the corners of her eyes. She hadn't realized how lonely she had been.

Afterward, Jason hiked himself up on one elbow to look down at her lying on the floor of the meeting room beside him. His hair still fell over his eyes, but some of its flyaway quality had been dampened with sweat. She reached up and brushed it back, but it promptly fell into its place. She laughed.

"Hey, you can laugh!" he said, tickling at her ribs until she squirmed. "I can hear your voice when you laugh. It's lovely." His fingers touched her ear, then traced down her neck until they found the chain she wore there. She reached up a hand to stop him, then changed her mind and let him pull the locket out of her dress.

"May I?" he asked, fingers poised at the clasp. She nodded. He opened it, leaning closer to see the picture inside. "Oh. I was expecting your fellow. Is this your baby?"

Akeli shook her head, then nodded, then shook her head again. She sat up, closing the locket and holding her hands over it.

"Was that your baby?" Jason asked in a softer voice.

Akeli nodded.

"How? Well, I guess you can't tell me. Did she get sick?" She shook her head. "Accident?" Nodded. "Oh God, did she fall?" Akeli nodded again, clutching the locket tightly in her hands and willing the tears not to come. It had been such a long fall. It had seemed to take even longer for her to disappear through the clouds than it had for Kahlil with his parachute.

Jason put his hands over hers, gently opening them and then undoing the clasp on the locket so that it lay open on her palms and he could look once more at the picture within. "She looks like you, but so young. Not even two, I'd say." Akeli couldn't bring herself to nod again; she kept her face turned away. But she didn't pull the locket away from him.

"What was her name?"

She looked up at him, his eyes bright and friendly under that unruly mass of hair. His hands on hers were warm.

"Karishma."

"Karishma," Jason said, smiling at her as he closed the locket and slipped it back down the neckline of her dress. "Lovely. I wish I could have met her."

They stayed there a while longer. The feeling of companionship only grew stronger, the two of them beside each other, not talking or touching or even sleeping, just being close and listening to the distant beat of the music.

Then the beat stopped.

"I guess it's time for me to go," Jason said with a sigh. They got up, and Jason helped her smooth out her dress. She tucked the hair that had worked free from her braid behind her ears. She would have preferred to look thoroughly ravished for her uncle's benefit, but the two of them together rejoining the others at the loading area would have to be proof enough.

"The guys on the airship say sometimes we dock for days, but I guess we won't be doing that here since so few of our crew have wives in this village. But maybe we'll be back here soon. I hope." He caught her arm, pulling her to a stop in the middle of the corridor just outside the loading area. They were no longer quite alone; other couples were farewelling all around them. "Akeli. I'll write to you, but letters take so long to move from ship to ship. Please don't think I've forgotten you. I really would like to see you again."

Akeli looked down at the end of her braid twisted in her hands.

"We could marry—"

Akeli shook her head sadly, touching a hand to her belly.

"Oh right, baby first. I'd forgotten that was the rule. Well, maybe, yes?"

Akeli twisted her braid.

"Can I kiss you good-bye?"

Akeli nodded, letting go of her braid to turn her face up to his. It was worse than dancing; everyone's eyes were all over her.

Jason smiled at her, kissed her softly one more time, then turned to walk down the ramp to his airship. Akeli didn't know where to look. She didn't want to watch him go, she didn't want to see her mother or the other women of her family smiling at her, and she especially didn't want to see Uncle Hyman looking at her.

She turned and walked away from the others, away from the noise and the stuffy warmth of the room. Then she found herself walking faster, past her room, through the garden rooms, running down the length of the pods and struggling to hurry through the doors.

The *Parjanya* was nearly free when at last she reached the railing she had watched its approach from. One last line was tethering it to the village, but even as she watched the crew were casting it away.

A sudden gust of wind nearly knocked her off her feet. She grabbed the railing with one hand, trying to catch her spinning braid with the other. Too late, the glittering butterfly was gone, and she had not even seen it fall.

Then something slapped her in the belly and she instinctively caught it. The last mooring line, torn from some poor crewman's hands. Akeli wondered briefly what was at the other end, her village dock, or the airship?

It was like flipping a coin, wasn't it? There were worse ways of making a choice. Grasping the rope tightly, she jumped over the railing and fell.

The wind made it impossible for her to keep her eyes open. It drowned out her hearing, numbed her body to the sensation of anything but the rope in her hands. She was alone with her thoughts for long enough to begin to wonder whether the other end was tethered to anything at all. Her brother had landed somewhere in South America. Karishma had landed somewhere in the Indian Ocean. She tried to remember the last time she had checked the charts. What was under her now?

Then she came to the end of the rope. It nearly jerked out of her hands before she started to swing. She knew she should be climbing up, but it was all she could do to hang on.

It was very cold, in the wind.

The sound of voices shouting brought her out of her head, and she opened her eyes. The airship *Parjanya* was above her. Several of those beefy-armed men were pulling together to reel her in, and Jason was working his way down along the outrigging to meet her.

"Are you crazy?" were his first words to her once he'd nearly cracked her ribs hugging her.

"Take me with you," was all she said in return.

"Where?"

"Up. Or down. Anywhere."

"I'll get booted off this ship, you know," he told her. "Dumped at the next port. Both of us."

"Oh."

"I'm not saying no," he said, squeezing her tighter. "Just, that's what's going to happen."

"Then what?"

"Well, what do you think of Mars?"

There is sensitivity that weakens, and sensitivity that strengthens. When a woman has the former kind, she cannot be a warrior. But when she has the latter kind, she can fight for what she believes in.

SILENT WHISPERS

by Karen Elizabeth Rigley & Ann Miller House

Surrounded by noise and clatter, Julia Hedrick stood holding her tray, gazing around the mess hall. Few glanced up, and those who did quickly averted their eyes to avoid sending mistaken messages of welcome. She noticed the Roamer sitting alone, a fellow outcast, and crossed the room to his table.

"Mind some company?" she asked.

Hand frozen halfway to his mouth, he looked up from his dinner as she sat down across from him. "Ah . . . no." He was obviously surprised. "Not at all. Glad for it."

He took a small bite and chewed, watching her with his large doe eyes, deep brown as rich chocolate. The caste mark at the corner of his right eye, a dark irregular star shape, proclaimed him to be of a clan on the Great Northern Continent of his world.

"You're dSavalo Ki?" Julia spooned up a bite of stew.

His full lips hinted at a smile. "How do you know such things about my culture?"

"My job." Julia didn't smile easily, but she allowed her own mouth to curve into an answering one. "I'm the Xenologist, a walking depository of alien trivia."

"You're the Zeenie, huh?"

"Yep. I can recognize several of the more prominent

dSavista caste marks, including dSavalo Ki." She took another bite of her stew. "Mmm, amazing. This actually tastes good."

"Not so amazing. If you don't feed miners well, they don't work."

"True. But I didn't expect the food to be this good. Or accommodations to be so comfortable."

"Must be your first assignment to a mining crew." Roamer pushed his empty plate aside and sipped his drink.

Julia nodded, glancing at her dining companion. She'd known he was dSavista from the first moment she'd spotted him on the jump ship. Not merely from the caste mark, which could pass for a scar, but from his overall beauty. He had a slim, well-formed body, and the most beautiful face she'd ever seen that wasn't feminine, framed by soft dark hair. Not a blemish marred his dusky complexion except for the caste mark. Sure, she'd known he was dSavista, but not why he was here.

"You know the significance of my caste mark," he said. "So do the silver rings you wear in your ears denote such about you?"

She shook her head, setting the earrings into motion. "No, just personal decoration."

"Attractive." His smile returned, more full fledged, but Julia read no flirtation in his expression. A relief; she'd had to fend off her share of passes from the other miners. At least until they'd discovered she intended to perform her duties vigilantly. *That* changed their attitude in a hurry.

"Tell me, Roamer. Why are you working in a mining crew? It's unusual for dSavistas to leave the home planet for extended periods of time, isn't it?"

He sighed, looking away from her, then stared down into his mug momentarily before meeting her gaze again. "I'm shais ranah."

She cocked her head questioningly.

"Shais ranah. Always noisy. Don't you possess that bit of alien trivia?" Roamer asked, a bit ironically.

"Guess not. Enlighten me."

As if by signal, they both rose, carried their trays to the depository and left the mess hall. They strolled to the edge of the camp and sat on a boulder still warm from the sun. A canopy of stars arched overhead. Night sounds hummed in the shadows.

"You know my people are telepathic," Roamer began, finally breaking their silence. "Our thoughts enhance our verbal communication rather than replace it. Like speech, it is controlled. For most people. But not for those like me. I cannot shut out others of my kind. Their thoughts and feelings fill my head, bombard me ceaselessly. In turn, I bombard others just as ceaselessly. So those of us who are shais ranah must become wanderers. We can't live near our own."

He sounded so sad, Julia had to restrain herself from reaching out to him. "And that's why you're called the Roamer?"

"Yes."

"But you *can* shut out other races?"

He nodded. "I form a mind barrier—a mental curtain of white noise." He waved a hand back toward the mess hall. "They all think I read their minds. That they can keep no secrets from me. I know that's why they ostracize me. Believe me, it's the *last* thing I want, to dabble in their thoughts. It can actually be painful to me."

Julia gazed up at the starry expanse above them. "I know what it feels like to be ostracized. Seems no one likes the Project Xenologist."

"A Zeenie has the power to shut down a dig." He raised a brow. "Miners do get real hostile when it comes to sacrificing profit."

"You don't act that way, Roamer."

He shrugged. "For me, this is only one way to make a living. If I don't do this, I'll do something else. I just can't go home."

In sympathy, Julia rested her hand on his shoulder as he

cast her a melancholy smile. She understood his isolation, since her job forced her to be an outsider. And they were *both* a long way from home.

ෞ෬ぷ෬ଓ

Warning sirens faded after signaling another accident. Only four days on this world—only two actually entering the caves—and already they'd suffered the third accident. So far, nobody had been killed, but the accidents grew progressively worse.

Julia moved outside to study new report. Like the others, this one proved inconclusive and unsettling. The Project Xenologist received instant readouts and reports on *everything* concerning a job. Dissatisfied, she snapped her infodisk shut and slid it into her pocket. A Zeenie had to determine if any sentient life existed on a world scheduled to be exploited. So far, she'd found no evidence of it here. Yet, like a gossamer shadow, something seemed to hover just beyond reach. It's not like she *wanted* to find something, she assured herself.

Restless, she walked toward the caves, donned a helmet and stepped into the mouth of the main cavern. Her helmet light activated, sending shafts of brightness to illuminate the cave's eternal night. She left the "twilight zone" beyond where light of day did not penetrate, picking her way along a cool corridor toward the first mineral chamber.

Each time she entered a mineral chamber, it took her breath away. Delicate, lacy formations crusted the walls, and glittering stalactites and stalagmites stretched to touch one another. Some had joined, becoming columns. A group of miners worked under bright lights on one side of the chamber chipping away at the crystal formations.

Caves riddled these hills; caves filled with rare and valuable minerals just waiting to be harvested. No need to actually dig—no blasting, no boring. Simply chop down the formations and haul them out. Instant riches. With this find, the discovering Energy Scout could retire to a life of ease. And Diversified Energies Development would add a huge plus to their financial statement. No, DED wouldn't appreciate a Zeenie coming up with a negative ecological impact report. This dig would make them all rich. Except for Julia. The Project Xenologist could never collect a percentage. And Julia was not an employee of DED, but of the Galactic Federation itself. After all, the promise of riches might cause a Zeenie to blink at questionable sentience.

Julia didn't care about getting rich. She was paid well and enjoyed her work while traveling throughout the galaxy. Since she was somewhat of a loner anyway, the ostracism shown a Zeenie didn't really bother her. Her true passion was discovering new life forms.

She passed the mining crew and climbed up to a small tunnel on the far wall. Crawling into it, she inched along commando style for several yards, then rose to hands and knees to crawl several more yards. She reached a larger chamber and sat down on a smooth formation, stretching cramped muscles while looking around. Mineral crystals sparkled on the walls and ceiling in "popcorn" formations. Smooth crystal floored the chamber, interspersed with humps like the one Julia sat on. She gazed around, wondering what formed the crystals. For that matter, what had formed the caves themselves? They didn't conform to other caverns on any other known worlds.

The caves fascinated Julia. She'd been in others, had done some caving on Earth and on a couple of other planets, and thoroughly enjoyed each experience. But this . . . this was different. She almost felt drawn to push farther and farther, to probe deeper. Reaching up, she snapped off the automatic switch on her helmet light, plunging herself into total darkness.

At first, the silence of the cave dropped around her like a cloak, but after a few moments cave sounds whispered and sighed in the blackness. Sliding down the formation, she settled on the cave floor and leaned back against her former seat, opening and closing her eyes, noting no difference in what she saw. Occasionally, if she sat in the darkness long enough, faint lavender starbursts would entertain her like distant fireworks.

A scuffling sound behind her sent chills rippling up her spine. She listened a moment, then snapped back on her helmet lamp. She swung her head around toward the sound's origin, and the light illuminated a man's form.

"Oh!" Julia scrambled to her feet, nearly bumping her head on the low ceiling. "Roamer?"

"Got me." He grinned. "Why are you back here in the dark?"

"I like it. Why are *you* here?"

"I like it, too." He crossed the small chamber, stooping slightly to keep from hitting his head, and stood before her. "Want to explore with me?"

"Explore where?"

"I plan on following this left passage a ways. Want to come along?"

"Sure."

"Ready check." He snapped on his helmet lamp. "How many sources of light are you carrying?"

"My helmet and a handbeam. And you?"

"The same. That makes four sources between us, so we're good."

"When I went caving before, we abided by the Cavers' Three Rules of Three." Julia ticked them off her fingers. "Always cave with three others so if someone gets hurt, there's one to stay with the injured and two to go for help. Always carry three independent sources of light. And everybody tell three interested parties where you're going caving."

"Close enough." Roamer dropped to his hands and knees and crawled into the narrow passage. "So you've done this sort of thing before?" His voice drifted back to her as she copied his actions.

"A few times. I enjoy caving. Is it popular on your

world?"

He chuckled softly. "About like it is on yours, I suppose. Claustrophobia must be a cross-species affliction, because some dSavistas suffer from it. Fortunately, I don't."

"Me, either. Ouch! These crystals growing on the floor are sharp and I'm not wearing kneepads."

"The passage is narrowing." With that announcement, Roamer dropped to his belly and began commando crawling. "If this doesn't widen fairly soon, let's back out."

Julia wriggled along behind him, his booted feet a couple of yards ahead of her. Instead of widening, the tunnel became tighter. It also smoothed out, much to her relief. She knew she'd scratched up her elbows, arms and knees already. Oh well, these weren't the first cave wounds she'd earned. Probably wouldn't be the last.

"Aha! A chamber," Roamer announced. "Be careful, these formations are delicate."

Emerging from the tight passage, Julia turned her head this way and that, oohing and ahhing with Roamer at the fragile beauty before them.

"It just doesn't seem right," she said, and he glanced down at her.

"What doesn't?"

"The mining. Defacing all this. They just break the crystals out, just break them out . . . and who knows how long it took to form them? Or even *how* they were formed? These caves aren't formed by water, seismic activity or volcanoes. So how did they get here? Where did all these beautiful mineral formations come from? I feel so uncomfortable allowing the mining to begin, but I have no reason to prevent it." She sighed, a tiny frown creasing her brow.

Roamer stared down at her, then looked around the chamber once more. "We should get back. We'll come again when we're better prepared and equipped, okay?"

"Sounds like a reasonable plan. After you, sir."

Less than a week later, Julia placed a stack of six accident reports on Sam Doakes's cluttered desk. The beefy superintendent frowned at it, then glowered up at her through bushy brows.

"Now what?" he grunted.

"This job has been underway barely ten planet days, and we just had the sixth accident."

Doakes rubbed a hand over his bristly hair. "What happened?"

"A column fell and trapped two miners."

"Injuries?"

"Charlie's leg is broken, and Ace has a mild concussion."

"Kincaid's crew again. His second accident."

"*Every* crew has had at least one accident. Tyler's crew had its second yesterday. So far Blas's and Shugley's crews have only had one accident apiece, but that could change any minute, the way things are going." Julia took a deep breath. "I want to shut down the dig and investigate."

"Shut down the dig?" Doakes glared at her, heaved his bulk up out of his chair and stomped over to the window. He stared out at the caves, then turned to face Julia again. "Impossible. You can't call shutdown just because miners get careless."

"I don't see any indication of carelessness. The formations that fall on the miners aren't the ones they're harvesting, but others. Charlie and Ace were on break, sitting away from the work site, when a very large stalactite fell on them. Ace says it felt like a deliberate attack."

Doakes grew very still. "What are you saying, Hedrick? That someone . . . or *something* is causing this?"

"We need to investigate. What if our activities are destabilizing the caves?"

"We can shore up." Anger rumbled in his voice. "Listen, Hedrick. You've run around looking for resident Bug-eyed Monsters and found *nothing*. So don't try cooking up some goofy tale just to prove you're earning your pay. Investigate the accidents all you want, but we're *not* shutting down. Is that clear?"

"Quite clear, Mr. Doakes. Please allow me to clarify a point as well. If I discover sentient life on this planet endangered by mining, you will shut down." With that, Julia whirled and marched from his office. That jerk wouldn't care if everybody got killed, just as long as he racked up his percentages.

Fuming, Julia stormed to the caves, snatched up a helmet and entered, settling it on her head as she walked. Then she heard the commotion. Peering ahead at the brightly lit work area, she saw what looked like a fight. She broke into a trot, trying to remember caution but when she realized Roamer was involved, the trot became a run. She raced up just as one of the men, Hah'kree, lifted a flailing Roamer away from another swinging miner. Two other men restrained him from wading back at Roamer.

"What th' *hell* brought this on?" demanded Tyler, the crew foreman.

"Stop. You've got to stop it," Roamer sobbed, fury twisting his features.

"Stop what?" Tyler turned to the other man. "What were you doing, Jones?"

"My job. I was chipping away at this column when that crazy dSavista jumped me. Started raving at me to stop. Hell, I don't know what I did. He probably read my mind." Wiping a trickle of blood from the corner of his mouth, Jones glared at Roamer, who'd gone almost limp in Hah'kree's grasp. "Found out what I really think of him." Jones spat into the crystal dust to emphasize his opinion of the telepath.

Tyler crossed to Roamer. "I don't know what's with you, but I won't tolerate this kind of crap on my crew. You haven't worked worth a damn the past couple of days anyway. Then you start a fight here in the cave. You want to cause another accident, you idiot? Shape up or you'll find your ass on the next jump ship out with any pay you got coming confiscated to cover your room and board."

Roamer stood in silence, letting his boss berate him until Hah'kree released him. Then he turned without a word and walked from the cave, Julia in pursuit. She fell into step beside him as they exited. Placing their helmets on the rack, they continued walking until they left the camp behind and reached a small stream that meandered across the meadow. They dropped onto carpeting grass beneath a feathery tree. Roamer plucked a strand of grass and drew it between his long fingers.

"What happened, Roamer? What caused the fight?"

"I'm not sure." He clenched his jaw muscles and knotted his hands into fists. "I felt panic. Maybe I'm going crazy. Sometimes an outcast shais ranah will go mad. It's difficult for a dSavista to be separated from our people."

Julia placed a hand on his shoulder and felt his shuddering sigh of misery. "Why do you think you're going crazy? Please tell me."

"I've started hearing things when I'm working in the caves."

"Like what?"

"Nothing clearly audible." Taking a deep breath, Roamer stared up at the sky that was rapidly deepening to twilight. "It's like whispers. Silent whispers inside my head. There are no words, just . . . whispers. It hurts."

He dropped his head into his hands and Julia rested her arm across his shoulders, her own heart twisting. Could some anguish be so great that it crossed species? Whatever, she desperately wanted to alleviate it.

"Roamer, you're aware of the accidents?"

"Right." He nodded, meeting her gaze, his dark eyes liquid in the fading light.

"They all seem to happen the same way. Formations fall on miners. Not in the work areas, but away. Yet, it's not random, since the formations don't fall unless someone's under them. It's almost a pattern. Those whispers you hear—is it possible the crystals are trying to contact you?"

Frowning, he considered the question, choosing a pebble to skip across the gurgling stream. "Maybe. You suspect the crystals might be intelligent?"

"Now you're asking me something I don't know. I told Doakes I'd like a shutdown to investigate further, and he all but threatened me. I can't order a shutdown unless I have something fairly concrete to back it up. Since you're hearing whispers, will you assist me?"

"Yes. Gladly. Tyler wasn't kidding. I'll get shipped out. If the foreman tosses me, you can bet nobody else will take me on their crew. Besides, I don't think I can force myself to mine the crystals anymore."

"We need evidence. Help me get it?"

"You trust me to help? I'm so messed up, I can't even remember jumping on Jones. For that matter, about all I recall about the fight is feeling like my head would burst when Jones chopped at that column, and then hanging there in Hah'kree's hands."

"I trust you." Julia playfully squeezed his tight neck muscles. "I must admit shock at seeing you fight. My store of alien trivia shows dSavistas as a peaceful species."

Roamer grinned. "True story. dSavistas rarely resort to physical violence to settle disputes. However, we are capable of holding our own if necessary."

"As you so clearly demonstrated with Jones." Julia gazed around at the advancing night. "We should head back to camp. Nocturnal carnivores hunt in this area."

"Right. I don't wish to test my physical prowess against a hungry beast with razor-sharp tusks." Standing, he offered a hand to Julia and pulled her to her feet. Then, as they started toward camp, he draped his arm across her shoulders.

"Thanks, Julia, for becoming my friend. I'd forgotten how nice it feels to have one."

"My pleasure. I don't find it easy to make friends myself. I tend to throw up barriers—rather like your mental ones. It gets lonely, but I'm somewhat of a loner. Maybe that's why working as a Zeenie suits me." She smiled up at him. "But you're right. It does feel nice to have a friend."

⋘⋙

Julia joined the staff meeting the next morning to update them about the accidents and to request Roamer's transfer to her.

"Take him," Tyler snorted. "He's not worth a damn as a miner anyway."

"I don't get it," Shugley put in, a frown creasing her forehead. "He was in my crew in the ore mines on Magathon. One of my best workers. I'd thought about asking you to trade someone with me for him." She barked a harsh laugh and looked at Julia. "But not anymore. Good thing you're taking him. I don't think any of us wants him now."

While the other foremen muttered agreement with Shugley, Julia secured Doakes's authorization so that Roamer would receive his pay. It wouldn't really scrape any skin off DED's back, since the wages of an employee appropriated by a Galactic official would be reimbursed to the company. Julia was just glad she didn't need to argue about it. She zipped away to locate Roamer.

"Do you think it'll bother you to go into the caves?" Julia asked as she and Roamer put on helmets and entered the mouth of the main cavern.

"I don't know," he replied, taking the lead. "We'll soon find out. Actually, at this moment it's what I want most in the universe. The *mining* is what bothered me, not being in the caves."

Julia glanced across the chamber to where Shugley's crew was setting up for the day. "At the staff meeting this morning, when I requested you as assistant, Shugley mentioned you'd worked in her crew on Magathon. Said you were a good worker there. So have you been mining long?"

"Yes, as soon as I got old enough to qualify for a work permit. I was fostered on Earth Colony Nine when I began showing signs of shais ranah. Nobody mistreated me, and my family provided well for me. When DED hired me, I wanted to repay my family for their sacrifices. I can do two things for my family—stay away and send them money. Mining pays well, and I'm not trained to do anything else."

"It sounds like a lonely life."

He shrugged, stepping around a formation. "Oh, well, it beats what happened years ago, before there was interstellar travel. Back then, when anyone manifested the shais ranah tendency, they were taken to the Desert Lands on the Lesser Southern Continent and left there. Most committed suicide at an early age. Couldn't stand the isolation, but couldn't stand each other, either."

"Well, you sure add interesting tidbits to my alien trivia store."

Roamer chuckled softly and started climbing up to the passageway they intended to explore, careful not to break any formations. "Be careful," he warned. "It's slippery today."

Julia noticed the water trickling from the passage. It had a faint green tint, reflecting the particular mineral it carried. The last water she'd seen coming from this very same passage had been gold. She'd collected and analyzed several different samples of water found in the caves, and all had proved free of harmful bacteria, but were heavily mineralized. She couldn't resist touching her tongue to the pale green liquid. It tasted metallic.

She followed Roamer on hands and knees through the moist coolness of the passage. After that first encounter in the cave, they'd always come better prepared for caving. They both carried two handbeams stowed in deep trouser pockets in addition to their helmet lamps. They wore kneepads. But they did continue violating two of the Rules of Three because they had no one else to invite along on their expeditions, and, due to the hostility from the others, they hesitated to say where they intended to go. They both carried a small supply of nutrient wafers in case they did get lost, but Roamer had displayed an unerring sense of direction in the caves. Julia felt total confidence in him.

They rested in a small chamber, admiring the pristine formations. "I like seeing things no one else sees," Roamer said. "I like the process of getting here. I like the darkness." With that, he snapped off his helmet lamp.

Julia turned hers off, too. "Yes. It's so intimate, as if you become part of the cave. You experience the cave the way it wants you to." She heard faint drips, soft sighs. "Roamer, do you hear the whispers?"

For a long moment he didn't answer. Then, "Not right now. Just cave sounds. Nothing in my head. Frankly, I'm trying not to."

"Maybe you should."

"No." He snapped his lamp back on and disappeared into a narrow passage. Wordlessly, Julia followed.

Their way grew tighter. She had to turn her head sideways so her helmet wouldn't wedge. Liquid trickled along the bottom of this tunnel, too, but the surface felt smooth. She inched along, pulling with her elbows and pushing with her toes, wondering how Roamer could manage to drag himself through such a squeeze when it gripped her so firmly. Though slim, he was still bigger than Julia.

When her fingers touched the bottoms of his boots, she stopped. Her breath whooshed in her own ears from exertion and all she could see was the passage wall, centimeters away. She tried to turn her head upright but her helmet jammed against the ceiling, preventing it. As her own breathing calmed with rest, she could hear Roamer's harsh gasps.

"Roamer? Hey, are you all right?" She worked her way forward enough to grasp his ankles. "Are you stuck?"

"No. I can't. . . . I can't. . . ."

"Can't what? Roamer, dammit! Answer me."

"I hear. It hurts. I can't stand it."

His words emerged in eerie sobs, muffled by the cave. Julia tugged on his ankle. "Listen to me, Roamer. You must calm down." Moans of agony answered her. "I'm convinced something is attempting to communicate with you. You need to accept it. Let it come."

"It's been so long since I've lowered my barriers. So long. It hurts."

"Maybe it's the *message* that hurts." Julia took a deep breath. "Lower your barriers. Shut off that mental white noise you told me about. Accept this. Please, Roamer. Share it with me."

"You don't want it."

"Yes I do! This might provide the answers I've been searching for. Can you reach your helmet lamp?"

"Yes."

"Let's turn them off, experience the cave as it is meant to be." She switched off her lamp, then gripped his ankles with both hands. "We're together within the embrace of the cave. Listen to the whispers and share them with me."

Pain. Anger. Grief. Confused suffering constant ripping tearing destruction agony unrelenting why why why why?

Her own weeping brought Julia back to reality, her tears mingling with the waters of the cave. "Roamer?" she rasped. "Are you okay?"

"Yesssss. . . ."

"You understood the message?"

"It's alive."

"We've got to get back. I'm calling for an immediate shutdown."

⋞⋗⋞⋗

"Shutdown?" Doakes roared, rising from behind his desk. "Get real, Hedrick. No way in hell am I shutting down this dig."

"Oh, but you *will*," Julia insisted calmly. "I've discovered indigent sentience."

Doakes shifted his glare to Roamer. "Is this crazy mind reader claiming those crystals are sentient?"

"No, the formations are part of the organism. The *caves* are alive, Mr. Doakes. The caves themselves."

"You have proof?" the superintendent sneered.

"I don't need proof, per se. The life form communicated with us. So I have what I need. Roamer is telepathic, as you well know. He received the message from the caves and passed it to me. That's enough to call in other dSavistas to document the caves' sentience."

Doakes laughed, an ugly sound that made his fat belly jiggle. "Intelligent holes in the ground, eh? Well, we'll clean 'em out and they can grow more crystals."

"No way." Julia shook her head. "It's murder. The mining operation is killing them. Imagine if tiny creatures invaded our bodies and started carving away our cells. This must stop immediately."

The whoosh of his door opening drew Julia's attention. All four crew bosses entered. Roamer stepped closer to Julia, sensing danger. She looked back at Doakes, knowing he'd signaled the foremen. His expression froze her blood.

"The Zeenie and the mind reader are trying to shut down our dig," Doakes announced to his foremen. "They claim the caves are alive and sentient. I say it's a bunch of crap they're making up to look important. And to get back at the rest of us for not making 'em our bosom buddies. Do we want to give up our percentages of such a fantastic dig just on the word of a couple of weirdos?"

The crew bosses all glared at Julia and Roamer. "Hell, no," Kincaid growled, and the others snarled agreement.

"You'll have no choice when I file my report," Julia pointed out.

"You ain't filing a report, Hedrick. Grab 'em!" Doakes roared.

Once more Julia witnessed Roamer's fighting ability. He spun like a ninja, lashing out with feet and hands, then grabbed Julia by the arm and crashed out of the office. Groups of miners standing outside parted to allow the two outsiders through.

Breathing hard, they raced across the camp and dashed into the cavern. Lights of a crew working in the main chamber illuminated their way enough to reach their special passage and scramble up into it. Darkness enveloped them. Roamer snapped on a handbeam. A frown creased his handsome face and he shook his head.

"They intend to follow us. They'll kill us and claim it was another accident. Come on. We can make it into passages they can't squeeze through. We know the caves."

"And the caves know us." Julia pulled out her own handbeam and dropped to her hands and knees to follow Roamer.

After scrambling through various passageways, they stopped in the small chamber of their first encounter and doused their lights. Julia felt her heart pounding wildly.

"Only Doakes and Kincaid are still following," Roamer murmured. "Blas, Tyler and Shugley stopped in the main chamber, working to avoid suspicion. And to avoid participation in our murders. They don't consider it right to kill over a dig, no matter how rich. Even Kincaid isn't really convinced, but Doakes sure is. Greedy man. Loves no one. Ahhh . . . got to shut them out. All their thoughts clamoring, banging around inside my head."

"Do it. We don't need to read their minds now. Shhh. I hear them coming."

"Me, too." Roamer flicked on his handbeam momentarily. "Quick, behind this stalagmite."

Moments later, Doakes and Kincaid crawled into the chamber, their helmet lamps slicing beams of light through the darkness.

"Where the hell did they go?" Doakes grumbled. His breath whistled raggedly.

"There!" Kincaid yelled, just as Roamer dived into a narrow passage with Julia on his heels.

"Let 'em go," Doakes snorted with a laugh. "They just crawled into their own grave. We'll seal this tunnel up and let 'em die. Claim they croaked in a cave-in. Everybody knows they're always crawling into some hole. We can say we tried to save 'em."

"I don't like this," Kincaid protested. "Do we have to kill them?"

"You coward, of course we have to kill 'em."

Julia heard the whine of a mining laser and chunks fell from the passage ceiling. Roamer's agonized keening rose above the laser whine. Then, above it all, great rumbles and crashes interspersed by cries of pain filled the cave. When silence returned, Julia tugged Roamer's ankle and began backing out. She had to kick away debris before sliding backwards into the small chamber. Roamer emerged beside her and they flicked on their handbeams to survey the damage.

A sharp stalactite pierced Doakes's chest, pinning him to the cave floor. His glazed eyes and lolling tongue proclaimed him to be quite dead. Kincaid groaned amid crystal shards. As they crossed to him, Roamer took Doakes's helmet and set it on his own head, pocketing his handbeam. He and Julia knelt beside Kincaid.

"My arm's broken," Kincaid moaned.

"We'll get you out of here," Roamer said, but Kincaid seized the dSavista with his good hand.

"I didn't want to kill anybody."

"We know," Roamer said, ripping Kincaid's sleeve to rig a sling.

"So did the cave," Julia added.

୧୯୧୧୨୦

Bright morning sunlight shone down on the busy camp as miners loaded equipment onto shuttles for transport to the jump ship. Finished with her packing and the report filed, Julia perched upon a large boulder and watched the bustle. Roamer walked over, and she patted the rock beside her as an invitation. He sat down and dusted his hands, squinting back at the caves.

"Amazing," he murmured.

"Everything okay?"

"Yeah, but I'm reluctant to leave. It feels like I'm deserting a friend."

"It'll be safe. We'll quarantine this planet and place it under intergalactic protection. Roamer, how attached are you to mining?"

"I told you, it's a way to make a living. Why?"

"Apply for a position on my research team. I'll recommend you for my assistant."

"They won't want me."

She smiled, feeling a kinship with him. "I bet you get the assignment. As a Zeenie, your telepathy will prove a gift; not a curse. This could become your first step toward certification as a xenologist."

His gaze shifted back to the caves. "I have no schooling or training."

"Not yet. But your personal experience with these caves counts for a lot. *You* established contact. If not for you, this unique life-form might've been destroyed. I detailed your part in my report. It'll carry weight, believe me."

"Shuttle up in five!" The announcement rang across the meadow and Roamer slid off the boulder.

"You really think it's possible?"

"Sure thing." Julia hopped down beside him and tucked her hand through the crook of his arm. "In this universe, there are *always* possibilities.

ᗱᑎᘓᑎᘓ

I am this place
I forbid you to enter
Depart
or I'll crash down upon you.

Human beings have always been willing to give what President Lincoln called "that last full measure of devotion." When Lincoln said it, he was referring only to men. But women give that measure, too, at times because there is nothing else they can give.

BENEATH THE ALIEN SHIELD

by Z. S. Adani

A scarab scuttled by on the wall of Habitat A, a purple streak of alien menace. Kestra stiffened, ready to defend herself, but the creature ignored her and disappeared around the corner.

"Speak waves, meaning," said the head that stood in the middle of the corridor, eyes darting left and right. Its lips quivered, and bloody saliva drooled on its chin.

Kestra suppressed a shudder. There was something infinitely obscene about a human head connected to alien nerve ganglia and mounted on a green sphere. Grateful she hadn't known the person the head belonged to before the Hermit murdered him, she examined the face, searching for anything human in it. But only blank eyes stared back. The young man had been a Belter, like everyone trapped on this asteroid.

The head telescoped higher from its spherical base, the slack face inches from her own. "Speak waves, meaning," it said again. Trace molecules of confusion wafted to Kestra's hair sensors, biological devices composed of super skin cells, perfectly natural, only enhanced. But as she silently analyzed the biochemicals from the nerve ganglia, the dense alien proteins and ancient lipids didn't yield further understanding.

"What are you saying?" Kestra asked. In the more than 50 years she'd been a Special Ops agent for Defense and Intelligence, she'd never hated an enemy as she hated this alien, and she'd never failed in carrying out an assignment. She had defused the Moon colony uprising with minimum loss of life, rooted out the bio hackers hiding in the old Martian domes, led the team that unraveled the insidious plan hatched by the Arctic Enclave, which could have killed millions if she had failed. On that mission, she had nearly died and had spent months in regeneration tanks and rehab—but she had not failed. Kestra had come to believe she could pull off any mission, and that was why DI had sent her here. But on Ursa she had accomplished nothing since her arrival. *Whatever you are,* she thought at the head, *I came here to kill you.* She would try to communicate, but only to learn the alien's weaknesses. It had to have some.

The coil of green nerve ganglia fused to the neck stump lit up at places, flickering intermittently. Translucent gummy flesh throbbed, encasing tubes like veins and arteries. "Match, join," the head said. A trace of chemicals that implied puzzlement or curiosity reached Kestra's hair sensors.

"Match what?" Anger made her reckless, but she also needed to test the alien's understanding of human language. "Analyze this," she said through gritted teeth. "You will *join* the denizens of hell if I have to *match* my templates to the power grid."

The head cocked to the side. "Hell . . . hello?"

She nodded, momentarily unable to speak. The gesture was so human a mannerism that she held her breath and looked for the darting of the eyes that she'd been told signified Hermit confusion. But it didn't come.

"Do," whispered the head. Face muscles contorted, then turned slack, but the fading expression was pleading.

Kestra closed her eyes for a second. This was the first indication, in her four days of exploring the upper part of the asteroid, that a remnant of human awareness still existed within a head. And the young man had understood what it meant to send the Hermit to hell. That he could still wish for it filled her with horror—it had been bad enough when she thought the heads were not aware of their situation. But maybe this one could help bridge the gulf between the Hermit and herself and bring about the beginning of a negotiation.

To achieve that, she went on, "Perhaps we can come to a peaceful understanding. In our corner of the universe, what you're doing is wrong. Killing sentient beings is a crime. You must stop—"

"Sound stop," said the head, eyes darting from side to side. It telescoped down to its base, the long fleshy tube wrinkling like a soggy hose. The head rolled away from her, nerve ganglia flickering and sliding into the rubbery sphere. She felt disappointed at her inability to communicate, but not surprised.

Her orders had been clear: Evacuate the civilians, gather intelligence on the alien, and most importantly, find out how to destroy the Hermit. Even without knowing the gruesome details on Ursa, it was not difficult for DI to conclude that the Hermit's hostility called for extreme measures.

Two human hands rolled by; the eyes implanted in their palms regarded her with animosity before they escorted the head along the corridor of the habitat, toward the dropplates that led downward, to the control center, where the Hermit itself resided.

Shoulders slumped, Kestra turned and headed for the commons. The 81 survivors were holed up there.

The young Belter she knew best, Jason, stepped out from the doorway of a vacant living quarter and joined her. He had been the one on watch duty topside when Kestra arrived, and it had been he who had quickly and calmly filled her in on the situation on Ursa and led her to the commons for the first time. His quiet strength and sharp intelligence impressed her, and the awkward movements caused by his missing left arm made her wince. Jason was only sixteen and had somehow come to represent the grandson she had never had. Victor's deep laughter rang in her mind—memories forty years in the past, still fresh—the smell of salt in his hair, and their long walks on the beaches of Mafia Island. They had toyed with the idea of settling down and raising a family, but their dreams had been cut short when Defense and Intelligence recalled her for yet another urgent mission. Her skills were needed; always, and by now, she understood that so well that it had come to dominate her life.

"Don't challenge it, Kestra," Jason said. "I peered out and saw the hands watching you from the corner."

"I know." The hands served as spies and guards for the Hermit; the scarabs were its weapons. Kestra wondered if Jason had ever recognized *his* hand among the dozens roaming the corridors of Ursa. And then there were the heads, so jittery—speech confused them and sound irritated them. Yet the Hermit kept sending human heads out—why, if there was really no way to communicate with the Belters? She might never know.

She had arrived at the asteroid on the exact trajectory of a previous DI ship that had been drawn in through the caul-like energy membrane that shielded the Hermit from attack and held in the thin air. But unlike the agent aboard that ship, who had tried to plant a bomb on the Hermit's ship and died for it, Kestra carried no detectable ordnance. DI would not make that mistake again.

A few hours after the Hermit's ship had landed, the alien closed off Ursa by the caul—hence, humans gave it the name "Hermit." During the next seven months, the Hermit had atomized several DI ships equipped with dirty missiles and resonating pulse beams, and their shield deflected any missiles fired from distant platforms. In retaliation, or as a warning to stay away, the Hermit had vaporized five small nearby asteroids, all inhabited. With the 4000 Belters lost on Ursa, the Hermit had killed over 30,000 people. Kestra could not let that continue.

As soon as she and Jason entered the commons, they were surrounded by the survivors. Kestra shook her head. "I'm sorry. I was unable to communicate with the Hermit part that controls a head."

An unfamiliar sense of failure filled her. Most of these Belters had already suffered the Hermit's maiming. A brother and sister in their late 20s, Mark and Helga were both missing their legs, dragging their torsos along by their arms. Once the Hermit had spun the asteroid to .36 gravities for itself, the disabled ones suffered; the near-weightlessness of Ursa would have been kinder to them.

"The head, that was Tom," said Gordon, an older Belter still in possession of all his limbs. "Tom went to check out Habitat B and never came back. He insisted on going because he was intact."

"Tom . . . is still aware," Kestra said. *But for how long?* The Belters had told her that none of the heads retained function for long, which was a blessing, as it cut short their needless suffering, and also a curse, because the alien would take more humans to replace them. It had taken fewer lately, however, and Kestra guessed it was because as it was able to convert more of the Belters' robots to whatever purpose it used the heads for.

"God help him," Helga said. Tears ran down her face.

"God won't help him, or us," said one of the men. His face was pale, and his one remaining hand was shaking.

Kestra deactivated her hair sensors through the augment. She didn't want to read these people's pheromones. It was too easy to feel their despair. The reality of being trapped under an alien shield, with the certain fate of being dismembered, was not something she could have imagined before this mission. She shoved her hands into her pockets to hide their trembling. "I tried to talk to the alien through Tom when I saw the awareness, but I doubt the Hermit understands the meanings behind most words, let alone concepts like morality."

Gordon nodded, face muscles twitching. "They seem to understand human anatomy and biochemistry, but not the mind. That's what Petrov said. He was a psychoanalyst, before he volunteered for the Acid Squad."

"Acid Squad?" Kestra raised her eyebrows.

Jason swallowed and explained, "Six of us scrounged up acid from various assemblers and went into the control center to try to kill the Hermit. The first squirt made the Hermit mound smoke. The second squirt just sizzled on its hide, and the third it neutralized. The acid just slid off. Then the scarabs attacked and cut the others to shreds. Terry and I barely made it out."

The young woman named Terry blinked and looked off into the distance. "The Hermit, the main mound, is an extremely robust organism," she said. "It adapts to adverse situations quickly. I can't imagine the world it evolved on, but it must be a vicious world."

"Well, we're clever little monkeys." Kestra forced a smile. "We'll find a way to defeat them." She thought she believed it—after all, so far the Hermit seemed unable to detect the organic weaponry DI had equipped her with. The situation might be bleak, but she was here to stop the carnage, and she had to believe she could do it. Her hand stole to her right side, with its regrown pelvic bone, femur, one lung, one kidney, and half her ribcage crushed during the Arctic mission when she was caught in the dome collapse. DI had pulled her back from the edge of death, and it wasn't for the first time. It was no secret among the Special Ops commandos that DI had been preparing for the possible arrival of hostile aliens.

Since the Hermit had sealed off the research sector and taken over the main computer, the survivors had lost their ability to use equipment to study the alien. Only visual observation remained, so the remaining Belters had to sneak out of the commons to see what was happening.

Now the latest one to venture out came in and closed the door behind him. "None of the pods left yet. They're still under the shield, and that's good. But there are 63 of them now."

"Two more since yesterday," Jason said. "It must be ready to start sending them out." He glanced at the food storage bins that contained the dry nutrient bars that were all the food they had left to live on.

The Belters had told Kestra that after the alien ship had landed, the Hermit and its helpers had consumed the contents of the hydroponics chambers, both crops and nutrient tanks sucked dry within a few weeks. Perhaps it was converting that mass to produce offspring now.

She could delay no longer—the Hermit must not be allowed to spawn. That threatened Earth itself. "I'm going to the control center." She turned and walked toward the door.

Jason came after her. "I'll come with you."

"No."

"Here, take this then." Jason removed his cap and gave it to her.

"Thanks." Kestra looked down at her boots, deeply touched by the boy's concern. She put the cap on her head; usually no one but DI cared if an operative lived or died.

Walking along the deserted corridor, she activated the T-cam in her upper left molar. Water-based micro lenses held in electrostatic fields and the sonar imagers responded to her subvocalized command, interfaces with her visual nerves and augment, and began recording.

Two hands fell in beside her at the next bend, rolling along on their gummy spheres. They turned at the wrists this way and that, fingers splayed and ready to squirt poison through the nails. The turquoise eyes embedded in the palms and the back of the hands glared malevolently. Robots rolled by, creepers and uprights, their logic centers ripped out and replaced with Hermit nerve ganglia. They all carried large pieces of the greenish alloy the alien was using to assemble sections of the pods.

A human leg unit with Hermit manipulators mounted on the hip pushed a cart, the bruised legs uncoordinated, stumbling on purple feet. A faint smell of decay wafted from the thing.

The indignity of it clawed at her sanity. Her rage threatened to spill forth; she wanted to smash them with her bare hands. But that would accomplish nothing; the thousands of dead Belters who had attacked the Hermit attested to that.

Energy weapons, projectiles, and flechettes didn't work; the Hermit mound absorbed or rejected everything.

A blast of cold air greeted her at the door. The acrid smell of the alien sent a burst of data to her augment: superconducting proteins folding in unfamiliar ways, strange lipids and microtubule production, metallic and crystalline molecules, and several unidentifiable compounds.

Around the frame of the open door, clusters of Hermit nerve ganglia clung, various colors and shapes. They pulsed inside transparent casings, extending ropy appendages down into the doorway. One brushed over her face. Kestra passed through quickly, grateful for Jason's cap perching on her hair sensors. What would the Hermit make of those? One of the reasons she had postponed visiting the control center was that she couldn't afford any scrutiny that might stop her from carrying out her orders.

She stared at the main bulk of the Hermit squatting near the asteroid's hexagonal control column, a pale green, teal, and pink mass of pulsing muscles, spikes, and ridges. Extended portions of it filled most of the open spaces. According to the Belters, it had grown thrice its current size since it arrived on Ursa.

On its top perched a giant translucent organ, vaguely flower-shaped, fleshy petals quivering wetly around the cluster of purple nerve tendrils that extended into hair-thin jell-like strands wrapping around and reaching inside the twenty-meter wide hexagon that housed the main computer. Through a pulsing hole in one section, dog-sized purple scarabs emerged.

Kestra stiffened, ready to bolt or defend herself, but the scarabs ignored her. They landed with a metallic clatter, shook themselves, and scuttled out of the control center. One of the hands that had accompanied her rolled inside another hole in the mound.

A biochemical factory, she thought, studying the convoluted bulges and recording everything. With quick motions, she touched the rippling flesh at several places, imprinting it for the ThermNites. Her fingers tingled from its coldness or from its strangeness, but she managed to snag a few alien cells for her report—*if* she could send it.

In a hollow place on the Hermit mound, upright rows of muscular ropes caught her attention. The blue trellises undulated, each one gripping a human body with Hermit tendrils. She realized the bodies were still alive. Some were partially flayed; others displayed slashed abdomens, the organs missing and replaced by alien tissues. Organic tubes carrying blue ichor were connected to each human. One of the victims was headless. She glimpsed a woman whose eyes followed her, mouth open but no sound issued from it as a tendril from the trellis wrapped around her arm. The rope tightened and exuded a sour stench, then pinched off the arm, which dropped onto the mound. Two star-shaped creatures shoved it into a hole.

Kestra looked away, blinking. It was her job to end this, no matter the price.

No matter the price, echoed in her mind. She wiped her eyes and continued studying the alien.

Below the trellises, four hands—not human, but made of green Hermit tissues—stood ready, rubbery fingers fluttering. She walked around them. An irregular opening pulsed once, twice, and spat out a miniature Hermit. The hands caught it and carried it to a transparent tube, then pushed the thing inside. Her gaze followed the tube to one of the corridors that led topside.

To the waiting pods near the alien ship. The Hermit could release the pods at any time. She had to act. She quickly calculated the heat her ThermNites would yield if she were to activate them here. No, the minute spark her body's mass would provide was not enough to consume this monstrosity. And the pods might escape through the shield. She couldn't allow that; to ensure that the Hermit and its pods were destroyed, she needed Ursa's power source and the mass of the asteroid itself. That would generate enough heat but just barely. Although Ursa was a main belt asteroid, it was of low mass, hollowed out by the Belters over the years.

Kestra squatted and peered underneath the alien to see if it had fused parts of itself to the floor. She saw hundreds of short legs—various stumps, appendages, metallic and bony spikes supported the giant bulk. And some did penetrate the floor.

But perhaps she did not have to activate the ThermNites. From her meager arsenal, she selected the packet of pricor, insidious prion corrupter molecules designed to mimic the host's proteins and coax them to fold wrong, then turn the surrounding proteins into necronites. *It just might work; if it does, I might be able to save the asteroid.* She nudged her augment to activate the dormant pricor packet, and another subroutine sent an impulse to the inside of her cheek. A tiny slit opened and squirted the microscopic mucus-encased lipid capsule into her mouth. Kestra collected saliva around it, straightened and, angling toward one of the openings of the Hermit, she spat the pricor inside.

As she stepped back, she accidentally swiped a passing hand. Whose? For a split second, the nightmare image of Jason's severed arm flashed in her mind. The hand smacked to the foamsteel floor, its arm section rippling with the blue ganglia inside, one side of its eye flattening and leaking a clear fluid.

Damn. Kestra dashed to the door. From her peripheral vision, she saw that two blue lozenges detached themselves from the Hermit mound and dragged the injured hand through an open hole. She ducked under the undulating appendages and hurried into the corridor, heart pounding. She dared not glance at the hands that appeared next to her, but kept her enhanced senses alert for attack. They simply escorted her to the commons, and Kestra entered.

At least she had done something, because the past days spent topside checking out the remains of the Belter ships had been a waste of time. Her original plan had been to repair them and evacuate the survivors, but all the ships had been scrapped by the Hermit, just as it had her own ship as soon as she had arrived. Jason had told her that some Belters had attempted to steal back the ship engines, but the scarabs had intercepted them and sliced them up, armor and all. Still she had to try, because evacuating the survivors had been the first phase of her mission. It seemed less and less likely that she would be able to accomplish that.

∽◌❀◌∾

Two hours later, eight of the scarabs and two hands appeared in the doorway of the commons. The survivors shrank back and stared at the lump of Hermit tissue one of the hands threw on the floor. Scabs on it leaked blue ichor, and then it shriveled up and turned into powder.

Kestra's stomach lurched; the pricor hadn't worked. Worse, the Hermit had discovered it and excised the infected tissues. *I should have known. Its technology is based on biochemistry.*

The scarabs moved suddenly and in unison, one group of four toward Terry and another group toward one of the men. Metallic carapaces shifted with grating sounds, and glassy purple antennae stung each human along the lower spine. Terry cried out and the man stiffened, their faces carved in pain.

Kestra took a step toward them, but Jason, Gordon, and another man grabbed her and held her back. She struggled with the men, but they held her tightly, and she watched with horror as the hands led their victims away, surrounded by the scarabs. Someone closed the door.

"You shouldn't have restrained me," she said to the three men.

"The scarabs would've killed you," Jason said. "And you're the only hope we have left."

A few Belters glanced in her direction, then away, their expressions full of bitterness, which she read as an accusation. Helga burst into tears. Her brother dragged himself to her on his arms and embraced her.

Kestra had to turn away. "I'm sorry." Not only she had failed to mount a rescue mission, she had made their plight worse. But Jason was right; commando training or not, she was no match for eight scarabs, even if, with a bit more effort, she might have overpowered the three men. Instinctively, she hadn't, and she realized now it was because her mission was more important.

Gordon put a hand on her shoulder. "The Hermit doesn't assign blame to individuals. Judging by its actions, it must consider us all one organism."

"I think," Jason said and moistened his lips, "we're all going to die slowly and painfully. I can't tell you how much that frightens me." He looked at her and continued, "But we have a chance now to prevent that. Right, Kestra?"

She nodded. Kestra was suddenly uncertain whether she would be able to complete the mission, because this time everything she knew and could do might not be enough. Subconsciously she had known that soon after her arrival, but she'd been hoping to prove herself wrong, so she'd tried her other options, limited as they were. But the Hermit was too alien. Extreme as her final solution was, the alternative—dismemberment—was infinitely worse. She shuddered, stiffened her spine, and faced Jason. "Absolutely. I can prevent that."

"I think Space Force has given up." Helga said, her voice bordering on hysteria. "You're the best they can do?" She gestured at Kestra. "Don't repeat our mistakes. We tried everything possible. Why aren't you working on disabling their shield?"

Kestra swallowed and didn't say that the Hermit shield was as yet beyond humanity's technological wherewithal. Space Force had lost several ships trying to penetrate the shield, so they *had* given up on the Belter settlement. But DI had sent its best commando. If she succeeded in getting data on the shield and the Hermit back to DI, they could study it to improve defense technology.

Jason scowled at Helga. "Go tend your garden." The Belter insult used to chastise brats who were too immature for serious responsibilities quieted her. Then he turned to Kestra, his blue eyes steely. "If you need help, I'm at your disposal. Anything, just name it."

Kestra met the boy's gaze, grateful. Just as he was, she was terrified, not of dying, but of the unrelenting mutilation.

"Count me in," said Gordon.

Another man hit a variform with his one remaining fist. "Nothing would give me greater pleasure than to hurt those fuckers."

Several other Belters offered to help.

Kestra shook her head, partly to clear her mind of the fuzzy thoughts and partly to restore her self-discipline. "What I have to do is best done alone. Less chance the Hermit will catch on. But I could use a good map of the lower levels. The Hermit could have altered the architecture. I need to know the shortest route to the power grid."

Since they couldn't interface with the computer to call up schematics—and the scarabs had consumed all the smart papers—Jason took off his shirt, spread it on the dining table, and began to outline the details with ketchup.

Kestra studied the sketch for a while, then nodded. "I'll find it," she said and headed for the door.

Voices behind her wished her luck, even Helga's.

Jason followed her. "I'll walk you to the dropplate."

Along their passage in every corner lurked a cold living fear. Whether human parts or Hermit tissues, they watched emotionlessly. Ursa hummed with the controlled fervor of alien biomachines bent on production. *Reproduction, rather*, Kestra thought, as she recalled the miniature Hermits birthed by the monster and installed in the waiting pods, secluded under the shield and ready to be sent forth.

"I have a half-sister at Clarke Station," Jason said quietly. "Her name is Katy, and she's brilliant. Only twelve and already passed the fourth level of robotics." He smiled, face alive with pride. "She lives at Clarke with her mother. Katy's not a Belter brat, but we shared a father. She adores him and doesn't know he's dead. He . . . Dad died trying to kill the Hermit after my arm was taken. I . . . I want my sister to survive."

The words cut through her, and Kestra almost stopped, but thought better of it; no need to attract the attention of the hands. She took a deep breath and exhaled, then said in a low voice, "She'll survive, Jason."

"I know. I knew when I first saw you getting out of your ship."

They reached the dropplates and chose a small one that wasn't in use by scarabs or robots manhandling pod sections and tubes. Kestra forced a smile and extended her hand. "Thanks for all your help."

Jason shook her hand. "It was nice knowing you. Make it good, Kestra." Then he turned abruptly and left.

She stepped onto the dropplate and started to descend, blinking from the haze that suddenly obscured her vision. She sighed with uncharacteristic sadness. *Evacuate the survivors.* Failed. But she might still accomplish two out of three of her mission imperatives: *get the data to DI; annihilate the Hermit and all its pod-selves before they could spread.*

When the dropplate stopped at the lowest level, Kestra stepped off. She rounded the winding corridor in the belly of the asteroid, following the memorized path. Her augmented vision traced the conduits of the power distribution grid, a faint green glow under the thin plazoy walls.

She glanced at the hands rolling behind her. If they had been accompanied by a head, she would have started singing to confuse them. As it was, she slapped her own hands at the walls, marking the strongest nodes of the grid by leaving behind a few cells. The ThermNites would read her DNA and suck power from the grid nodes, speeding up the process of reaching the main Hermit mound, the pods, and the ship.

Before the Hermit takeover, Ursa had had an efficient production setup, the Von Neumanns chewing small asteroids and converting them into alloys, then into ship hulls, bulkheads, engine housings, and life support machinery. Engineering specialists and technicians assembled parts of the life support systems and engines, overseeing the testing and analyses. Everything now had been reconfigured to produce Hermit pods.

She passed large pieces of alien equipment and translucent bubbles before she entered another down-sloping tunnel. Her IR vision drove back the shadows in front of her as she proceeded, but the darkness still seemed to swallow her. *I'm old*, she thought for the first time. *I'm letting emotions get to me.*

She reached the door of the power chamber and began to turn the mechanical lock when a metallic clatter caught her attention. Kestra pivoted and dodged as a glassy proboscis stabbed at her.

A scarab streaked by. It turned sharply, careened into the wall, then came at her again. She jumped aside, but the wall was in her way, and the creature's razor-sharp claws swiped the back of her wrist. Pain flowered in her, and blood squirted. She swayed and, through her augment, released a dose of painkillers and medchines to stem the blood flow. Her wrist hung by a few tendons, bones protruding. Kestra watched the scarab getting ready for another assault. When the creature ran at her again, she jumped high, twisted in the air, and landed on its carapace. It cracked with a satisfying crunch. For good measure, she stomped on the head with her boots until it was just a purple stain on the floor.

Panting, she turned back to the door and opened it one-handed, then quickly stepped through and locked it from the inside. She ripped off the sleeve of her coverall and wrapped it around her wrist. As the lights came on, her eyes followed a green rubbery conduit snaking out of the ceiling and connecting to the power source's housing.

The Hermit was sucking power for its reproduction and pod assembly. No one had told her the alien was so completely entrenched in the asteroid, but she was glad. That would make it even more vulnerable.

Placing her uninjured hand on the housing, Kestra initiated the release through her augment. Following strict protocols, the ThermNites that were scattered throughout her body began to rush toward her hand. Fast-burning structures assembled into microscopic gossamer webs using her body's carbon, potassium, phosphorus, and the implanted nanoscopic plasma elements. She swayed, her blood pulsing from the accelerated metabolism. Perspiration drenched her, and she shivered; her palm felt hot as the skin sloughed off and curled into a lump of programmed death. The lump turned cherry-red and began to burrow into the housing of the power source.

Light-headed, she leaned against the wall and pulled a dry nutrition bar from her pocket. She bit into it and washed it down with water from a bulb. It was a far cry from the last dinner she had shared with Victor on Mafia Island, real steak and champagne. Her mind tried to pull her into the happy past, but she banished the memory and called up the energy-mass ratio on her retinal screen; fourteen minutes until the ThermNites converted enough mass to critical heat.

After she finished her lonely meal, she returned to the hub by the tube access. She left the tube and headed toward a girder near the shield. She had selected it two days ago, as farthest from the control center, because she needed just enough time to launch the message capsule after the shield fell. She refused to think about the possibility that it might not. During the short wait, she subvocalized a personal addendum and attached to it Jason's recorded words. It was a message to Katy Newman of Clarke Station, informing her that Jason and her father died bravely.

Though she would rather have returned to the commons and spent the final minutes of her life among the Belters, it was imperative that DI receive her data on the Hermit and its shield, and this was her best chance to send it.

Her wrist had stopped bleeding, but it throbbed with a dull ache. Kestra grabbed a strut one-handed and climbed as far as she could on the angling metal. She stopped a meter from the shield when she felt a minute vibration through her boots.

It's almost time. She attached a line to the strut so she wouldn't be thrown off prematurely. Activating her T-cam, she recorded the energy from the shield. From this close, the caul looked pearly, turning pinkish in the distance. No stars showed through.

In the back of her mind, she realized that she had somehow accepted the inevitability of death. It had become the better alternative. She felt a tremor, and the shield rippled, then righted itself. Below her was a heaving lump of crimson lava, but the ThermNites hadn't reached critical mass yet. When they did, they would destroy the control center, the main Hermit mound, the pods holding the miniature Hermits, and the alien spacecraft. The shield would buckle. It had to.

Kestra dislodged the T-cam from her molar and formed a propulsion tube around it. She checked the compressed air implanted in her cheek and waited, ready to shoot the capsule out as soon as the shield collapsed. She needed to shoot it far enough to escape the immediate heat, then the micropile inside the T-cam would power the nanorockets and carry it out of harm's way. DI would home in on it.

Perspiration drenched her. Leaning against the support strut, she brushed her hand over her rebuilt side. She had courted death long enough, and she had extracted much from the courtship by way of countless successful missions. Now, at the end of her most important mission, death had become her ally.

Another tremor shook her perch, and she almost lost her footing, but the line held.

Then a white worm of plasma surged below, growing rapidly. The shield rippled and began to turn dark, sections opening on black space. *The Hermit is dying now; the pods have melted.* Kestra smiled and felt another jolt, followed by a sharp pain in her back. She threw herself toward the collapsing shield with all her strength and shot the message capsule outward.

Mission accomplished, Jason, she thought. Her lungs exploded in the vacuum.

Some men try to use women for their own purposes; if the women let
them, there are consequences for all concerned. And those
consequences may be unanticipated by the women as well as the
men.

RAINFIRE BY NIGHT

by DJ Cockburn

The women's voices filled the room as they sang praises to
the naked goddess. Rainfire sang with them and despised
them. She hated hearing her voice swallowed by voices that
never spoke a kind word to her. She watched the women nearest
the fire sway with their eyes closed and vowed to die before she
gave up her own thoughts like that. She had already found that
she preferred having warriors wanting to beat her than to marry
her, and her fifteen winters made her the oldest unmarried
woman in Doune.

Yet she had been waiting for those closed eyes because
they showed her that the women were absorbed by their songs
and not paying attention to each other. She edged back to the
wall, where the shadows of the singing women became one with
each other. No one was guarding the doorway because not even
Rainfire had ever dared leave the keep while the men were in
council. *But I am Rainfire and I do as I please.* She could barely
sit because of a beating from a warrior who saw her watching
him with his new bride two days ago, but her father's short
temper over the last few days told her something would happen
in this council that she wanted to see.

The women's voices faded as she ran up the stone
staircase to the top of the keep. She heard men shouting and
knew that whatever her father had anticipated was happening,

but she could not see it because the only window looked along the battlemented wall that surrounded the courtyard, rather than into the courtyard itself. The single light was from the fire in the courtyard, so no one down there could see her slip through the window and huddle against the wall of the keep. A cold wind bit through her shift, but Rainfire was ready to endure far worse to see her father, Keenblade, in council.

Keenblade sat on a steel throne that was slightly inclined toward that of the Director. Their backs were taut, as though they were about to leap to their feet. The fifty-two warriors of Doune sat on the ground on the other side of the fire from them, looking equally tense.

The Director was yelling, "You're a fool, Keenblade! You'll get us all killed and still give Doune to the enemy!"

"A fool?" Keenblade spoke quietly, but Rainfire heard more menace than if he had bellowed.

"Yes, a fool! Only a senseless fool would think we can stay here and live!"

Rainfire held her breath for the moment of silence that followed. She released it when her father stood up. She might not have witnessed a council before, but she knew there was only one reason for a man to stand.

"Then I speak for all the *fools* among us." Keenblade shrugged off his cloak.

The Director hesitated, then stood. "It's taken you long enough to find the courage." Rainfire heard the waver in the sneer he tried to put into his voice. Keenblade had earned his warrior name several times over.

The Director's sword scraped from his scabbard and sliced at Keenblade. Keenblade's sword swung into a parry. A clash of metal echoed around the castle walls. Rainfire clapped her hand over her mouth to stop herself screaming at her father to stop before he was killed.

The heavy, two-handed swords glinted in the firelight as they hacked at each other. The blades were crudely battered out of the detritus of Before, and Rainfire knew that handling them was more a matter of strength than skill, but a well-placed blow could still be deadly.

The Director stepped back to avoid a blow rather than parrying it, shifted a hand in front of his hilt and lunged while Keenblade was still on the backswing. Rainfire screamed aloud, her voice lost in a great sigh from the watching warriors.

Keenblade stepped to one side, parried with impossible speed and smashed the Director's fingers against his own hilt. The Director wailed, his manhood deserting him. His point dropped to the ground. Keenblade pulled his sword back and drove its point so deeply into the Director's throat that it nearly severed his head.

After the blow, Keenblade thrust his sword into the ground in front of him, angled so its edge faced the two Peoples, as did the insignia of a three pointed star enclosed in a circle that was welded to the back of the guard. His gaze raked the now silent warriors. "I, Keenblade of the People of the Mercedes, claim the Directorship of the Two Peoples of Doune by right of combat. Does anyone else claim the same right?"

Rainfire smirked at the thought of any of the warriors trying their luck while Keenblade's face was still streaked with the Director's blood.

Keenblade stepped back from the sword and smiled. All of the Peoples could see the smile, but Rainfire pretended it was for her and her alone, his way of celebrating his promotion with her. He half turned and waved at the picture presiding over the council. "Then our lady goddess has smiled on me. I hope I'll be worthy of her honor."

The naked goddess of Before smiled back. Rainfire did not know how long the Peoples had been bestowing their praises on the image, but anyone could see she was a goddess. She lay on a soft bed of Before, her glowing skin bared to the cold air that kept the Peoples wrapped in leather and wool. Her impossibly large breasts and parted legs suggested the reward a successful warrior could expect from the women he would claim.

Keenblade knelt before the goddess and kissed the scratched plastic that covered her. He stood again and thrust the Director's sword into the ground next to his own, so that the rhombus insignia on the hilt faced the Peoples.

He sat behind his own sword. "Before we continue the Council," he said, "we must find a new Manager for the People of the Renault. I suggest Nightcloud, son of Steelfist."

A murmur of surprise hummed through the Peoples, and Rainfire had to think for a moment to remember that Steelfist was the late Director's warrior name. The real surprise was the name of Nightcloud, who had yet to grow his full beard and whose warrior name referred to the dark night when he killed his only Stirling warrior to earn it. Yet nobody dared speak against the blood on the naked blade, so Nightcloud made his way to the front of the Peoples. Rainfire saw the falter in his step.

Keenblade embraced Nightcloud, leaving his tunic smeared with the blood of his father. Both men sat down on the metal thrones of the Board Members.

Keenblade spoke again. "Before we honor Steelfist, we must resolve the matter that he and I quarreled over. Had he not insisted on leaving this castle, he would still be alive. I say that we have our herds and our homes here and cannot leave because we've lost a few skirmishes to the enemy of Stirling, whom we outnumber. What do you say, Nightcloud of the Renault?"

Nightcloud looked around as though he thought the question was directed at someone else. Rainfire smiled at her father's wisdom. He had pushed the boy into the only position from which a Director could be challenged. *My father*, she thought, *the greatest man in Doune.*

Nightcloud found his voice at last, and spoke as though he were reciting one of his childhood lessons. "We can't fight them, because their arrows kill us before we're close enough to use our swords."

Keenblade regarded him in silence. Nightcloud glanced at his father's body. "Director."

Keenblade nodded. "It's true that our swords and slings can't match their bows on *open ground*, in *daylight*."

He swept his gaze across the Peoples to remind them that he had fought their enemies when Nightcloud was waving his wooden sword and bragging to his mother of the great warrior he would be. Did her father's eyes flick toward Rainfire, or did she just wish they had? "There are other ways of fighting them, ways that will make us masters of the valley rather than refugees from it, as Steelfist wished."

Rainfire's imagination filled with ways by which she herself could fight the enemy. She would serve her father as he had never been served before, if only he would let her. She sighed. What use would a warrior have for a girl?

The moment ended. "Now we must honor Steelfist. Call his wives to prepare him for the feast. Let my own wives prepare the fires to cook it. Steelfist has led us long and wisely, and let us pray to the goddess that he may pass some of his strength and wisdom to us, along with his flesh."

Someone ran to call the Director's wives. They huddled together at the door of the keep when they saw their husband's corpse.

"Don't be afraid," said Keenblade. "Come to him."

Steelfist's senior wife broke away from the huddle and strode across the courtyard. The four co-wives held each other as they followed. The senior wife took Steelfist's broadsword and crouched by his head. She closed his eyes and kissed his lips. Her hand lingered on his cheek.

"Don't delay," barked Keenblade. "His spirit needs release."

The senior wife stood up and thrust the broadsword into Steelfist's heart. It was only then that Rainfire realized that the decision to stay in Doune had been taken without any discussion at all.

ೞ෴ಞ

Rainfire dipped her horsehair brush in blue dye and touched it to the Mercedes she was painting on the wall. A sound startled her and she spun around to see Keenblade standing behind her. "Father! How long have you been there?"

"A while. I like to watch you paint."

Rainfire felt her cheeks flush. She wanted to tell him how she treasured such words, but she could not find words of her own.

Keenblade stepped forward. "I see these are the warriors of the Peoples with swords, and these are the enemy of Stirling lying dead with their bows. But what are these beasts that our warriors are riding?"

Rainfire flushed again when she saw the streak of blue she had made when he startled her. "They're Mercedes, father. The legends say they used to travel faster than any horse. When you said you could find a way to rule the valley, I thought. . . ."

Her voice died as she realized how foolish she sounded. The Mercedes were just hulks of metal like the Renaults and Volkswagens and all the others. Whatever the legends said they once had been, they were only good for feeding the smiths' forges now.

Keenblade did not look as though he thought she was foolish. He nodded. "Good idea. But where are their wheels?"

"Wheels father? I've never seen one with wheels."

"That's because we've used them all for our wagons, but they had wheels once. The question is what animal they used to pull them so fast. We'd have to ask the goddess about that."

"So you can't use them against Stirling?"

"Not unless the goddess answers, which she never does. But she's given us an easier way to beat them. Not a way for a warrior, but a way for a woman. A young woman anyway." He looked straight at Rainfire.

Rainfire could not hide her amazement. He was actually asking her for something. "A woman like me?"

"Exactly like you, Rainfire."

Rainfire backed up to a doorless cupboard. She could not believe that the day after her father had become the greatest man in Doune, he had come to compliment her painting and ask for her help. His smile really was only for her, because they were alone. Was she worthy of what he wanted of her? The thought slapped the smile from her face. "What do you want me to do, father?"

He became serious. "You know where Stirling's power comes from?"

"From their warriors' bows?"

"Their fighting power comes from their bows, yes. But we don't know how they learned to make them. We've tried it and we can't make anything throw an arrow more than ten paces. Their arrows are deadly at a hundred. So what should we be asking?"

Rainfire quailed before Keenblade's question. If she didn't know the answer, she was inadequate for the task he was going to give her. She clawed for a reply. "How do they know how to make the bows?"

She hated herself for showing her foolishness with such a question, but Keenblade nodded. "Exactly. And now we know how."

"We do?"

"We got it out of one of their women. She seemed anxious to help us when we offered her a quick death." His smile invited Rainfire to share the joke.

She smiled back. "I hope you didn't give it to her."

"We did. Eventually."

Rainfire savored the joy of sharing laughter with her father.

"But she had a lot to tell us first," said Keenblade. "They have some very strange customs in Stirling, but the most important thing is the Cedrom."

Rainfire tried the word. "Cedrom?"

"Their chief advisor keeps it in the castle. It's the source of their knowledge."

"What is it?"

"It's not much in itself. A disc small enough for any child to throw. It's what it contains that's important. The knowledge of Before."

Rainfire drew breath slowly. So she was not only to beat the enemy of Stirling; she was to secure the knowledge of Before for her father. "How can I get it for you?"

"By joining the enemy and taking advantage of their strange customs."

Rainfire's fingers tightened on the top of the cupboard. She felt as though he had asked her to cut off a limb. "I must leave you, father?"

"Just for a day. If you can't do it by then, you won't be able to do it at all. But when you come back with the Cedrom, all of the Peoples will fall at your feet."

Rainfire found herself reliving a memory of two winters ago. One of Keenblade's wives had tired of her disobedience and accused her of stealing food from her children, and Rainfire's own mother was dead, so there was nobody to speak for her. She had not heard a kind word for a year, but the worst of it was that Keenblade himself had pretended she ceased to exist.

Even a day among the enemy would be worse than that year. At least she had been able to see Keenblade then. She looked up to see him cut off a few strands of his brown hair with his sword.

"Show me your ankle," he said.

Rainfire knelt and rolled the hide of her left boot down. Keenblade knelt in front of her to tie the hair around her ankle. The touch of his fingers sent a thrill singing up her leg.

Keenblade drew back. "Now I'll be with you all the time, and they won't see me under your boot."

"Yes, father." Something in Keenblade's eyes told her she hadn't sounded as brave as she hoped.

"Here's something we can ask the goddess about. Let's see how many ravens she's sent to bless our plans."

Keenblade took Rainfire's hand and led her through the rotting doorframe. A raven was sitting on the house opposite them and cocked its head to watch them.

Rainfire looked around her. "I can only see one raven."

Keenblade pointed upward. "There are several up there, watching us. See?"

Rainfire squinted into the grey sky. "I can't see them. Your eyes are so much sharper than mine."

Keenblade squeezed her hand. "Now that we have the goddess's blessing, let's talk of what we must do with it."

∞

The movement of Keenblade's back against Rainfire's arm stilled as he reined in his horse.

"From here we walk," he said.

Rainfire, who was riding sidesaddle, slid straight off. Nightcloud climbed off his own horse and tethered it beside Keenblade's. He turned to the warriors who would guard them. "You look after them properly unless you want to lose a few teeth."

Rainfire sighed loudly, and he glared. He had only been a Manager for a couple of days and he was already so full of his own importance that Rainfire wondered where he put his food. Taunting him was a privilege of the Director's daughter, and one she had learned to enjoy.

Nightcloud's bombast left him as he followed Rainfire and Keenblade up a streambed that led into the pine forest above the trail. "I don't know why we had to meet them in here."

"That's because you've never seen what their longbows can do on open ground," said Keenblade.

Rainfire cast a mocking smile over her shoulder, and Nightcloud's crestfallen expression made her laugh aloud. He had not recovered before Rainfire saw gaps between the branches ahead, where the stream flowed out of a clearing. Keenblade turned and placed a hand on Rainfire's arm. "Are you ready, daughter?"

Fear crushed Rainfire's heart. She didn't know whether she was more afraid of failure or of success. She made herself smile. "Yes, Father."

She unlaced her cape, and it fell open to reveal the thin white shirt beneath. It was a relic of Before, made of a single strip of cloth that swept down from her shoulders to cover her torso while hiding very little of it. The shirt showed its age in places, but nothing that the Peoples' weavers could make came close to matching it. Rainfire felt like a demigoddess of Before, who could show her skin to a friendly sun whenever she wished. Keenblade had told her she could not fail with the power of such a relic to aid her, and she knew he was right when she saw Nightcloud's gaze. She didn't know what it was about breasts that so obsessed men, but she had seen the effect that they had. Usually without being noticed herself.

"Nightcloud." Keenblade frowned at him. "Come in front with me. Remember, keep your mouth shut and don't look surprised at anything." He did not need to give Rainfire any last-minute advice.

Her step was firm and confident as she followed the men into the clearing. She saw two enemies stand to greet Keenblade and Nightcloud. She had never been this close to the enemy before and was surprised at how ordinary they looked. One had a full head of grey hair, and his gait was awkward. Rainfire wondered how he defended his position, as he did not look like a dangerous swordsman. The other was only a few years older than Nightcloud, with broad shoulders and a red beard. He was the Director whom Keenblade had described, and she had to suppress a smile when she saw him already looking at her. She met his gaze and lifted her chin as she knelt in the coarse bracken.

Keenblade rapped out his introduction. "I am Keenblade, Director of Doune and Manager of the People of the Mercedes. This is Nightcloud, Deputy Director and Manager of the People of the Renault. May the sun shine on our meeting."

The red-bearded enemy was still looking at Rainfire. Rainfire allowed a smile to creep across her lips. Some instinct warned her not to smile too openly. The greybeard coughed, and the redbeard's gaze snapped to Keenblade. Neither of the enemy spared Nightcloud a second glance.

"I am Rannoch, Chief Elect of Stirling. May the sun shine on you," said the redbeard.

"I am Gealag, Advisor to the Chief Elect. May the sun shine on you," said the greybeard.

They sounded as portentous as men always did, but Rainfire knew she had already stolen the redbeard's attention. She wondered why he called himself a Chief Elect, whatever that was.

The four men sat down on logs that had been arranged to face each other. Rainfire saw Gealag the greybeard staring at her pointedly. She could not resist smiling back.

Keenblade spoke first. "We're here to discuss the depredations that you have carried out against us. You've stolen our sheep and cattle, leaving our larders bare, and killed several of the People in the process."

Rannoch the redbeard's eyes stole back to Rainfire. She met them and held them while her father spoke on. Fingers of cold found their way through her shirt and stroked her breasts, but she ignored them and allowed the cape to slip back and reveal her shoulders.

Keenblade's voice fell silent. Rainfire had to struggle to contain her smile of triumph when she realized Rannoch had not heard a word Keenblade said.

Rannoch jerked his attention back to Keenblade, and he didn't look like the warrior who had driven her people behind the walls of Doune, but a youth caught picking his nose during sword practice. "Yes I hear your words, Keenblade, but we—I—must consider that, er. . . ."

Gealag leaned forward and spoke in a deep voice that belied his feeble body. "What the Chief Elect wishes to say is that we attacked your people to recover goods that you stole from us. If your warriors were killed, they shouldn't have tried to stop us taking what is ours."

Rainfire watched Rannoch edge away from Gealag. His hands knotted in his lap. He looked like Nightcloud when she laughed at him, and she suddenly felt she knew Rannoch. He was no longer the enemy Director, but another warrior boy who could never match her father.

Gealag was still speaking. "You've made it very clear by your constant theft of our cattle and sheep that we won't be safe until you're out of our way. We're quite willing to annihilate you in battle if you wish. If not, we'll allow you to move south of the River Forth, where you may do as you please."

Rainfire kept the slight smile on her lips while she seethed. She was angered less by the outrageous demand than by Gealag's tone. Steelfist had died for speaking to her father like that.

Keenblade spoke to Rannoch as though he didn't take Gealag seriously. "Of course we can't leave our homes to cross the Forth. Doune Castle has belonged to us since Before and we can't abandon it now. However, we would be happy to confine ourselves to, say, a quarter of the distance between Doune and Stirling."

Gealag snorted, and Rainfire twitched her shoulders to throw the cape even further back. She saw Rannoch's eyes flick toward her, and Gealag looked at her as well. Rainfire delighted to see not only hatred in his eyes, but a touch of fear as he recognized what she was doing to Rannoch. She had seen how obviously men wore their feelings many times, but never realized how easy those feelings were to control.

Rannoch was struggling for words again. "I, well, perhaps we should consider. . . ."

Gealag leaned forward. "What the Chief Elect means is that your suggestion is ridiculous. You dare not graze your animals this side of Doune as it is, so why should we accept a guarantee of what we already have? Your choice is simple: leave Doune or we'll throw you out."

Rannoch's hands clenched in fury at his advisor rather than his enemy. He looked at her again. She smiled back and allowed her tongue to slide between her lips.

Keenblade spoke as though Gealag's threats meant nothing to him. "Of course we won't ask you to accept a guarantee without a pledge. That's why I brought my daughter, Rainfire." He waved a hand at her. "I offer her to you as a wife. So that you'll know we're sincere."

Gealag and Rannoch both looked at her and Rainfire saw the desire in the way that Rannoch's whole body shifted in her direction. Gealag must have seen it too, because what she saw in his eyes was near to panic. He started to speak, but Rannoch cut him off. "Your offer is acceptable, and I accept your—your pledge."

Gealag ran a hand across his face, which had lost all of its keen intelligence and just looked old. He swayed as he stood up. Rannoch's eyes never left Rainfire for more than a moment at a time. Keenblade turned and held his hand to her. She stood up. Her joy at her success vanished as she realized what it meant. She would have to leave with the man whose eyes probed where his hands would surely follow, and the man who would kill her if she gave him the chance. She found she could ignore the cold no more and pulled her cape around her. Keenblade guided her hand into Rannoch's, and she shuddered at the calluses on his fingers from drawing his longbow.

Her father had asked it of her, so she let Rannoch lead her away from him. She would not look back. *She would not look back.* But when she did, Keenblade had already been swallowed by the pines.

⋅⋅⋅⋅

Rainfire laid her head against Rannoch's shoulder and watched Stirling Castle loom over his chariot. It was huge, several times larger than Doune, and built on a high cliff that no man could climb. She could not imagine how even Keenblade could hope to attack it. Except with her help. She smiled to herself and nestled closer to Rannoch, who took it for affection and put an arm around her without letting go of the reins.

Rainfire thought about what to say to make Rannoch even more devoted to her. "How many wives do you already have, sir?"

Rannoch pulled away so he could look at her, and his gaping mouth made Rainfire wonder what she had said wrong. He threw back his head and laughed. "You don't know much about us do you? In Stirling, we only take one wife."

"But what do you do when she gets old?"

"It's simple. We love her. As I love you."

In Doune, only women pledged a lifetime with the word 'love,' and Rainfire was astonished to hear the enemy Director talking like a woman.

Rannoch took a hand off the reins and placed it on hers. "And when we love someone, we like to hear our name on their tongue. I'm called Rannoch, not Sir."

Rainfire's world lurched with the chariot. She had spent her life giving her love to her father, and neither asked nor received more than an occasional kind word or touch in return. Now the enemy was offering more than she would ever get from her father or anyone else in Doune.

Rannoch smiled at her bewildered look. "I know it's a bit different to what your people do, but believe me, it saves a lot of blood. While your men were fighting over your women, we were working on these." He patted his unstrung bow. "It took years to work out how to make them and use them, and we'd have given up before we started if we'd had to watch to see who was slipping back to someone else's women. Like you do in Doune."

Rainfire remembered her father telling her about the Peoples' efforts to make bows. Was Rannoch saying their failure was due to the Peoples' marriage system? And if a man of Stirling had to behave like a woman in a marriage, how did a woman behave? She tried asking a question as directly as a man would. "How do you know so much about us?"

She half-closed her eyes for the blow she would have received in Doune, but Rannoch just nodded. "You're not the first woman to prefer us to your own people."

Rainfire remembered what her father had said about the enemy having strange customs. She fell silent as she absorbed how truly strange they were.

Rannoch's chariot led Gealag's around the castle's hill, then up a steep road through the broken-down houses of Before that had once been the town of Stirling. The horses strained at the climb until the road leveled out and the grey stone of the castle itself blocked their way, pierced by the open drawbridge beneath the gatehouse towers. Rainfire could see that if the drawbridge was closed, the walls would be as unassailable as a father's decision. She shuddered at the idea of her father leading the Peoples against those walls. She must not fail.

Rannoch stood and lifted his bow over his head as they crossed the drawbridge. "Prepare a feast, sons and daughters of Stirling! Rannoch Longbow has found a wife!"

Rainfire looked up at the towering warrior, who had shed all his resemblance to the petulant youth who had stammered his way through the meeting. The black bow reminded her of why she was here. Cheering people swarmed in the gateway and leaned over the battlements. Rainfire remembered when some of those happy young men had sent a shower of arrows over the walls of Doune Castle, picked off the warriors who rode to meet them and galloped away. The memory made her want something solid and friendly to hold onto, and Rannoch at least offered that. She wrapped her arms round his waist as the enemy jostled around him to slap his back and shake his hand. Rannoch took Rainfire's hand and helped her down. He led her to stand beside Gealag, who was sitting in his chariot and scowling. "Our valued advisor disapproves," declaimed Rannoch. He dropped his voice and spoke seriously. "Tell us what's wrong, wise Gealag."

Gealag looked startled. "This is hardly the place."

Rannoch laid a hand on Gealag's arm. "You've been my friend and advisor since I was a child, and I want you to be happy today. Please tell me your thoughts."

Gealag sighed. "As you insist. Keenblade sent this girl to distract you, and he succeeded. He got you to agree to far less than we planned to demand and left us no stronger than we were yesterday. It doesn't put me in the mood for celebration."

The enemy surrounding them looked less happy, and angry looks sent Rainfire shrinking closer to Rannoch. His arm slipped around her, but his smile did not slip. "You're probably right. I was certainly distracted, but what of that? I've found my bride, so I don't complain. As for allowing them to keep a quarter of the land between here and Doune," he held up his free hand to still the muttering. "If they won't keep that bargain, they wouldn't have stopped attacking us from across the river. The difference is that now we know where they are, and we don't have to cross the river to counterattack. I'm sorry, Gealag, I know you want peace, but I want them where they are if we're going to have to finish them off."

Gealag's face softened a little. "Maybe you're right. You're a better battlechief than any other I've known."

Rainfire felt cold again. She had made a mistake to compare Rannoch to Nightcloud. The look that Gealag shot at her as he climbed off his chariot did nothing to make her feel better.

Rannoch raised his voice again. "Now we must show my bride that the feasts of Stirling are as unsurpassed as our archery!"

A cheer answered him and the enemy dispersed, laughing and talking. Rannoch turned to Rainfire, and his breath warmed her forehead. She didn't want to look at his face, but his finger nudged her chin upward, and she didn't dare resist. She tried to control his smiling blue eyes as she had at the meeting in the bracken, but she could not even control her own feelings. These eyes belonged to the man who could destroy Keenblade, and to a man who had already given her more than Keenblade ever would. Confusion blocked her throat and stung her eyes, and she was horrified to find herself assailed by weakness now that she was where her father intended her to be. Rannoch pressed his lips to her forehead and she found she could fight the weakness that those eyes brought when she could not see them. She dropped her gaze so that when he pulled back, she saw nothing but her feet.

"I'm sorry," he said. "I couldn't help myself."

He seemed to be waiting for something, so she took one of his hands in both of hers. He squeezed gently. "Come on, let me show you Stirling Castle."

He kept hold of her hand while he led her over the towers and battlements, and she looked for anything that might be useful to Keenblade. It was not difficult as long as she avoided looking at Rannoch's face, though she could not be as resentful as she wanted to be when she compared the large rooms that the warriors of Stirling enjoyed with the damp dormitories of Doune.

She noted the ease with which the enemy could watch their herds half way to Doune, or send their chariots to sweep down on any marauders. Yet she noticed that although ground immediately beyond the drawbridge was open, the remains of the town sprawled for thousands of paces beyond it. There were hiding places for hundreds of warriors in there, and Rainfire saw why the drawbridge was only lowered when it was necessary. She hid a smile at the thought of how seriously men took themselves when it was so easy to think like a warrior.

"But I haven't shown you our best," said Rannoch.

He led her inside the castle to a door guarded by two warriors with short swords strapped to their belts. Both men embraced Rannoch. "We heard the news," said one of them. "Just our luck to be on Cedrom duty at the great moment."

The word 'Cedrom' cleared the clouds from Rainfire's head, and she took careful note of the heavy wooden door, with its lack of bolts.

"Don't worry, you'll be off in time for the feast," Rannoch said to the guard. "Just a pity for whoever's stuck here."

Two guards outside this door tonight, thought Rainfire.

Rannoch took a large key from a pouch on his belt and opened the door. "Our smiths spent ages making the parts for a proper lock," he said.

Rainfire looked at the lock closely as Rannoch lifted a burning candle from the wall in the corridor. The Peoples' smiths had given up on making working locks.

Candlelight flickered on stone walls and over something on a table in the middle of the room. Rainfire caught her breath, then saw it was an ordinary metal box. Rannoch put the candle in a holder on the wall of the Cedrom room and undid a clasp on the box, opening it. He reached in, and Rainfire gasped. Blades of red and green and blue chased each other around a silver disc Rannoch's held up. He turned it over, and Rainfire saw its other side was coated in indecipherable runes. Rannoch held it out to her. She moistened her lips and took it between the tips of her finger and thumb.

The smooth texture of the disc set her whole body trembling. This was the reason for leaving her father and coming to Stirling. If only she could run, and keep running until the gate of Doune closed behind her, and never have to fight the dangerous thoughts that chipped at her resolve. She would never get past the door, but she wanted to try so much that her knees nearly folded with the effort of keeping herself upright.

"I can see you've heard of our Cedrom," said Rannoch.

Rainfire ordered herself to think and act as Keenblade's daughter. "Is it true that this is the wisdom of Before?"

Rannoch sighed. "We think so, but we don't know for sure."

Rainfire turned it over to watch the dance of the colors.

"It came to us a long time ago," said Rannoch, "in my grandfather's time. There were still a few who could speak the runes then, and they said these runes say the word 'Britannica.' I don't know what that means, but they said it's some sort of store of knowledge."

"How does it tell you the knowledge?"

"It doesn't, and we don't know how to make it. Perhaps it's a key, but we don't know where to find the lock it goes into. Perhaps it needs a key of its own, to go through the hole in the middle, but we don't know how to make one."

"So you have the knowledge of Before, but you don't know how to get at it?" Rainfire didn't know how she kept her disappointment out of her voice.

"No, and I'm not sure that's such a bad thing. For all we know, the knowledge of Before may not be any help to us now. It didn't do the people of Before much good. We should be thinking about what to do with the future, not what was done with the past." He took the Cedrom and returned it to its box. "We didn't need it to make our longbows, and we should be thinking of what else *we* can do instead of what it might do. I'm sorry to say this, my love, but your people's problem is that they worship Before to avoid thinking about now. If I wouldn't lose my head, I'd throw that box into the River Forth before we make the same mistake." He snorted with laughter. "Sorry, my tongue runs away with me in here. Let's go before the feast starts without us."

He took her hand and led her out of the room. Rainfire felt she had left something behind when he locked the door.

಄ಅ౨౪ಅಲ౪

Rainfire was losing a battle with her own weakness. Every mouthful of sharp wine made his hand on her waist feel stronger and more pleasurable. Rainfire even enjoyed being whirled around the courtyard in a dance that made her feel foolish until she found herself laughing. In Doune only the men drank and danced. Keenblade had warned her about this particular strange custom, but she had expected to endure it rather than enjoy it.

Rainfire tried to concentrate on the voice in her mind telling her that with half of Stirling's warriors unable to stand and the rest soon to join them, the enemy would never be so weak. She tried to see Keenblade and his warriors making their way through the cover of the ruined town, but it was so easy to lay her head on Rannoch's shoulder and pretend that all was as he thought it was. A faint glow rose over the battlements and a few threads of moonlight forced their way through the ever-present cloud to tell her it was time to act. She didn't want to act; she wanted to stay here, in the island of warmth and calm that she found herself marooned on. She closed her eyes.

Rannoch's voice was muffled by her hair. "Are you tired? Shall we go to my chamber?"

Rainfire's stomach tightened as she silently shouted that she didn't want to go anywhere ever again. She found herself nodding and allowing herself to be taken by the hand. Cheers and laughter washed over her, and she felt she was watching from outside herself, curious to see whether Rannoch or Keenblade would prove the stronger.

She watched herself standing beside Rannoch's bed as he bolted the door, and watched while his mouth engulfed hers.

He was breathing fast. "I've waited all my life for this."

Rainfire watched her own surprise at his uncertain eyes and shaking hands. This man had actually become a Director without ever having had a woman. The marriage system of Stirling must be more strongly observed than she had imagined.

She giggled at her own blank expression at his nakedness. She had seen an enemy, a warrior and a husband in him today, but naked and panting, he looked as absurd as any of the young warriors of Doune fumbling with their first woman. She was naked now, and his chest hair tickled her as he laid her down on the bed and climbed on top of her. Gusts of breath blew across her face, and his weight pressed on her own breathing.

His leg brushed the bracelet of hair on her ankle, and she was not watching any more because he grated into her and hauled her back into her half-stifled body. His weight crushed her and stopped her from crying out as he rocked back and forth. She felt her nails dig into the hard mass of his shoulder, and she tried to match her breathing to the rhythm so she could get some air into her lungs. The grunting crescendoed into a sighing groan and the weight rolled aside. She pressed her legs together. A hand closed around hers and a voice breathed, "I love you."

"I love you." She was lying by any meaning of the word. She turned her head to see the stone walls and ceiling that enclosed her and thought of herself surrounded by layer upon layer of stone until she came to the outer ramparts and the closed drawbridge. Then she saw her father and his warriors hidden among the ruins. She was Keenblade's daughter. She was Rainfire.

She waited until she heard snores from the enemy beside her. She swung her legs off the bed. She winced at the soreness between them, but pulled on her shirt, skirt and cape. She found the key in Rannoch's belt and pulled an arrow from the leather bag beside his bow. The rough feel of the shaft made her stand up straight and look down at Rannoch. She could ignore her soreness when she thought how helpless he was before her. She held the arrow with her thumb along the shaft, the way

Keenblade had shown her how to hold a dagger, and looked down the point to Rannoch's open mouth. She imagined thrusting it home, putting an end to her father's enemy forever. Then she imagined the grate of steel on bone, and the blue eyes that would fly open for one last look at her. Perhaps it was not time to kill Rannoch. She would not be able to move freely through the castle if she were soaked in blood too soon. And he might scream. She was still thinking of reasons when she tucked the arrow under her cape and closed the door behind her. She pulled the hood up to hide her face. She didn't want anyone to recognize her and wonder why she was roaming the castle.

She jogged through the candlelit corridors of the castle, but at first she could not find the way to the Cedrom room. She imagined the moon taking its light back below the horizon while she scampered through the stone maze. She stepped out of a flight of stairs to find herself ten paces from the Cedrom guards, sitting on the floor with their backs against the wall. She nearly ducked back into the staircase, but one of them was already looking up. She angled her body toward the hand holding the arrow, so her face was in shadow and she looked as though she were clutching a wound. "Help me! Help me!"

A young guard started toward her. She found her eyes focusing on the wispy beard that lightly covered his chin. "There was a man! A warrior! I found him with a dead man, and he's right behind me!"

The beard turned as the guard looked back to his companion, who nodded. Rainfire heard a blade leaving a scabbard, and the warrior with the lightly covered chin was gone. She wished she had learned how easy it was to control men years ago. She staggered toward the older guard, seeing alert eyes darting around him beneath gray-streaked hair. *He may as well be blind drunk if he can look straight at his enemy without seeing her*, she thought. She sank to one knee with a groan. The guard leant over her, mouth open in concern. The part of the throat that Keenblade had told her about was straight over the arrowhead. All she had to do was flick back the cape, jam the arrow upward and back away from the warm blood splashing her face.

She stood up and savored a power she had never imagined. Power to make a man who had defeated the best warriors of the Peoples drum his heels on the floor and spray the wall with blood. Power to light fires of impotent rage in his eyes when she showed him the key. Power to smear the Cedrom itself with bloody fingertips and slide it under her cape.

She knelt beside the dying man and sent a scream echoing through the castle. She made sure her face was smeared with enough blood that she wouldn't be recognized unless anyone looked closely and screamed again, summoning the lightly covered chin back, hunting for an enemy to run his sword through. "He was here," she sobbed. "He's got the Cedrom!"

Now was the time for the man to ask a question, if he would only stop gaping at the open door and ask it. Wasn't there any way of willing him to use his brain? "Where did he go?" he asked at last.

Rainfire stared at him as though the thought had never occurred to her, then scrambled to her feet and ran back up the stairs. "This way!"

The lightly covered chin panted after her, but could not get past her until they were standing in the empty corridor above. Her hood fell back, but she could taste the blood that disguised her face. The chin showed no sign of recognition.

"Did you hear that?" asked Rainfire.

"What?"

Rainfire was already running up another flight of stairs and hoping hoping hoping that she was where she thought she was. She shouted with relief when she emerged on to the battlements.

"What?" The chin was still on the stairs.

"There he is! Stop him!"

She pointed at the tower at the end of the wall.

"Who's there?" A guard on the wall.

"Where is he?" The chin.

"He's gone! Over the wall!" Rainfire led the chin along the wall. "Here! He went over here!"

The chin leaned over the wall. "Can't see anyone. But then I could disappear in this light too." He turned to the guard running along the wall. "Alarm! Call the Chief Elect! The Cedrom's been stolen!"

Rainfire felt a surge of elation. The chin was standing next to Keenblade's daughter, yet he had convinced himself that he had seen a nonexistent thief because it had not occurred to him that a girl like Rainfire could have killed his companion. He crouched by one of the crenulations. "Nothing here. He must have doubled his rope around it. Then he could take it with him and we'd never know how he got out."

Rainfire put a hand over her face to hide her smile. She had been ready with that explanation, but the chin was telling her lie to himself.

The chin seemed to come back to himself. "We'd better get to the courtyard. We'll have to get after him before he gets too far."

He grabbed her arm and pulled her down the stairs. Rainfire cursed to herself. She had hoped to slip away and leave the enemy to confuse themselves, but there was no slipping out of that grip. She used her free hand to pull her hood up.

Men were running around the courtyard like ants whose nest Rainfire had poked with a stick. Here was a man hopping up and down as he fastened a boot while his wife tried to buckle on his sword. There was a man shaking a comrade who was still unconscious from the feast. Was this the enemy her father was so afraid of?

Rannoch forced his way through the crowd and seized her hands. Rainfire's stomach tightened. She had still hoped she could avoid being recognized until she could disappear. "Rainfire, my love, you're covered in blood! Are you hurt?"

Rainfire faced the power behind those eyes. She would need everything she had learned today to beat it. She allowed her jaw to tremble. "Hurt? No, I. . . ." She broke off with a sniff and fell into his arms.

She heard his voice echo through his chest as he spoke to the chin. "What happened?"

The chin hung in astonishment as the young warrior realized who Rainfire was, but he pulled himself together at Rannoch's question. "Somebody chased her through the castle, Chief Elect. Lucky for her she ran into me and Iolair guarding the Cedrom. I went after him, but he got 'round me, and I found Iolair with an arrow in his throat and the Cedrom gone."

Rainfire decided she could not have picked a better man.

"The Cedrom? Then what?" Rainfire felt Rannoch's grip tighten on her arm.

"We chased him up to the battlements of the west wall, and he got over the side. Must have had a rope. That was when I called the alarm."

"You said Iolair was killed by an arrow?" Rainfire recognized Gealag's deep voice, and sounded as though he had not been drinking. "Was he one of our own?"

"I didn't get a good look at him," said the chin. "She— the Chief Elect's wife might have done."

Rainfire clung to Rannoch even harder now that the moment when she would have to speak bore down on her. She would not fail. She was Rainfire.

"Rainfire?" Rannoch's hand felt slimy in her blood-soaked hair. She allowed him to tip her head back. "What did you see?" Rainfire turned to meet Gealag's glare. "What exactly?" Gealag's hand hovered over his sword, and she knew he would never believe her. She had to make the enemy act before Gealag could make them think.

She swallowed and remembered Keenblade's voice. "Don't answer them directly if you have to lie. Don't try to make up a story they can trip you up on. Be frightened and confused, and let them work it out for themselves."

"I don't know!" she wailed. Gealag rolled his eyes. "There was a man! He ran after me! He killed him in front of me! He took the Cedrom!"

Gealag's voice was drowned by a surge of questions.

"Someone's taken the Cedrom?"

"Iolair's dead?"

"My platoon's ready to get after him, Chief Elect!"

"The Cedrom?"

Rannoch lifted his arm from Rainfire, and she could feel him waving for silence. Warriors hunched forward for answers. Their eyes saw straight through her to Rannoch. Only Gealag realized they were doing her bidding, but they would work it out quickly enough if Rannoch made them wait long enough to think. She gripped Rannoch's cloak and drew a sobbing breath. Every muscle urged him to take action before it was too late, and she knew the warriors around them would see it. She forced words out of her mouth, praying to the naked goddess that they would infect the enemy with their urgency. "*He killed Iolair and took the Cedrom!*"

"Let's get after him," shouted someone.

"We'll lose the moon if we don't get out there now!"

"He'll be half way to Kildeen!"

Rainfire felt Rannoch's fists crumple her cape and she felt Rannoch being torn between Gealag's sense and his warriors' will, and still he did not see the power of Rainfire's presence as she clung to him and sobbed. Rannoch stepped away from her, shedding his indecision like an ill-fitting cloak. He organized his men into groups and gave each a part of Stirling to search. Rainfire saw why Keenblade feared Rannoch even as he led his men where she had sent him.

The malice in Gealag's eyes burned into her, but it was the malice of a man caught in a flood, unable to stem the tide that would wash him away. Rannoch ordered him to take command of the castle guard and his eyes dropped away from her. Rainfire slipped into the keep and found a window where she could watch the drawbridge. She saw the enemy find their discipline as warriors gathered in their platoons. The moon would give enough light for swords, but not bows, Keenblade had told her. "And we know who the best swordsmen are, don't we, daughter?"

Her fingers tightened on the sill when the drawbridge clanked down. Enemy warriors jogged across it and disappeared. Rainfire's breathing sang in her ears.

Keenblade murdered the silence with yells and clashes of metal. Any moment now, the picked men he had told her about would sprint round the main battle to seize the gatehouse, and she would be Keenblade's daughter again. She found herself waiting for the joy the thought should bring. She tried to imagine the pointless orders she would use to torment the women who had spat on her, but it all seemed as drab as the winter sky compared to this moment; the last moment of the enemy whom she had sent to their deaths.

Movement on the drawbridge. Silhouettes tumbled into the gatehouse. Arrows blurred down from the battlements. Smashing swords flooded into the courtyard.

Rainfire felt like the hidden girl at the Doune council again, watching the men make the decisions.

The last Stirling warrior in the courtyard fell. She heard screams inside the castle. Larger objects than arrows were tumbling from above her. Clothes. Furniture. A child.

A man crashed into the room. Bared teeth and bared sword glinted in candlelight. Rainfire shrank away even as she recognized Fleetfoot of the Mercedes. One hand grabbed her hair and the hand holding the sword tore her cape aside.

"Fleetfoot!" she screamed as he ripped the shirt of Before to her waist. "Fleetfoot! It's me! Rainfire!"

He looked at her face, seeing her clearly for the first time, and hauled her outside. She wrapped her cape around herself.

Keenblade was directing a small group of warriors in the gatehouse, checking that the warriors coming in were all of the Peoples. Seeing him again was like a cloudburst that washed away a painting before it dried.

"Director," called Fleetfoot, "I have your daughter."

Keenblade looked round, and back again at a cheer from his men. Nightcloud ran into the gatehouse, dangling Rannoch's head by the hair. "Their Director's head!"

Rainfire looked at the head and knew she had crushed her weakness when she felt nothing. She looked at Nightcloud more closely. The challenge in the way he brandished the head at Keenblade showed that someone else had learned to see the world differently today.

Keenblade clapped Nightcloud's shoulder; the image of a benevolent Director praising good service. "A fine trophy, Nightcloud. We'll sing your courage tonight, as we'll sing the cunning of my daughter who gave us Stirling castle."

"Your daughter!" Nightcloud held up Rannoch's head beside his own. "Your daughter who you gave to be defiled by this half-man!"

Rainfire stepped forward and took the Cedrom out of her cape. It captured every eye in the gatehouse, glinting in the light of a fire that had started in the keep. Rainfire gave it to Keenblade without taking her gaze off Nightcloud. Nightcloud's head jerked toward her as though he never wanted to look at anything else again. Rannoch's head sank to the level of Nightcloud's waist.

Rainfire thought proudly that none of these strutting warriors could have got their hands on the Cedrom, but then she felt a stab of dismay at the thought of telling Keenblade that the enemy had not known how to take the knowledge that the Cedrom carried. With every eye on the Cedrom, she raised her own to Keenblade's face as he took it. Keenblade was not looking at the Cedrom but at Nightcloud, and she saw a shadow of a smile through Keenblade's beard. Her breath sighed through her lips. She found Keenblade's thoughts as obvious as any other man's. He did not care about the knowledge of Before any more than Rannoch had. He had only cared that the enemy's reverence for the Cedrom could be used to force them into a foolish decision, just as he only cared about her reverence for him because it made her the only woman he could send into Stirling who would not be seduced by the enemy's kindness. She had seen and learned so much that she felt as though she had been blind and deaf until she knelt in the bracken yesterday.

"Don't be so quick to judge, Nightcloud," said Keenblade. "A warrior must use all his weapons, don't you agree?"

Rainfire painted a look of adoration on her face and reveled in her new freedom of thought. *You want me to be the weapon that will cripple Nightcloud as I did Rannoch, don't you, Father? You think that with me in his bed, he'll be under your control and won't challenge you until you want him to. Well, you go on thinking that, Father, because I'll be in his bed before long. But you'll trust me as much as he will. And we know what happens to men who trust me. Don't we, Father?*

ABOUT THE AUTHORS

Jennifer Brissett is a writer, artist, web developer, and former bookseller. A Jamaican-American (born in London, England), she moved to the US when she was four and grew up in Cambridge, Massachusetts. For three and a half years, she owned and operated a storefront bookstore. She currently lives in Brooklyn with her life partner Geoff and their cat Dudley. Her website can be found at www.jennbrissett.com.

Ian Whates has seen some 30 of his short stories published over the past three years, appearing in various venues including the science journal *Nature* (twice) and subsequently the 'best of' collection *Futures from Nature* (Tor Books, 2007). One of his stories, "The Gift of Joy," was shortlisted for the BSFA award, losing out to Ken MacLeod's story from his own anthology, *disLOCATIONS*. Ian is currently a director of both SFWA and of the British Science Fiction Association, for whom he also edits the news and media webzine *Matrix*. He is also the proprietor of independent publisher NewCon Press, which he founded in 2006.

Ian is currently busy compiling and editing *The Mammoth Book of Alternative History Stories* as well as writing the first of two novels commissioned by Solaris books. His debut short story collection, *The Gift of Joy,* was released in April 2008.

Jennifer R. Povey is in her mid thirties, and lives in Northern Virginia with her husband. She writes a variety of speculative fiction, whilst following current affairs and occasionally indulging in horse riding and role-playing games.

Ardath Mayhar is a member of SFWA and has had novels published for thirty years, by Doubleday, ACE, Atheneum, Zebra, TSR, many more. Most recently her short stories appeared in anthologies *Redshift* (Fungi) and *Cross Plains Universe* (Pillar in the Mist). In 2008, SFWA chose her as their Author Emerita.

Leslie Brown is a research technician working in the Alzheimer's field. She has previously published stories in *On Spec, Strange Horizons,* and in several anthologies including *Thou Shalt Not, Loving the Undead* and *Sails and Sorcery.* She is a member of Lyngarde, an Ottawa Writers' Group. Her website is at www.leslie-brown.com.

Lee Martindale's first professional fiction sale was to Marion Zimmer Bradley in 1992. Since then, her work has appeared in numberous anthologies, magazines, and online venues. Most recent sales include stories in the Martin Greenberg/Janet Deaver-Pack anthology *Catopolis*, Esther Friesner's *Witch Way to the Mall* (coming out from Baen sometime next year), and another Friesner project, *Turn The Other Chick.* In addition, she edited Meisha-Merlin's first original anthology, *Such A Pretty Face.*

Sarah Ellender writes science fiction, fantasy and horror. Over the last year, she has become a flash fiction enthusiast, and posts a story every fortnight at http://www.plotmedics.com/friday-flash.html. She is an ardent believer in the helpfulness of a good writing group, and a long-term member of the London-based T-Party. She has spent most of her working life as a software engineer. Every now and again she throws up her hands and runs away screaming. On those occasions she has taken a foundation course in art and design, travelled around the world for six months, studied as a potter's apprentice in Italy, interned in the art department of a TV production company, and become the proud holder of an NVQ level 1 Wood Occupations certificate. It's all material.

Michael O'Connor's stories have received 'Honorable Mentions' in the 10th and 13th editions of *Year's Best Fantasy and Horror,* and others were successful in the 1998 Department for Education Cancer Research Campaign competition (First Prize) and the Camberley Writers' Circle 1998 Competition (Highly Commended), as well as in the 1997, 1998 and 2001 Lewis Wright Competitions and the 1996 Redcar Writers' Competition. He has had stories and poems published in numerous UK/USA print magazines; he has also had work published online by *Bloodletters* (Canada), *Electric Acorn* (Ireland), *Gateway Monthly* and *The Errorist* (both UK) and *Lost In The Dark* (USA). He has an article on Dickens in the Urban Fox Press book *The*

Medway Scene and six stories and two poems in their sequels *New Art From North Kent* and *The Arts in Medway*, in addition to which Urban Fox published an anthology of sixteen of his short stories in January 2004 under the title *Where Do They All Belong?* His non-fiction book *From Chaucer to Childish: A Chronological Survey of Writers and Artists in the Medway Towns* was published by Medway Delta Press in September 2006.

Website: www.mpoconnor.co.uk.

Deborah Walker lives in London, with her partner Chris, and her two lovely, yet distracting, young children. After a twenty year period of procrastination she has, finally, started to write speculative fiction. She has had around thirty acceptances for her short stories and poetry, most recently from *Champagne Shivers, Scifaikuest* and *Outshine*.

She can often be found in the British Museum stealing ideas from ancient cultures.

Jeff Crook is the author of four novels in the Dragonlance universe. He has short fiction pending publication in *Murky Depths, Cat Tales,* and *The End of an Aeon* anthology. His stories have previously appeared in *Mallorn, Helix, Nature* (twice), *Nature Physics* (twice), *Horror D'oeuvres, Paradox,* and many others. He lives a life of relative peace and harmony in Olive Branch, MS, with his wife and two male offspring.

Catherine Mintz has appeared in *Warrior Wisewoman, Marion Zimmer Bradley's Sword and Sorceress XXII* and *XXIII,* and *Nature Magazine,* among many others. For a more complete list, see www.catherine-mintz.com.

David Bartell has a degree in Astrophysics, and a job as a manager at a high tech company. He has been writing SF for decades and has recently been selling a fair amount. He has a wife and four kids. His hobbies include music, photography, and of course, writing. He has sold a number of stories to *Analog: Science Fiction and Fact,* as well as a few to anthologies and other markets. One story, co-written with Ekaterina Sedia, won the Analog AnLab award for best short story of 2005, and also made the Locus Recommended Reading list. Two others were translated into Russian for *ELSI* magazine. For more information, visit http://www.davidbartell.us.

Kate MacLeod lives in Minneapolis, MN. Her work has previously appeared in *Allegory* and *Beyond Centauri* and is forthcoming in

Beneath Ceaseless Skies and *Fantastical Visions V*. She can be found on the internet at KateMacLeod.net.

Karen E. Rigley of Utah and **Ann Miller House** of Texas have been published in short fiction and nonfiction and have won numerous awards. They are long-time members of the Science Fiction & Fantasy Writers of America. Their stories have appeared in Andre Norton's *Tales of the Witch World* anthology series, Volumes 2 & 3 (TOR); *Catfantastic* volumes I, II, & III edited by Andre Norton & Martin H. Greenberg (DAW), *The Magic Within, Magic, Computeredge, The West Texas Sun, Vision, Grit, Strange Wonderland, Science Fiction Review,* and other publications.

Z. S. Adani has a background in biology and art. She started writing fiction in 2005, and is currently working on short stories and novel revisions. She lives in Florida with her husband and two daughters.

Sophy is a graduate of of the James Gunn Writers Workshop. She is co-editor of *Destination: Future,* an anthology to be published by Hadley Rille Books in early 2010. Her short stories appear in *Global Warming Aftermaths* anthology, *Something Wicked* magazine, *The Book of Exodi, Alternative Coordinates, The Writer's Eye Magazine, Murky Depths* magazine, *Desolate Places* anthology, and *Afterburn SF.*

One of her stories has been a Finalist in the Writers of the Future Contest.

Website: www.alnitak-z-orionis.com

DJ Cockburn's previous credits include publications in *Aeon, Aoife's Kiss, Paradox* and *Flashing Swords.*

LaVergne, TN USA
18 October 2009
161246LV00003B/23/P